P9-BYD-748

"By heaven, you belong to me now, do you understand?" he uttered close to her ear.

His voice, low and husky and brimming with barely controlled anger, sent a shiver dancing down her spine. She gasped when he forced her abruptly about to face him. *"You're mine!"*

She had no time to argue, no time to scream or struggle or even finish drawing in a deep, shuddering breath. He swept her close, his strong arms encircling her while his mouth swooped down to capture hers.

It was a fire, of course, a wild, intoxicating blaze of mutual passion that would not be denied. . . .

Also by Catherine Creel
Published by Fawcett Books:

WILD TEXAS ROSE

LADY ALEX

Catherine Creel

FAWCETT GOLD MEDAL • NEW YORK

Sale of this book without a front cover may be unauthorized. If this book is coverless, it may have been reported to the publisher as "unsold or destroyed" and neither the author nor the publisher may have received payment for it.

A Fawcett Gold Medal Book
Published by Ballantine Books
Copyright © 1994 by Catherine Creel

All rights reserved under International and Pan-American Copyright Conventions. Published in the United States of America by Ballantine Books, a division of Random House, Inc., New York, and simultaneously in Canada by Random House of Canada Limited, Toronto.

Library of Congress Catalog Card Number: 94-94410

ISBN 0-449-14786-X

Manufactured in the United States of America

First Edition: October 1994

10 9 8 7 6 5 4 3 2 1

With love to my sister, Carol,
who has at long last
found the happiness she deserves.

Chapter 1

New South Wales . . . 1820

" 'Tis a fine day to be bringing home a bride, Captain."

"Damn your eyes, you old Irish rascal."

"Aye, Captain."

"And tell Baxter to clean the stables while I'm gone."

"Aye, Captain."

Finn Muldoon grinned broadly—and unrepentantly—while he steadied the horses and watched his employer climb up to the wagon seat. Captain Hazard was in a foul temper, to be sure. Why, he looked every bit like a poor man taking himself off to fight a duel instead of just going to hire a new housekeeper.

Saints be certain, the small, gray-haired former seaman mused with an erudite shake of his head, there *was* always the possibility of a brawl whenever tangling with the daughters of Eve. Especially the sort kept under lock and key at Parramatta.

"Those Factory lasses are said to be a wild lot, Captain." He offered the caution solemnly, almost paternally.

"I'm well aware of that." Jonathan Hazard's rugged, sun-bronzed features became a grim mask, his green

1

eyes darkening with obvious displeasure. "But I've little choice."

"Have you not?" Muldoon challenged, with the privilege of both age and long acquaintance. "Well now, it strikes me you could head downriver to Sydney and have yourself a look-see at the new prisoners. Fresh off the boat, and willing to please they'd be."

"Blast it, man. I haven't the time!" Jonathan growled in response. And then, for the first time that morning, he allowed the merest hint of a smile to touch his lips. His gold-flecked emerald gaze brimmed with humor for the situation as he reached up to pull the front brim of his hat lower. "I've little doubt the woman I choose to employ will prove 'willing to please.' Her choices are, after all, considerably more limited than my own."

"Aye, Captain. And that would be the very reason you'll need to take care," said the Irishman, gently stroking a hand along one of the animals' sleek necks. " 'Tis likely she'll want nothing more than to find her way back to Sydney and the flash houses there. Many a Jezebel from that place has made use of her charms, such as they be, to gain her ticket-of-leave and then forget as how it was her husband that got her her freedom." He frowned and shook his head again before adding, "Brazen they are, Captain. Brazen and coarse— and like as not to cut a man's heart out if given the chance."

"I'll bear that in mind," Jonathan replied dryly, raising a booted foot to the wagon's front rail. "But since matrimony is not *my* intent, I doubt my own heart will be in any real danger." He gave a curt nod, at which the older man obediently released his grip on the horse's bridle and stepped back. "I should return well before noon. God willing, we'll have a decent meal this very night."

"Aye, Captain," Muldoon responded, though his tone lacked any real conviction. "God willing."

Jonathan felt a sudden impulse to say more, but decided to ignore it. With a simple, practiced flick of the reins, he drove the wagon away from the house and soon left the well-shaded grounds behind.

The cloudless summer sky was brilliantly ablaze with sunshine, the morning air heavy with the mingling scents of eucalyptus and honeysuckle. Only the ghost of a breeze stirred the leaves, while somewhere in the near distance the mocking laugh of a kookaburra joined with the more lyrical outpourings of brightly colored tropical birds. The day promised to be another one of Australia's infamous scorchers; already, a vast, shuddering array of insects blended into the stillness and secrecy of the ground to escape the coming heat.

The handsome young master of Boree Plantation tossed a swift, irritated glance heavenward. The last thing he'd wanted to do was pay a visit to the Factory. He had avoided the place like the plague up until now. But as he had told Muldoon, he had very little choice in the matter. Either he took his chances there, or risked losing a whole day by traveling to Sydney. And even then, there was no guarantee that he'd be able to find a more suitable woman. No guarantee at all.

He swore beneath his breath and gave another flick of the reins, thereby hastening the horses' progress along what passed for a road in that part of the country. The look in his eyes grew thunderous again as he reflected upon the task before him—*and* the stroke of ill fortune that had made it necessary.

It had done him little good to hire freewomen thus far. Three housekeepers in a row had traded their hard-won independence for the bonds of marriage. Nary a one of them had been what even the most charitable of men would term either young or attractive, yet they had certainly never lacked for suitors. Given the fact that men still outnumbered their feminine counterparts by so great a margin, it should have come as no surprise when nature took its course.

"Nature," Jonathan muttered contemptuously. Nature be damned.

In a sudden, angry movement he dragged the hat from his head and flung it aside. The sun's rays, filtering softly downward through the ever-present canopy of the trees, set fiery gold to his thick, dark brown hair. The throbbing croak of a cicada reached his ears, but he took no notice of it as he shifted his lean, hard-muscled hips on the uncushioned wooden seat. He impatiently loosened his neckcloth, cursing the fact that society—of which he was a reluctant member—demanded so many clothes in such a sweltering climate.

Turning his eyes toward the west, he caught a glimpse of the Blue Mountains, their rugged, sterile sandstone peaks in stark contrast to the tangle of greenery below. A country of extremes, he mused absently. The landscape was a far cry from any other he had seen ... certainly different from the flat and marshy plains of the Maryland coastline.

He felt a rare wave of nostalgia hit him. For a few moments, his thoughts drifted back to home.

Home. His features tightened anew, and the curse he breathed this time was directed toward himself. Australia was his home now, by heaven, and had been so for two years. There was nothing to be gained by thinking of the past.

He drove onward, forcing his mind elsewhere. His mood had seen no real improvement by the time he reached the settlement of Parramatta—"plenty of eels" the aborigines had called it—and slowed the horses to a walk.

Even at that hour of the day, Parramatta was bustling with activity. It was a good-sized town, but nothing to compare with Sydney. Jonathan was glad of that.

His gaze traveled absently over the odd collection of buildings nestled on the banks of the river. The Government House, with its classical porticoed lines, seemed out of place amid the more simple stores and taverns. The twin-towered St. John's Church looked as though it might have been transplanted from any one of England's villages. The entire town, with its orderly streets, quaint cottages, and placid greens, was something in the English character, yet distinctly *un*-English at the same time. Like everything else in Australia, it was a peculiar blend of the old and new.

Offering a silent, preoccupied nod in response to the greetings directed his way, Jonathan continued down the cobbled width of the settlement's main street. In the clearing just ahead, a short but satisfactory distance from the more respectable elements of Parramatta, lay his final destination. The temptation to call the whole thing off grew stronger with each rotation of the wagon's wheels.

But he would not allow himself to turn back now. Drawing the team to a halt, he set the brake, snatched up his hat, and climbed down. Before him stood the Female Factory, so named because it was where the women prisoners wove the coarse cloth used to make the convicts' winter clothes.

The Marriage Market. His mouth tightened into a thin line while he surveyed the infamous compound. The main building was a surprisingly pretty, three-story Georgian structure, boasting of both a cupola and a clock. It was surrounded by a handful of single-story outbuildings. Around the entire area stood a stone security wall, intended more to keep men out than women in.

Prison though it was, Jonathan told himself with a frown of remembrance, the place was a damn sight better than its predecessor. Until a few months ago, the Factory had been nothing more than a scene of disgusting squalor, a cramped, filthy loft above a jail. A full two-thirds of the prisoners had found it necessary to find lodging with the local settlers. And since they'd had little to offer in the way of payment, most had been forced to raise the money in a manner known locally as "buttock-and-twang." Their main clientele had consisted of male convicts; when the men couldn't raise the meager compensation in an honest manner, they had resorted to thievery. A vicious circle, to be sure . . . Was it any wonder that Parramatta had gained a reputation as a modern day Sodom and Gomorrah?

Thank God, all that had changed now. Whatever other indignities the women still suffered, they at least had sufficient housing. *And* the chance for a better life.

Steeling himself for the unpleasant task ahead, he raised the hat to his head and strode forward. He knocked at the heavy, iron-banded door. In a matter of seconds, it swung open to reveal a buxom, drably attired woman whose appearance, he concluded with an inward scowl, would have stopped the face of an eight-day clock.

"Yes?" the imposing matron demanded. Her eyes flickered over him with a well-earned wariness. She was nearly as tall as he, and looked entirely capable of defending her honor should the need arise. He doubted it ever would.

"I've come to choose a woman," he proclaimed tersely, removing his hat.

"A bride, you mean?"

"No." *God forbid.* "My purpose is employment, not marriage."

"Employment?" Her gray, hawkish gaze narrowed in obvious suspicion. "And what sort of employment would that be?"

"I am in need of a housekeeper." Cursing the fact that she was treating him more like a callow stripling than the well-seasoned man of thirty that he was, he frowned again and added, "Nothing more than that."

"I see." Still, she looked dubious. "Well then, have you a letter from the Reverend Marsden?"

"I have." He reached into his coat pocket and withdrew the required missive, which had been duly signed by the colony's self-annointed champion of morality. The black-haired giantess took the letter, subjected its contents to a close examination, then finally swung the door wide. Her demeanor was only slightly less inaffable as she stepped aside to allow him entrance.

"I be Mistress Burke. And I've heard of you, Captain Hazard." Her voice, never pleasant to begin with, held a note of indictment when she added, "You're the American, aren't you?"

"One of many," he shot back, his own tone dangerously low and level. He gave an impatient nod toward the main building. "If you don't mind, I'm in a hurry."

"You and all the other gents," she said, sniffing. Pivoting about, she began leading the way across the grounds. The large bunch of keys at her waist jangled with each of her heavy, ungraceful steps.

Jonathan followed in her wake, his fingers threatening to crush the hat in his hands. He was shown into a central yard, instructed to wait there, and left alone to cool his heels beneath the sparse shade of a pine tree while the matron took herself off to summon the prisoners.

The wait was a mercifully brief one.

He watched as a group of women, perhaps thirty in all, filed out of the main building into the narrow, sunlit yard. They lined up in total silence, dutifully presenting themselves for inspection.

"These here be our 'merit' prisoners, Captain," the matron announced, moving forward to take her place at his side. She directed a faint, superior smile toward her charges. "The least troublesome, they are. Six months of good behavior, every one of them, and none in the family way."

Jonathan offered no immediate response. He allowed his piercing gaze to sweep over the women, surprised at how young the majority of them were. Clad in their coarse, gray flannel dresses and white mobcaps, they looked like schoolgirls, not hardened criminals. But then again, he reminded himself with a cynical half smile, appearances were often as not deceiving. A woman could at once possess the face of an angel and the heart of a strumpet. By damn, he had certainly learned that much.

Murder, thievery, prostitution . . . Whatever the reason for their banishment, he couldn't help feeling a twinge of compassion for them. They were far from home, and would likely spend the rest of their lives in Australia.

The seconds ticked by while his silent, critical appraisal continued. Muldoon's warning rose in his mind again; he wondered if they really were the worst of the lot. Some of them were pretty, some were not. At least two appeared to share his distaste for the proceedings, he noted wryly. They glowered back at him, their eyes promising swift, and possibly murderous, retribution if he should dare to set his sights on them. Many of the others, however, smiled enticingly. He doubted they'd last a month at Boree.

"Mayhap you'd care to have yourself a closer look, Captain," the matron suggested. It was clear that she found his lack of enthusiasm annoying. "If there be any here that suit your fancy—"

"No." He shook his head. His instincts told him that he had not yet found the woman he sought. And his instincts had only rarely misled him. "Are there no others?" he demanded quietly.

"There be others right enough, but—"

"Then take me to them."

The matron visibly bristled at his commanding tone. She was not accustomed to being ordered about, particularly by an *American*. But duty was duty.

"You'll find none better," she predicted, with a brisk, condescending air.

"There's a great likelihood of that." He offered her a faint smile, to which she responded by drawing herself haughtily erect. She turned away and signaled to the group of prisoners. Some of the women, disappointed at the outcome, cast wistful glances at Jonathan as they returned inside the main building. It wasn't every day that such a fine specimen of manhood came to the Factory. No indeed, the usual "bridegrooms" were either old or ill-favored, or both. Fate, cruel as it had ever been, had tempted them with a glimpse of paradise that day, only to thrust them back into misery once more.

"This way," Mistress Burke directed. Jonathan followed in her wake again. She marched toward a row of long, low-roofed outbuildings, her ample backside swaying beneath her brown woolen skirts. "We keep the 'incorrigibles' here." Her mouth curled into what looked suspiciously like a sneer when she advised, "You'd best have a care to yourself."

Selecting a key from the bunch at her waist, she unlocked the massive outer door and led the way inside. A narrow hallway ran the length of the building, with still more doors marking the solitary cells. Jonathan caught the unmistakable scents of straw and pine oil as he paused briefly to let his eyes adjust to the semidarkness.

"These be the devil's own darlings," Mistress Burke remarked in a caustic tone. Her own eyes gleaming with certain triumph, she unlocked the first door they came to and pushed it open.

Jonathan stepped forward, his tall frame filling the doorway. The floor of the small, airless cell was covered with straw. There was a narrow bed against one wall, a tiny window high above it, and a bucket for "convenience" in the corner. A woman of indeterminate age sat huddled on the bed, refusing to acknowledge their presence. Her hair, probably blond at one time, had been cropped short. She was quite pale and reed-thin.

"On your feet, Cora!" snapped the matron, sweeping inside. "You've a visitor."

Jonathan's heart, though usually well guarded, stirred with compassion again. He watched while the poor creature before him finally raised her head. Her eyes were dull, the expression in them hopeless, much the same as a wild animal that had been kept in captivity too long.

"Stand up, I say!" Mistress Burke angrily prompted once more. She raised a menacing hand toward the prisoner.

"Leave her be!" Jonathan ground out, his gaze glittering harshly. "I've seen enough."

"Save your pity for them that deserves it," she told him, with another gesture of contempt. "Why, this little

dearie here would cut your throat from ear to ear the
minute your back was turned."

"That may well be true, but—"

He got no further. Without warning, Cora suddenly
sprang from the bed and launched herself at him. He instinctively raised his hands to seize her wrists—
otherwise, she would have plunged her dirty, ragged
nails into his eyes. She was in truth like a wild animal
now, kicking and writhing and letting loose with a
string of Billingsgate oaths that would have burned the
ears of a lesser man.

Jonathan was surprised at her strength. Still, he managed to subdue her quickly. Mistress Burke offered neither comment nor assistance as he wrapped his
powerful arms about Cora, and, lifting her bodily, deposited her back on the bed. All the fight seemed to go
out of her then. She cowered atop the threadbare blanket, her knees drawn up toward her chin and her hands
covering her face.

Staring down at her in mingled pity and bemusement,
Jonathan resisted the urge to lay a soothing hand on her
shoulder before he finally spun about and strode from
the cell. He retrieved his hat from the straw on his way
out. His features were taut with anger when the matron,
after closing and locking the door behind them, turned
to meet his gaze.

"Why the devil didn't you tell me she was mad?" he
accused, his deep-timbred voice whipcord sharp.

"You said as how you wanted to see the others."
With a smirk on her face, she ambled blithely past him
and continued on her way down the corridor.

"Play me for a fool again, Mistress Burke, and you'll
be seeking new employment." It was no idle threat.

The matron appeared to realize that, for the next several interviews were conducted without incident. All of

the prisoners were considered sane yet notorious. Two of them sat combing wool placidly in their cells, another was carding in the meager sunlight that streamed in through the single window above, while still another scrambled to her feet with a grinning, openly vulgar invitation to Jonathan the minute the door was opened.

Few of them looked capable of committing the crimes for which they had been transported—although there was one who muttered something about men being the "sons of Satan himself," and thereby deserving to have their "bollocks roasted over a fire." Jonathan could well imagine that she had wreaked havoc upon English mankind.

Finally he was shown into a common room in an adjoining building, where another group of inmates sat weaving the Parramatta cloth. A good many of them were obviously with child; the rest were either crippled by injuries or recovering from illness. None would be suitable for the job he had come to offer.

"There be no others," Mistress Burke informed him smugly.

He gave a curt nod and headed outside. Wondering if he had come on a fool's errand after all, he was ready to abandon his quest altogether when he caught sight of a door to his right. He stopped and turned back to Mistress Burke.

"What is in there?"

"Nothing to interest you, Captain."

His eyes narrowed in suspicion at the woman's evasiveness. Gripped by a sudden, unexpected curiosity, he tried to open the door. It was locked.

"Have you the key?" he demanded.

"No." He could see that she was lying.

"Then I suggest you find it."

"We've orders to leave the girl be," she confided reluctantly. Compressing her lips into a thin line, she shook her head and sliced a glance toward the room in question. "A real she-devil, that one is."

"I'd like to form my own opinion," persisted Jonathan. It was quite possible that he'd find himself facing another madwoman like Cora. Still, something compelled him to find out. "Since we've had little luck thus far—"

"You said as how I was to tell you—"

"I'll take full responsibility," he assured her, with another ghost of a smile.

Mistress Burke visibly wavered, her plump, ruddy countenance reflecting her indecision. She favored him with a hard stare, looked toward the door, then back at him. When she capitulated at last, it was with an ill grace.

"Have it your way then, Captain. But it will do you no good. She'll not go with you."

Her words only served to fuel his interest. He watched as she miraculously produced the key and jammed it in the lock. She opened the door to reveal a cell much the same as the others he had seen. Except this one held an angel.

An angel. Jonathan's eyes widened in disbelief, for the young woman who whirled to face him was the most beautiful he had ever seen.

Her thick auburn hair had been cropped short. Instead of making her seem less feminine, however, it actually heightened her beauty. A white cap was perched atop her head, but delightfully wayward tendrils escaped to curl about her face. The coarse, ill-fitting gown she wore could not disguise the womanly perfection of her curves. Her breasts were full, her hips slender yet well rounded. With a mouth that seemed to beckon the loving touch of a man's, features as lovely and aristocratic as any true lady's, and a smooth, flawless complexion that bespoke her Saxon heritage, she was the very picture of flowering English womanhood. And her eyes—By heaven, her eyes were the color of the sea, their luminous, blue-green depths full of fire.

She stood proud and defiant before him, looking for all the world as though she were in the midst of an elegantly furnished drawing room instead of a cramped, dingy prison cell.

His deep emerald gaze burned across into the brilliant turquoise of hers. A highly charged silence rose between them. The redoubtable Mistress Burke, standing forgotten off to one side, wisely held her own tongue while the seconds crawled past.

And then, finally, the angel spoke.

Chapter 2

"What is the meaning of this intrusion?"

Jonathan stared at her with a mixture of surprise and wholly masculine appreciation. She certainly didn't speak the way an angel would. Her tone was clear and angry and imperious, her eyes hurling invisible daggers at his head. He was certain that, under different and decidedly more advantageous circumstances, she would have gladly employed a real weapon.

Intrigued, he allowed himself the luxury of a more thorough appraisal. His blood ran hot as his gaze traveled slowly, intimately, over her. She was unlike any of the other women he had seen at the Factory. . . . She was unlike any he had seen in Australia. How the devil had such an exquisite-looking creature come to be imprisoned in such a place?

"This gent here is looking for a housekeeper," Mistress Burke drawled, with a smile of perverse satisfaction. She folded her arms across her ample bosom and waited for the fireworks to begin.

"A housekeeper? Why, I—I am no servant!" the young woman sputtered indignantly. Two bright spots of color rode high on the silken smoothness of her cheeks; her chin lifted to an even more rebellious angle while her eyes shot to the matron. "Did you not tell him who I am?"

"Lady Alexandra Sinclair, so she says," Mistress Burke remarked to Jonathan. Her rejection of the claim was apparent as she gave a scornful little smile and added, "We call her 'Lady Alex.' What with her la-di-da ways, she—"

"Insult me all you please, you ill-favored harpy. I *am* Lady Alexandra Sinclair!"

"Lady?" Jonathan echoed, his brow creasing into a thoughtful frown. His eyes narrowed while he regarded her steadily. There was no denying the air of refinement about her. She both looked and sounded well born. But, an English noblewoman among the convicts? No, there had to be some other explanation.

"I'll wager she was on the stage," the matron put forth as though she had read his mind. "Actresses are a clever lot. But not *too* clever, eh, dearie?" she taunted Alex. Then she turned to Jonathan and said, "Transported for thievery, she was."

"I was falsely accused!" Alex proclaimed.

"You and everyone else on these godforsaken shores!" the older woman shot back derisively.

"Whoever you are," said Jonathan, flinging the matron a quelling look as he took a step forward, "I would imagine you'd be grateful for the chance to get out of here." His gaze caught and held Alex's again.

"If it's gratitude you expect, sir, then you would do well to search elsewhere!" She planted her hands on her hips and charged, "I have little doubt that the duties of your 'housekeeper' include a good deal more than the traditional domestic endeavors!"

Alex took a deep, steadying breath. Her show of bravado was in direct contrast to the turmoil he had created within her. She was doing her best to ignore the wild beating of her heart and the strange warmth spreading throughout her body. Good heavens, what was happening? She had never felt this way before. The man (an American, of all things, from the sound of it) was handsome, devilishly so . . . but it was more than that. Much more.

Unable to prevent her eyes from straying up and down the whole magnificent length of him, she swallowed hard. He was quite tall, his body lean and powerfully muscled. The dark blue coat he wore was tailored along simple lines, yet fit his broad shoulders to perfection. Above the snowy whiteness of his linen shirt, his features looked tanned and rugged. Tight-fitting doeskin breeches molded the hips and thighs of an athlete, while the lower half of his long legs were encased in a pair of black leather knee boots. The overall effect was one of undeniable masculinity, of a self-confidence that bordered on arrogance, and a mastery of whatever—*or whomever*—he set his mind to.

Her eyes flew back up to his face. A rosy blush stained her cheeks when she glimpsed the unholy smile of amusement playing about his lips. Was the rogue laughing at her? she wondered in angry confusion. The possibility sent her temper flaring to an even more perilous level. Although she resisted the sudden urge to strike him, she fixed him with a withering look and balled her hands into fists at her sides.

"Get out!" she ordered as haughtily as a queen.

"I told you as how she wouldn't go with you," Mistress Burke took pleasure in reiterating. She started out the door, only to halt in surprise at the sound of Jonathan's voice.

"Perhaps you should consider the alternatives before you make a decision," he suggested to Alex, moving even closer to where she stood glaring at him with fiery outrage.

They were separated by mere inches now. He towered above her, his gaze raking over the stormy, up-turned beauty of her countenance, while her breasts rose and fell rapidly beneath her coarse gown—and the dull ache in his loins became near torturous. An invisible current passed between them; though unseen, it was no less palpable.

A warning bell sounded in Jonathan's brain. What the devil was he doing? This flame-haired little spitfire was far too comely for the job and he knew it. Once word got out that she was at Boree, he'd probably be forced to keep guard over her night and day. No woman was worth that much trouble, he told himself sternly. His purpose in coming had been to find a housekeeper who wouldn't be lured away by kisses and compliments and broken promises. And by heaven, the last thing he needed was a woman who made *him* want to throw caution to the four winds and sweep her into his arms. . . .

But it didn't matter. For all the many reasons he could think of to turn and walk away, he knew he wouldn't be leaving Parramatta without her.

"My name is Jonathan Hazard," he declared in a low tone. "My plantation is only a few miles from here. We've a large number of workers living at Boree, but your duties would be confined to the main house. There's only myself and one other to cook and clean for. We receive few visitors."

"I told you: I am no servant!" Alex protested, with far less vehemence than before. She could literally feel the heat emanating from his body, and the way he was looking at her sent an inexplicable tingle dancing down her spine.

"Perhaps not, but you *are* a prisoner."

He gave her a brief, thoroughly disarming smile. She caught her breath on a sharp intake of air.

"What I am offering you, 'Lady Alex,' " he pointed

out, with an inordinate degree of patience, "is the opportunity to improve your lot in life."

"To improve *yours*, you mean!" she retorted in a flash of spirit. She watched as his green eyes darkened to jade.

"I give you my word you'll be treated with both kindness and respect." His deep, splendidly resonant voice was laced with steel.

"And why should I believe you?"

"Because you have little choice."

Alex could not deny the truth of his words. She stared up at him with eyes wide and full of perplexity a moment longer, then abruptly whirled about. Her pulse was more erratic than ever, her head was spinning, and she was seized with the alarming urge to accept Jonathan Hazard's offer. Closing her eyes, she offered up a silent prayer for guidance. The decision she faced might well mean the difference between life and death. And she very much wanted to live.

"We've wasted enough time here, Captain," Mistress Burke insisted. "Even if the girl was willing, she'd not be allowed to go."

"Why not?" he demanded.

"We've orders to keep her here."

"Orders?" He frowned as he turned to confront her. "Whose orders?"

"How should I know?" she replied in a defensive huff. "Her papers said she was to come straightaway to the Factory and stay here. Why else do you think she was sent upriver? There's thieves aplenty down in Sydney, and far worse. Hellcat she may be, but what with her looks, she'd have been snapped up for certain the minute the ship dropped anchor." Her lips curled into another sneer when she said, "I'll wager she'd be earning a pretty penny for some 'husband' on the waterfront right about now. Yes, and spending plenty of time on her high-and-mighty back doing it."

"Wait outside," Jonathan suddenly ground out.

"But I—"

"Outside."

The matron grew red-faced with anger and opened her mouth to object. But the almost savage gleam in Jonathan's eyes cautioned her to push him no further.

"It will do you no good," she muttered, nevertheless beating a hasty retreat.

Once Mistress Burke had gone, Jonathan impulsively raised his hands toward Alex's shoulders, only to force them back to his sides again. His gaze moved over the graceful curve of her back, and he couldn't help noticing the way the narrow stream of sunlight set her short titian curls aglow. Once again, he was struck by the unexpected quality of her beauty. Whoever she was, whatever she had done, she didn't belong at Parramatta. Any fool could see that.

"Do you wish to go with me?" he asked quietly. He was satisfied when she spun about.

"How can I?" she responded in a tremulous voice, her own eyes bright with sudden tears. "You heard what Mistress Burke said. I am to stay—"

"Yes or no?" He cut her off, not unkindly.

"I . . . I was under the impression that freedom from this prison could be gained only through marriage." Although she had been at the Factory for less than a week's time, she had heard the other women discussing the many advantages of being chosen as a settler's bride. But perhaps this particular settler was already married, she told herself. *One other,* he had said. Astonished by the keen sense of disappointment the thought provoked, she clasped her hands together in front of her and cast her eyes downward.

"I'm not looking for a wife," Jonathan denied.

"Nor a mistress?" challenged Alex, lifting her head proudly once more.

"I've given you my word on that score."

"The word of a gentleman, Captain Hazard?" More than a touch of sarcasm crept into her tone.

"I've been called many things, but 'gentleman' is not a term that comes readily to mind," he replied, with a faint smile of irony, then quickly sobered again. His gaze, steady and intense and penetrating, bored down into the flashing blue-green depths of hers. "Whatever else I may be, I am no liar."

"And *I* am no thief!" she exclaimed, only to gasp in fear and startlement when his hands came up to seize her upper arms in a firm grip.

"Blast it, woman, I don't care what you've done," he asserted, with a barely controlled fury that surprised them both. "You can either take your chances with me, or else remain locked up in this hellhole for the next seven years! There's always the possibility that some rough, foul-smelling scoundrel will come along and offer you marriage, but I doubt you'd be willing to trade your bondage for the sort of 'freedom' he'd have in mind!"

Shocked into speechlessness, Alex blinked up at him. His hands burned upon her flesh even through the protection of her sleeves, and she could have sworn her heart turned over in her breast. Why should this man care what happened to her? she pondered dazedly. And even more importantly, how could she know that he was even the least bit worthy of her trust?

Eight months ago, she would never have dreamed of placing her life in the hands of a stranger ... but eight months ago, before the terrible, endless nightmare had begun, she had still been free. Now, the privileged and pampered Lady Alexandra Sinclair was gone, and in her place was Lady Alex, a transported convict with a sentence of seven long years hanging over her head. No matter how desperately she wished otherwise, nothing would ever be the same again.

You have no choice. His words echoed within the turbulent recesses of her mind. Heaven help her, what should she do? Her soul cried out for deliverance, just as it had done every single day since she had been so cruelly snatched away from all she held dear. Perhaps her prayers had been answered at last, she thought, her eyes searching the man's face for any visible evidence of sainthood. There was none. Still, this tall, wickedly attractive American might have been sent by Providence all the same. It had always been said that God worked in mysterious ways.

"Yes," she finally answered, then nodded and confirmed in a stronger voice, "yes, Captain Hazard. I will come with you!" For better or worse, the die had been cast.

"Good." His features relaxed; his gaze warmed with obvious pleasure. He reluctantly let go of her arms and asked, "Have you anything to take with you?"

"Only this." She turned away again, hurrying across to the bed. She knelt beside it and retrieved a locket she had concealed beneath the hard, narrow mattress. "It is all I have left." Clutching it in one hand, she returned to Jonathan's side. Her eyes sparkled with a combination of excitement and apprehension. For the first time in months, she dared to feel hopeful. "What if they should not allow me to leave?" she whispered, glancing nervously toward the doorway. She was certain Mistress Burke would try and stop them. The woman had made no secret of her hostility, mocking and jeering at every turn these past few days. "What shall you do if—?"

"Never fear. We Americans have a long-standing aversion to defeat," Jonathan stated dryly. He took her arm and began leading her forward. "Stay close. And say nothing."

Alex nodded in agreement. She somehow knew that if anyone could rescue her, this man could. Indeed, it wasn't at all difficult to imagine him slaying dragons at every turn. The vision brought a light of amusement to her eyes—a light that had been too long absent. Drawing strength from her new protector's confidence, she quickened her steps to keep pace with his and sought to prevent her arm from trembling within the possessive warmth of his grasp.

The matron was waiting in the corridor, poised for battle, when they emerged from the cell. She looked more formidable an opponent than ever as she rounded on them with a vengeance.

"Here now, where do you think you're off to?" she demanded, then offered a shrill, bellowing threat. "I'll call the guards, I will, if you don't—"

"Call them, then, and be done with it," challenged Jonathan. His gaze flickered contemptuously over her. "I'm sure Governor Macquarie will be interested to know of your 'hospitality.' It so happens I'm to dine with him tomorrow night." Alex glanced up at him in surprise, but his fingers merely tightened about her arm.

"The governor?" Mistress Burke repeated, half to herself. She eyed him narrowly. "Even if that be true, orders is orders!"

"You have Reverend Marsden's letter," he reminded her in a brusque tone. "In it, I have been granted permission to choose from among the women here. And I have made my choice. Now you must make yours. Either allow us to pass—or call the guards and face the consequences of your misguided actions."

His warning earned him another look of wonderment from Alex. He spoke with such authority. . . . But that was quite natural, of course, given the fact that he had once been the commander of a ship. *Capt. Jonathan Hazard.* She had little doubt that he had been able to claim total obedience from his crewmen. God willing, she thought as she held her breath and shifted her wide, anxious gaze to the matron again, Mistress Burke would take heed of his iron-willed determination.

Mistress Burke did. With nothing even remotely re-sembling graciousness, the woman finally stepped aside. Her features, never pleasant to begin with, twisted into an ugly grimace.

"Have it your way, Captain," she hissed. "Take the girl. Take her and good riddance. But don't be blaming me when the little trollop leaves you drowning in your own blood!"

"Should such a fate befall me, I promise to lay no burden of accountability at your feet," he vowed, with a sardonic half smile.

He led Alex toward the outer doorway. She instinc-tively raised a hand to shield her eyes against the sun's brightness. A strange hesitance settled upon her when she crossed the threshold, but Jonathan urged her out-side and across the central yard. In silence, they trav-eled through the front gates of the compound.

Alex turned back to stare up at the high stone walls once she and Jonathan stood on the other side. A sud-den shadow crossed her pale, heart-shaped visage. The prison had only been her home for a few days, yet she had already begun to despair of ever escaping its op-pressive darkness. . . .

"There are many who think it should be burned to the ground."

Jonathan's deep voice startled her from her reverie.

Whirling to face him again, she saw that he was regarding her closely. A dull flush crept up to her face.

"Is that your opinion as well?" she asked.

"The place serves its purpose, I suppose," he said. His expression was inscrutable as he propelled her toward the nearby wagon. "It's time we were away, Lady Alex."

"Don't call me that!" She jerked free, her eyes impetuously ablaze. "My name is Lady Alexandra Sinclair!"

"You can call a halt to the performance now," he advised, with a stern frown. He could not help noticing how much her anger heightened her beauty; the warning bell in his brain sounded louder than ever. He swore inwardly and attempted to take her arm again, but she eluded his grasp.

"I am not an actress!" she denied.

"Nor a true lady," he retorted.

"If you have any shred of decency at all, Captain Hazard, you will listen to me! My uncle is Lord Henry Cavendish, and I was—"

"Enough!" His features tightened with displeasure as he jammed the hat on his head and reached for her. Ignoring her breathless protests, he conveyed her none too gently over to the wagon, seized her about the waist, and tossed her up onto the seat. Shocked and highly indignant, she tried to rise, but he imprisoned both of her hands with one of his large, work-hardened ones and forced her to remain.

"Let go of me!" she cried hotly, to no avail.

"We'll settle this matter here and now, Lady Alex—or whatever else you choose to call yourself," he decreed. His gaze smoldered into hers. "You are no innocent, and I am no fool. I'm well aware of the fact that only the most refractory female convicts are sent here to Parramatta. I don't want to know the particulars of your crime, for that is in the past and I am a practiced believer in second chances. From this day forward, however, you will deceive me at your own peril. You will obey me, you will be a good and faithful servant, or by heaven, I'll marry you off to the first moonstruck young simpleton who comes asking!"

"Why, you—you wouldn't dare!" She gasped in disbelief, her eyes growing very round. "You could not!"

Jonathan suffered a sharp pang of remorse for having uttered the threat. She was right, of course. He wouldn't. But he would be master of his own household, and she would have to learn obedience. She was far too proud and spirited for her own good. He'd probably live to regret his decision—or die for it, he mused with bitter irony, if Mistress Burke's prediction came true.

Breathing another curse, he released her hands and strode around to take his place on the seat beside her. He was acutely conscious of her furious, reproachful gaze upon him when he gathered up the reins.

"I was speaking the truth," she declared in a tone simmering with emotion. "My uncle *is* Lord Henry Cavendish, and I *was* falsely accused! Had I believed you to be anything other than an honorable man, I would not have come with you."

"As you'll soon discover, honor is rare in Australia." He shot her a look that struck trepidation in her heart. "And for better or worse, you're bound to me for the next seven years."

"Unless I marry," she countered.

"That is always an option." He turned his head to face her squarely, his eyes meeting and holding hers in a silent battle of wills. "But my consent is required. You see, I am responsible for you now—your guardian, if you will." Oddly enough, he realized, the prospect wasn't a disagreeable one. "You cannot go anywhere, nor see anyone, without first seeking my permission. If you try to leave, you will be caught and punished. Keep that in mind, and we'll have no—"

"What you are describing is nothing short of slavery!" protested Alex. Her initial relief had now turned to dawning horror. Merciful heavens, she thought while panic rose within her, what had she done? *Gone straightaway from the kettle into the fire,* an inner voice echoed.

"It's your country's system, not mine," he pointed out grimly.

He gave an abrupt flick of the reins. The wagon lurched forward as the horses strained at their harnesses. Alex gasped, and, solely on reflex, clutched at Jonathan's arm for support. He stiffened, clenching his teeth at the wildfire that shot through him when the fullness of her breast grazed against his side. Although she blushed and hastily moved away, the damage had been done. His every instinct told him that he was in very real danger, that he should turn back and forget he had ever set eyes on this woman. But he stubbornly defied his instincts; *this* was a danger he would not flee.

Alex rode in angry, thoughtful silence beside him as they drove out of Parramatta and into the fragrant shadows of the surrounding wilderness. Her preoccupied gaze swept over the ancient eucalyptus, and she was only dimly aware of the white cockatoos that flapped overhead, shrieking like a gathering of lost souls. The sights, sounds, and smells were not yet familiar to her, for she had recently spent precious little time out of doors.

She raised her face to the sun's warmth, while her eyes clouded at the sudden memory of the journey upriver from Sydney. It had been a miserable undertaking.

Traveling by barge, she and her sisters in misfortune had been treated with very little kindness. The wind had not set fair, so that the trip had taken a day longer than expected. They had been forced to spend the night at one of the ramshackle inns along the way, where the accommodations had consisted of nothing more than thatch-roofed huts. The food they had been given proved inedible, the beds only a few patches of straw, and the washing facilities nonexistent.

But the worst of it had come when the innkeepers, grizzled ex-convicts who were now free to engage in "honest" pursuits, plied the women with rum, assaulted two of them, and then robbed the others of whatever small possessions they had. If not for her own vigilance and refusal to drink, Alex recalled with a shudder, she might well have been among the violated. As it was, she had only suffered threats and verbal abuse before the barge constable had finally made his belated entrance upon the scene.

It was a miracle she had been able to escape harm thus far. A faint, ragged sigh escaped her lips. *Thus far.* Stealing a glance from underneath her eyelashes at Jonathan, she saw that his features were still set in a grim, unapproachable mask. He looked at once well-bred and rugged, as though he belonged in two different worlds. Or a world entirely of his own making.

What manner of man held her fate in his hands? she asked herself in bewilderment, still seething over his rough treatment of her. She had accepted his offer of employment because she had believed—foolishly, it now seemed—that he would help her. Something in his eyes had compelled her to trust him. He had rescued her from the Factory, true enough, yet at what cost?

Catching her lower lip between her teeth, she shifted on the hard wooden seat with a frown of discomfort and endeavored to stay as far away as possible from a deceptively impassive Jonathan. The silence between them stretched on, broken only by the soft creaking of the wagon springs and the peculiar symphony of the forest.

Alex toyed with the idea of scrambling down and taking flight, but she knew the impulse was a foolhardy one. Even if she could manage to elude her new "guardian," where would she go? She had no food, no money, and no earthly idea in which direction Sydney lay. Escape would have to wait for a more opportune moment, she conceded with another deep and highly troubled sigh. Common sense and caution, not a surrender to harum-scarum impulses, would see her on her way back to England.

England. A sudden, sharp pain sliced through her heart. Closing her eyes for a moment, she found her thoughts drifting back to the very beginning of her ordeal. Fate had turned cruel and capricious that long-ago day in London. . . .

Aside from one earth-shattering tragedy, her life had been a charmed one. She had lived with her aunt and uncle since the death of her parents some fifteen years earlier. She could not have asked for more permissive, doting substitutes. Never having been blessed with children of their own, they showered their attention on her, providing her with a superior education, a wardrobe befitting a princess, and, most important of all, the unheard-of freedom to follow her own heart. They were, quite naturally, proud and delighted when she became the toast of London society. Even after she had spent five years in the frantic whirl of matchmaking, they had not pressured her to choose a husband from among her immense circle of admirers.

She adored her uncle, of course. Lord Henry Cavendish was a well-respected peer of the realm, a man whose advice was often sought by other members of Parliament, and even by the king himself. He was quite outspoken in his views, which were unfashionably conservative, and had thus made more than his fair share of enemies. She and her aunt Beatrice had always feared some form of retaliation. No one could have guessed that it would ever be visited upon either of them.

But it was, and with terrifying results. One of her uncle's adversaries—the fiend had not revealed his identity to her—waited until her aunt and uncle were away from London for a few days, then seized the opportunity to carry out his evil, cowardly scheme. She was abducted by hired ruffians from the very doorstep of her town house, spirited across town in a carriage, and thrust into a cell within the walls of the notorious Newgate Prison. Desperately trying to convince her jailers of both her innocence and high station in life, she was met with the horrible, startling news that an "acquaintance" of Lord Henry Cavendish's, set upon revenge, was responsible for her fate. Nothing could be done. No one would believe her.

Everything happened with dizzying swiftness after that. Within the space of twenty-four hours, she was charged with thievery, convicted as a result of false testimony against her, sentenced to death, and, by the decree of a cynical yet ultimately merciful high magistrate, ordered to be transported to New South Wales instead of hanged. She had been aware of the government's practice of shipping convicts to faraway British colonies, but the subject had rarely been discussed among the elite.

There was no class distinction among the prisoners. Prostitutes, murderesses, pickpockets . . . it did not matter, for all were judged the same. She was taken aboard one of the convict ships and imprisoned below decks with more than two hundred other women. The ship set sail from Portsmouth Harbour on an early spring morning that seemed to mock them with its placid, sunlit beauty.

The sea voyage that followed was both long and perilous; the storms and months of confinement took their toll. Many died, many more were struck ill, and a heartbreaking number were preyed upon by the more unscrupulous members of the crew. She escaped that particular misfortune because of the captain's intervention. A fairminded older man with daughters of his own, he was impressed by her refinement and intelligence. She was granted the privilege of assisting the ship's doctor, who, though as skeptical as the captain when she related her incredible tale, promised to contact her uncle upon his return to England. If not for his kindness and the duties he assigned her, she was convinced she would have gone mad.

When the ship finally dropped anchor in Botany Bay, she intended to go ashore and plead her case with the governor himself. Her hopes were dashed, however, when the captain regretfully informed her of his specific instructions that she be transferred to Parramatta without delay. She could only speculate that it was due to a prior arrangement between her unknown tormentor and the authorities back home. Other women with money or evidence of property were given their ticket-of-leave upon arrival, and were thereby free to seek employment of their own choosing. The less fortunate were given over as servants—or wives, if both parties were agreeable—to the military officers and ex-convicts deemed respectable enough to be trusted with the "gentle element" of the overwhelmingly male, mostly criminal population. Lastly, those who were either pregnant or hardened sinners, sick, disfigured, or simply too old, were sent to the Factory at Parramatta. . . .

It was still difficult for her to comprehend the events of these eight months past. And now her life had taken yet another extraordinary (and alarming) turn. Here she was, heading deeper into the wilderness with a mysterious, green-eyed stranger who, in essence, owned her for the next seven years. He could turn out to be a brigand, a rakehell, or even a cold-blooded murderer. Who would know, or care, if she suffered untold horrors while in his possession?

A frown of self-reproach creased her silken brow. It would serve no purpose to allow her imagination such a wild flight of fancy. With anger and impatience, she dashed at the single tear coursing down her cheek. She had always despised weepy females. Tears were a sign of weakness, and as God was her witness, she would *not* lose courage now.

"We're almost there," Jonathan announced a short time later. Noting her valiant efforts to keep her emotions in check, he felt another twinge of guilt. It was followed closely by a fresh surge of irritation. He wasn't accustomed to feeling guilty. Damn it all, he had done nothing wrong.

"How far is your plantation from Sydney?" Alex questioned, with a studied attempt at nonchalance.

"Much too far for you to ever consider making it on your own," he replied tightly.

"Justice will prevail in the end, Captain Hazard," she prophesied. Then she turned the full, fiery condemnation of her turquoise gaze upon him. "And when it does, you can be certain you will regret having turned a deaf ear to the truth!"

"Am I to take that as a threat, Lady Alex?" His mouth twitched, while his eyes warmed with a glimmer of wry amusement. The redheaded little vixen was very good at melodramatics. But not good enough to make him forget where he had found her.

"Indeed, sir. You may take it any way you—" She broke off with an audible gasp when the wagon suddenly pitched to one side, throwing her against him. The intimacy of the contact made her face flame. More shaken than she cared to admit, she quickly pushed away and sought refuge in her anger once more. "I swear by all that is holy, you shall rue the day you set eyes upon me!"

"In that, you may well be right," he murmured. They fell into an uncompanionable silence again. It wasn't long before the horses, sensing the nearness of familiar surroundings, accelerated their pace. The sun was hanging almost directly overhead by the time the wagon broke from the cover of trees atop a hill. The air, warm and scented with a combination of woodsmoke, animals, and a dazzling array of subtropical flora, held the faint yet recognizable sounds of human voices.

"Boree," Jonathan indicated, with a nod.

Alex's gaze, following the direction of his, widened in amazement. The whole of the plantation was spread before her like some enchanting, fairy-tale kingdom. It wasn't at all what she had expected to find.

She saw fields, green and fertile, stretching as far as the horizon, sheep grazing peacefully in well-tended pastures, and cattle and horses dotting the gentle slopes in their own respective corners of the valley. A long row of small, cozy-looking cottages flanked a tiny lane beneath the shadows of tall, swaying palms, while a short distance away stood two massive, whitewashed barns and a low-roofed stable. Workers, both male and female, went about their duties with no discernible sign of mistreatment, while several young children laughed and scampered playfully about the grounds. Flowers bloomed in profusion everywhere, their wondrous blaze of color a perfect compliment to the agrarian tranquility of the place.

Stunned, Alex looked to where the plantation's crowning glory lay. The main dwelling, though only two stories high, was no simple farmhouse. Whitewashed, with blue shutters at the windows and a veranda running the length of the ground floor, it featured a high, sloping tile roof and narrow columns that gave it a distinctly American colonial air. An orderly tangle of shrubbery grew all around its latticed base, while several thick-limbed trees shielded it from the sun's rays. The whole effect was one of simple yet elegant charm. How could such a paradise exist in the godforsaken land called Australia? she mused, her head spinning anew.

"Welcome home," said Jonathan. There was an unmistakable note of pride in his voice.

She was nonplussed when she turned her head and met his gaze again. He seemed capable of seeing a good deal more than she would have liked. Swallowing a sudden lump in her throat, she impulsively masked her confusion with defiance.

"This is not my home and never will be."

"Never say 'never,' " he cautioned in a mellow tone, "unless you're prepared to make it fact."

"I am prepared to do whatever it takes to regain my freedom!" she avowed.

"Are you?" His eyes held a challenge as they traveled over the stormy beauty of her countenance. Resisting the sudden, powerful urge to find out if her lips were as sweet and soft as they looked, he forced his attention back to the road ahead and drove the wagon down the hill.

Chapter 3

"Sweet Saint Bridget, would this be herself then?" Finn Muldoon muttered aloud, blinking in true amazement at the sight his eyes beheld. He watched as the wagon drew closer to where he stood poised, arms akimbo, on the edge of the veranda. Judging from the look on his master's face, there was something amiss.

His eyes shifted to the woman, narrowed to mere slits, then grew round as saucers again. His mouth literally fell open.

"A redhead!" he gasped, hastily crossing himself. And an angel-faced young beauty to boot. It made no sense—no sense at all.

Moments later, Jonathan pulled the team to a halt directly before the house. He set the brake, secured the reins, and climbed down. Taking note of Muldoon's oddly stuporous presence, he flung him a dark look.

"This is our new housekeeper," he announced quietly, almost angrily. "Miss Sinclair."

Alex glanced at him in surprise. It was the first time he had accorded her the dignity of a last name. But she had no time to appreciate his courtesy, however reluctantly it had been bestowed, for the Irishman hurried down the front steps now to greet her.

"I bid you welcome, Miss Sinclair," he said, his lined, weather-beaten features splitting into a broad

36

grin. "I'm called Finn Muldoon, and it's happy I am to make your acquaintance." He reached up to help her down, and she found that she could not remain immune to the twinkle lurking in his pale blue eyes. A smile, albeit a weak one, tugged at her own lips.

"Thank you, Mr. Muldoon." She allowed him to swing her to the ground. He was unexpectedly strong for someone of his age and stature. She wondered if he, too, were a convict.

"We've waited many a day for a new housekeeper," he told her while she gracefully smoothed down her skirts. "The captain here is as good as his word, for didn't he say we'd have a decent meal this very night."

"A meal?" she echoed, with a sharp intake of breath. Coloring a bit, she confessed, "I—I'm afraid I don't know how to cook." She looked up at Jonathan as he came to join them on the other side of the wagon. Her gaze swiftly fell beneath the steady, piercing intensity of his.

"You say you cannot cook?" Muldoon appealed to her in disbelief. His heart fell when she shook her head in a silent confirmation.

"She'll learn soon enough," decreed Jonathan, stopping close beside her. Inwardly he swore and wondered what new game she was playing. "Tilly can teach her."

"Aye, Captain," said the Irishman, then turned back to Alex with an air that was both kindly and disappointed. "And can you not clean as well?"

"No."

"Do you mean to tell me, girl, that you were never taught anything at all in the way of a woman's duties?" he asked, eyeing her dubiously.

"No, Mr. Muldoon, I was not!" Angrily defensive, she shot Jonathan a quick, speaking glare before informing the older man, "I am in truth *Lady* Alexandra

Sinclair! I told Captain Hazard I was no servant, but he refused to listen!"

"Did he now?" Muldoon murmured. The grin spread across his face again, and his gaze was fairly dancing with mischief as it narrowed up at his stone-faced employer. "Well then, here's a fine kettle of fish. A housekeeper who isn't a housekeeper, a servant who isn't a servant . . . and a convict who's a highborn lady. Could be we're in for a time of it, would you not say so, Captain?"

"Haven't you any duties to see to?" snapped Jonathan.

"Aye, Captain, that I have." He gave Alex a conspiratorial wink before sauntering away. "I'll be telling our Tilly she's needed in the kitchen."

Alex stared after the wiry old Irishman in bemusement. The relationship between the two men appeared to be a curious one. Perhaps they were not simply master and servant after all.

"I'll show you to your quarters," Jonathan told her. He took her arm and began leading her toward the front steps of the house.

"My quarters?" she echoed, then paled as realization dawned. "You intend for me to sleep under the same roof as you?"

"I do."

"Absolutely not!" She jerked her arm free and rounded on him in a flash of righteous indignation. "I may be a trifle naive at times, Captain Hazard, but I am not a complete babe in arms! Indeed, my eyes have been most cruelly opened of late! I demand—"

"You're in no position to make demands," he pointed out in a voice that was dangerously low and level. His eyes were suffused with a fierce, unfathomable light as they raked over her. "If I *were* of a mind to have you in my bed, Lady Alex, your maidenly protestations would not sway me at all."

She crimsoned hotly at his bluntness.

"You have no right to speak to me like that!"

"I have every right." His mouth curved into a faint smile of mockery when he added, "And know that I am not deceived by your ladylike manner. You can proclaim your innocence all you like, but I've little doubt that you are not as 'untouched' as you would have others believe."

Thunderstruck, Alex could only stare up at him for several seconds until an audible gasp finally broke from her lips. Her temper, ever precarious, flared beyond control. Without pausing to consider either the wisdom or consequences of her actions, she raised her hand to slap his infuriatingly handsome face.

But he was too fast. His own hand shot up to catch her wrist before she could strike the blow. She cried out as his fingers tightened like a vise about her flesh, and she had no time to struggle before he suddenly yanked her up hard against him. His other arm slipped about her waist.

"Take care, 'my lady,' or you may well find the flat of *my* hand on your backside," he warned, his tone scarcely more than a whisper. His green eyes burned relentlessly down into the wide, luminous blue of hers.

Alex could not look away. Pressed against the length of his virile, hard-muscled warmth, she felt herself growing light-headed with both alarm and outrage—and with something else she dared not put a name to.

And then he released her abruptly, almost as though the contact had burned him. She stumbled backward, tripping over her long skirts before regaining her balance and drawing herself rigidly erect. Her cheeks flamed anew, but she refused to retreat in the face of his bullying. The look she gave him would have withered a lesser man.

"If you ever dare to touch me again, Captain Hazard, I will see you hanged!"

"Better dead than wed," he muttered under his breath, only to wonder why that particular retort had sprung to mind. He scowled to himself and reached up to jerk his neckcloth completely loose.

"I beg your pardon?" demanded Alex. Her angry bafflement increased tenfold as she watched his eyes darken.

"I've work to do. And so have you." He seized her by the arm again, and, disregarding her vehement struggles, pulled her forcefully toward the house. "You can accompany me of your own free will, Miss Sinclair," he ground out, "or be carried over my shoulder." His threat had the desired effect of calming her; she knew with a certainty that he would not hesitate to humiliate her in such a fashion.

The interior of the house proved every bit as charming as she might have expected—or would have proven so, if she had been allowed the privilege of more than a passing glimpse of it. Jonathan immediately propelled her up a wide, curved staircase to the second floor, along a carpeted landing, and onward to a room at the farthest end. Opening the door, he led her inside and finally released her arm, though he continued to loom ominously over her.

"This is where you will sleep," he said, his glance encompassing the surprisingly large, sunlit bedchamber. "I'll have Mrs. Howarth explain your duties to you."

"In England, the servants' quarters are below stairs," she saw fit to inform him, her eyes full of vengeance as she rubbed at her arm.

"We're not in England." His own eyes fell significantly toward her coarse woolen gown, and he frowned in obvious disapproval. "You'll need some new clothes."

"I will not accept your charity!"

"You will take what you're given and be glad of it. But it won't be charity. No, by heaven, you'll earn your keep just like everyone else." He turned to leave, but paused in the doorway to offer her one last bit of advice. "Remember what I told you—it's useless to try to escape. Accept your fate. It will go better for us all if you do."

"My 'fate,' as you call it, is a gross miscarriage of justice, and I would not be worthy of the name Sinclair if I did not seek to remedy it!" Remarkably, she managed to compose herself in the next instant, and her voice was only slightly tremulous when she told him, "The very least you can do is allow me to send word of my whereabouts to my uncle. Surely *that* can do no harm."

"Agreed," he consented. Another hint of irony played about his lips when he asked, "Do you really have an uncle?"

"Of course I do!"

Her blue-green eyes filled with fire again, her beautiful head lifting in the gesture of proud defiance he had already come to know—and admire, in spite of his annoyance with her.

"Lord Henry Cavendish," she continued, "is also my legal guardian. He is a very wealthy and influential man, which is precisely the reason someone arranged to have me imprisoned. You can be certain he will do everything in his power to find me and punish those responsible for—"

"I've never been to the theater in London," drawled Jonathan, "but I'm sure your performances were well attended." His gold-flecked emerald gaze was brimming with sardonic amusement. Alex was seized by yet another impulse to strike him. Her nature had never been a particularly violent one, but this man seemed to possess the ability to drive all reason from her mind.

"How many times must I tell you, I am *not* an actress!" she said, thoroughly exasperated.

"Some critics have no doubt said so as well."

With that, he took his leave. Alex glared after him in helpless fury as he closed the door. She impulsively looked about for something to hurl in his wake, but settled instead for muttering a most unladylike oath.

Whirling about, she stood in the center of the room and made a quick appraisal of its furnishings. It was quite lovely, decorated in soft shades of rose and cream—a woman's colors, she reflected with a deep frown. Lace curtains rustled gently at the two windows, a large cherry wardrobe stood near the doorway with a matching chest of drawers beside it, while a beautifully carved dressing table sat below a gilded mirror hanging in the center of one floral-papered wall. She spied both a washstand and a folding brocade privacy screen in the far corner. But it was the bed that held her attention. A wooden four-poster, with a rose velvet canopy and a coverlet of embroidered cream satin, it looked wondrously comfortable and inviting.

Her brow cleared, and she caught her breath as a sudden wave of nostalgia washed over her. It had been so long since she had slept in a real bed. So very long.

Heaving an eloquent sigh, she turned away, only to notice a second door, this one to the right of the dressing table. She hurried across to discover where it led, but found it locked. Her eyes kindled with burning suspicion at the thought that suddenly sprang to mind.

"You scoundrel!" she said, mentally consigning Jonathan Hazard to the devil. She had little doubt that it was his bedchamber that lay on the other side of the door. That would explain why he hadn't followed the usual custom of assigning her a room downstairs. He had wanted her close by.

Your maidenly protestations would not sway me at all. Her cheeks flamed while her heart thundered in her chest. God help her, the man was probably planning to take advantage of the "convenient" arrangement that very night. So much for his silver-tongued promises of respect and kindness!

She gasped in startlement when a knock sounded behind her. Tensing with a newfound dread as Jonathan's face swam before her eyes, she spun hastily about and found herself wavering between the urge to answer his summons with a scathing response—and the more tempting impulse to ignore it altogether. She was spared the necessity of a decision, for the door swung open without any further delay.

"Miss Sinclair?" a feminine voice called out softly. Flooded with relief, Alex watched as a pretty, dark-haired woman, perhaps half a dozen years older than herself, stepped into the room. The petite brunet's face wore a smile of genuine warmth, and her brown eyes were shining congenially. "There you be. I'm Mrs. Howarth, but everyone calls me Tilly. Captain Hazard said as how I was to show you about," she announced, with a distinct Cockney accent. Her blue cotton gown was stretched tight across her belly, which, although covered by a clean white apron, was noticeably round.

"You are with child?" Alex impulsively queried, then colored in embarrassment at her own lack of delicacy.

"My fourth," Tilly replied, with maternal pride. She did not appear in the least bit offended. "My Seth and I, we be hoping for a girl this time. We've three fine, strapping sons already. 'Tis time for a change." Her smile was replaced by a slight frown of compassion when she asked, "You've just come from the Factory, haven't you?"

"Yes," confirmed Alex. Though sensing in Tilly a possible advocate, she was nonetheless wary. She had befriended other young women during the voyage from England, only to suffer the heartache of loss when they died, or the pain of betrayal when they sought to use her to curry favor with the captain. The memory sent a sudden shadow across her face.

"I would have known so, even if Muldoon hadn't told me."

"How—?" she started to ask.

"Your gown, for one," Tilly supplied, with another brief smile. "Parramatta cloth's that easy to recognize. And your hair." Again her eyes were full of sympathy. "Poor miss. How you must have wept to see it cut."

"Some of the prisoners could be heard screaming when their turn came," Alex recalled, half to herself. She shuddered involuntarily. "We were told, of course, that it was to promote cleanliness, but few doubted that it was anything other than a means of intimidation." She had, indeed, shed a few tears of self-pity afterward. Aunt Beatrice had always remarked that her hair was her best feature. What would she think if she saw it now?

"That's all done with," Tilly murmured soothingly. "You be safe and sound at Boree. No one will harm you here."

"No one?" Her eyes blazed once more as she directed a swift, meaningful glance toward the connecting doorway. "I wish I were able to share your conviction of that."

"What do you mean, miss?"

"Only that Captain Hazard appears to be far less trustworthy than I originally thought."

"Why, the captain's a right true gentleman, he is!" the other woman hastened to reassure her. "A finer master could never be found. He took me and Seth in when we'd no place else to go. And plenty of others as well."

"Did my predecessor occupy this room?" Alex demanded pointedly.

"Predecessor?" Tilly echoed in confusion.

"The former housekeeper." She watched as a telltale flush rose to Tilly's face. Her voice was brimming with sarcasm when she asked, "Was she also privileged enough to sleep within earshot of your benefactor?"

"Benefactor, miss?"

"Captain Hazard!"

"No," admitted Tilly, looking uncomfortable. She immediately brightened again and speculated, "But the captain no doubt thought you'd be deserving of such finery after Parramatta. Maggie Denby—she was the housekeeper before you—was a freewoman, and a simple, plainspoken one at that." Remembering what Muldoon had told her about Miss Sinclair's incredible claim of blue blood, she felt her curiosity growing. The poor girl didn't look or act like a madwoman, but she *was* different, to be sure. Certainly a cut above the usual sort found at the Factory. Where might she have come about such quality ways?

"So I am being treated with 'special regard,' " Alex remarked in a seething, bitter tone.

"Yes, miss. I suppose you could say that."

"I see." She did see—all too clearly. Jonathan Hazard's rescue of her had been prompted by neither gallantry nor a domestic need after all, but rather by pure, unadulterated lust. She had encountered far too many of his kind these eight months past and should have known better. Yet he had seemed so strong and kind, so dashing and intrepid. But then, she told herself ruefully, a mistake of that sort wasn't so surprising, given her circumstances at the time. It was easy to see how her judgment could have been impaired. She had been shut away inside that awful prison for seven long days and nights; desperation had made her reckless.

She drew in a ragged breath as she thought of Jonathan's betrayal. *Escape could not be postponed.* She would have to find a way to leave that very night.

"We'll have plenty of time to talk," Tilly said, stepping forward now to lay a gentle hand upon her arm. "You must be fair worn out from the trip. Parramatta's not far, but 'tis a hot day. We'll away downstairs to the kitchen. You look as how you could do with a cup of tea."

"I am a bit tired," Alex murmured, averting her gaze. It was far from the truth, of course. She was feeling quite stimulated by both fury and determination. Her mind once again raced to formulate a plan. She refused to consider Jonathan's warning. Her one thought was to get away before the worst happened.

Aware of Tilly's eyes upon her, she looked back to the kindly brunet. Perhaps Tilly could help her . . . ? Perhaps if she knew the truth . . . ? But no, Alex concluded with an inward, disconsolate frown, the woman was obviously a loyal and trusted servant. She would never agree to defy her master. Still, there might be *some* way she could provide assistance, if only indirectly.

"I have not enjoyed a proper cup of tea since I left England," Alex declared, forcing a wistful little smile to her lips.

"Well then, miss, we'll set that to rights soon enough," Tilly asserted, with a soft laugh.

"Please, you must call me Alex."

"Alex? Why, 'tis a gent's name!"

"I know," she acknowledged, her mouth curving briefly upward once more. "But I am accustomed to it all the same. I fear my aunt is the only one who still insists upon Alexandra."

"You've family back in England?" asked Tilly, leading the way toward the door.

"Yes." She started to elaborate, but decided against it. "And you?" Although she gave no clue of it, Alex was paying close attention to her surroundings while she accompanied Tilly along the upper landing. *Twenty steps to the staircase,* she counted, committing it to memory.

"I've three sisters there. And a brother, too—though the last I heard of him he'd run afoul of the law one too many times."

"How long have you been in Australia?" The stairs would pose no difficulty, Alex decided, so long as she held fast to the railing. Her eyes darted furtively about, noting what she guessed to be the drawing room to the right of the entrance foyer and the dining room to the left. She wondered if any other servants occupied quarters in the main house.

"It be nigh on to ten years now," answered Tilly.

"Ten years?" Alex repeated in surprise, her preoccupation with escape momentarily forgotten. "Why, you scarcely look old enough—"

"I was but sixteen the day I boarded the ship." She sighed and unconsciously folded her hands in a protective gesture across her belly. Reaching the foot of the staircase, she turned back to Alex with an air of nonchalance that was at once puzzling and commendable. "Arrested for stealing food, I was, and never mind that we was starving. But you'll be hearing far worse than that. They say everyone has a tale to tell. I expect you've one of your own."

"None deemed believable." There was a noticeable catch in her voice.

"I be willing to listen all the same," offered Tilly.

Gazing across into the woman's open, honest features, Alex battled a powerful urge to confide in her. She wanted desperately to have someone believe her, to be able to plead for help and understanding without fear of contempt. Yet she had given her trust once that day already, and had seen it betrayed.

"Suffice it to say that, I, too, was a victim of injustice," she replied evasively, looking away.

Tilly stared at her a moment longer, then turned and continued across the foyer to the dining room. Alex followed in her wake, still making mental notes of all she observed. Once again, in spite of the gravity of her mission, she was pleasantly surprised at the tastefulness of the room's decor. Gold velvet draperies hung at the windows, a long mahogany table and twelve spindle-backed chairs, polished to perfection, held reign in the center of the room, while overhead, suspended from a high, frescoed ceiling, was a crystal chandelier.

"I thought Captain Hazard received few visitors," she recalled aloud.

"That he does," Tilly affirmed. "But he's not a man to be caught unprepared." Pausing at the far end of the room, she pivoted to face Alex again. " 'Tis not an easy task you've set yourself. There be fourteen rooms to be cleaned and kept, and three meals a day to be cooked, though the captain's not a great one for breakfast. Mind you, you'll be getting a hand from some of the other girls, and I'll be that happy to help whenever I can. At least until the babe comes."

"You seem more than capable ... Why is it you do

not hold the position of housekeeper?" Alex queried, musing that Tilly would no doubt compare quite favorably with any of the women who ruled the dwellings of the elite back in London.

"What with Seth and the boys, I've little time for it," Tilly explained. Her eyes shone with pride when she added, "I've my own house to look after. It's small, true enough, but I hold it as dear as if it were the grandest palace in all the world."

"Of course," murmured Alex. Flushing guiltily, she transferred her gaze to the gleaming wood floor. "I should have realized you were no longer bound to your sentence."

"You'll have a good life here as well, miss," the brunet reassured her. "There's none better to be found on these shores." Releasing a small sigh, she resumed her amble toward the kitchen. "Now, we've still that proper cup of tea to see to. And then I'm to help you get started with the captain's dinner. He's got a fearsome appetite, he does. Finn Muldoon, little though he is, can put away enough food for a man twice his size. Still in all, good plain cooking's what they're used to." She gave another quiet laugh. "Since Maggie Denby took herself a husband, they've had to suffer through on their own most days."

Listening with only half an ear, Alex followed Tilly through another doorway into the kitchen. It was a spacious room, its walls painted a soft white. Sunlight streamed in through two large windows, where red gingham curtains found themselves stirred by what little breeze could make its way through the trees. There was a sink with a hand pump for washing, a giant black cookstove along the same wall, and a wooden worktable in the center of the tiled floor. A glass-doored cabinet held all the necessary pots and pans and utensils, while the foodstuffs were kept in the cool darkness of a pantry.

Alex's eyes lit with sudden interest when they fell upon the door that led outside. It might well be that she would need to make use of that exit later. . . .

She was given no further time to think about it at the moment, for Tilly carried through with her determination to first prepare a pot of tea, then set about cooking dinner. Alex, even after once again confessing her ignorance of culinary pursuits, was assigned the task of peeling potatoes. She played the part of a willing student, all the while consoling herself with the thought that, if all went as she hoped, she would be doing so for that day only. In truth, it wasn't Tilly's instructions she resented—it was the knowledge that Jonathan Hazard would be the beneficiary of her efforts.

Within an hour's time, the master of Boree and his second-in-command were sitting down to a meal that, while not fit for a king, was at least hot and filling. Alex was mercifully spared the ordeal of facing Jonathan. Tilly, mistaking Alex's restlessness for exhaustion, had insisted that she return upstairs to rest shortly before the two men arrived, and had promised to see that she was given the opportunity to bathe later that afternoon.

"I mean no offense, miss," Tilly had commented, "but I'm that sure you could do with a real bath after being shut away in that terrible place."

Alex was only too glad to seek the privacy of her room, but she did not rest. She flew across to the window and gazed down upon the buildings below. The stable, she estimated, was no more than a hundred yards away. If she could manage to slip out of the house and across the yard, she could take one of the horses. And then—and then, God willing, she would somehow find her way to Sydney.

Folding her arms beneath her breasts, she spun away and began pacing distractedly about the room. There was nothing she could do until night fell, nothing but bide her time and hold on to her courage.

She would soon be able to forget she had ever set eyes on Capt. Jonathan Hazard.

I have made my choice, he had said.

"And I have made mine!" she vowed, her blue-green eyes shooting vengeful sparks as they narrowed toward the doorway.

Chapter 4

Several hours later, Alex was again alone in her room when she suddenly leapt to her feet.

She had heard the sound of footsteps, muffled by the carpeting yet discernible all the same, in the hallway outside her room. Her eyes flew to the door. While her heart set to pounding fiercely within her breast, she held her breath and waited for the inevitable knock.

It was both forceful and abrupt when it came, giving evidence of its perpetrator's impatience.

"Yes?" she called out. She congratulated herself on her calm, measured tone.

"I'd like a word with you, Miss Sinclair." Just as she had expected, the voice resonating through the thin barrier of the door was *his*.

"I happen to be busy at the moment, Captain Hazard," she lied.

"This won't take long."

She inhaled sharply when the door opened. Her gaze flickered anxiously toward the window, where only a short time ago she had stood watching the prayed-for night cloak the plantation in darkness. She looked back to Jonathan. His tall muscular frame filled the doorway, his green eyes burning across into the brilliant turquoise of hers.

"I did not give you permission to enter, sir!" she de-

clared hotly. Facing him again was not as easy as she
might have wished. She had not seen him since morning, for he had not returned to the house until quite late.
Tilly had generously offered to serve the second meal
she had helped to cook, leaving her free to seek the privacy of her room once more. She had half expected him
to summon her at some point throughout the day, but he
had not done so.

Merciful heaven, she thought while a sudden lump
rose in her throat, she had almost forgotten how wickedly appealing he was. Dismayed to feel her body grow
warm, she stiffened and raised her head to an even
more defiant angle.

"I trust you enjoyed your first day here?" challenged
Jonathan, the merest ghost of a smile playing about his
lips.

"Enjoyed?" She visibly bristled in the lamplight. "Is
a slave expected to enjoy her bondage?"

"Tilly said you were an apt and cooperative pupil. I
was glad to hear it. She has neither the time nor the en-
ergy to maintain two households."

"While I find your concern for her quite touching, I
must remind you that *I* was not the one who requested
her assistance."

"Perhaps not," he allowed, then frowned. "But your
ignorance of your duties—or refusal to perform them—
made her assistance necessary."

His gaze darkened as it traveled boldly over her. She
had bathed and exchanged her coarse woolen gown for
one Tilly had found for her. It was of pale pink cotton,
with a very high waist, short puffed sleeves, and a low,
rounded neckline. Though not exactly haute couture, it
was a vast improvement over her previous attire. Gone
as well was the white mobcap. Her short auburn locks

curled softly about her head, making her appear at once younger and more innocently seductive.

"You look much improved this evening," pronounced Jonathan, his deep voice tinged with a slight huskiness.

"Am I supposed to be flattered by your approval?" Alex shot back. She blushed fierily when his eyes fell to where her full, creamy breasts swelled above the gown's tight bodice. Too late, she remembered the light woolen shawl she had earlier flung atop the bed. Resisting the impulse to turn her back on him, she stood proudly erect and said, "Now that you've soothed your conscience with the assurance of my well-being, I insist that you leave me to my privacy!"

"It will be my pleasure," he replied tersely. In truth, he wanted nothing more than to stay. He cursed himself for the temptation, and cursed her for looking as she did. By damn, he was well deserving of this torment. And now he would just have to live with it. "You've eaten?" he asked at a sudden thought.

"How could I *possibly* be hungry?"

"You'll manage to work up an appetite sooner or later." He turned to leave, but her voice detained him.

"One more thing, Captain," she demanded. She swallowed hard when her gaze encountered his once more. "I should like to move to a room below stairs tomorrow. I find this one not at all to my liking."

"And why is that?"

"Need you ask?" Her beautiful eyes flashing, she gave a significant nod toward the connecting doorway. "Is it not true that *your* bedchamber lies through—"

"The door is locked," he assured her, his features tightening. When he spoke again, it was in a tone laced with sarcasm—and an anger he could not explain. "Your 'virtue' is perfectly safe."

"So you deny—?"

"The arrangement will remain as it is." His eyes gleaming dully, he subjected her to a hard look. "Believe what you will, it is for your own benefit. In time, when you have demonstrated the good sense to accept your position, I will consider your request." She could not be trusted to stay put. And he wanted to protect her from the many dangers of the bush—human or otherwise. "Until then, you will be safer here."

"Will I indeed?" came her cynical retort. For a moment, it appeared he would dearly love to set hands upon her—to do what exactly, she dared not contemplate.

"Good night, Miss Sinclair," he bade her quietly. With one last frown creasing his sun-kissed brow, he left her alone, closing the door on his way out.

"*Good-bye*, Captain Hazard," she whispered once he had gone. Her eyes flew wide in the next instant when she detected the sound of the key being turned in the lock. Filled with dread, she hastened forward to make sure her ears had not deceived her. They had not. She was locked in—locked in, dash it all, her plans thwarted by so simple a maneuver.

"Now what?" She sighed dispiritedly. She could hear Jonathan entering the adjacent room. Her face flamed at the thought of what could still happen.

Scurrying back to the window, she leaned close to survey the ground immediately below. A three-quarter moon cast its silvery glow upon the thick tangle of shrubbery. It didn't look so very great a distance. . . .

Her face brightened with renewed determination. *There was still a way!*

She wasted no time in blowing out the lamp and easing the window completely open. Catching up the borrowed shawl, she settled the curve of her hips on the windowsill and swung her shapely, stockinged legs outward. She saw no sign of anyone moving about the moonlit yard. While her pulse raced, she directed one last cautious, vengeful look toward Jonathan's room.

"Someday," she vowed underneath her breath, "you shall go down on your knees and beg for my forgiveness!" It was a highly pleasurable thought, and one that served to bolster her resolve as she rolled onto her side and carefully lowered herself from the window.

Her fingers loosed their grasp on the sill. She stifled a cry as she fell earthward. Landing unharmed in an inglorious tumble of skirts amid the greenery, she allowed herself only a brief moment to recover before scrambling to her feet. She hastily extricated herself from the fragrant, clinging bushes, sent a last glance upward, and set off toward the stable.

Her eyes darted furtively about as she raced across the yard, her skirts flying up about her ankles. She reached her destination in a matter of seconds. The certainty of success blazing higher within her, she unbolted the door and slipped inside.

The smell, a combination of hay and horses and leather, reminded her of the many enjoyable hours she had spent riding with friends. She paused momentarily while her eyes adjusted to the darkness, then made straightaway for the nearest stall. The horse neighed softly at her approach.

"Easy, boy," she murmured soothingly. Although she had left the door ajar, it was difficult to see. She dared not risk lighting one of the lamps hanging from the post above. Running a hand along the top of the stall door, she managed to locate the catch. She unfastened it, swung the door open, and moved to the animal's side. He snorted and pawed nervously at the hay-strewn ground. Several of the other horses followed suit, protesting the unknown intruder.

"There now," whispered Alex. "It's quite all right. But I need your help." Searching about, she spied a bridle on a hook. She slipped it over the horse's head and led him out of the stall. There would be no time to bother with a saddle. She had never ridden bareback before, but she would not consider turning back now.

Gathering up the reins, she entangled a hand within the animal's thick mane. He shied away, and she was forced to tighten her grasp to keep from losing her balance. She tried to mount, only to be repulsed once more. Finally she lifted her booted feet to the bottom railing of the stall and hoisted herself determinedly up to the horse's back.

"Slowly," she cautioned close to his ear. She touched her heels to his flanks in a gentle but firm command. He obeyed, carrying her out of the stable and into the cool, honeysuckle-scented night air. She stole a backward glance at the main house, satisfied when she glimpsed no light. Pulling on the reins, she guided the horse toward the beckoning forest.

"Now, *go!*" she urged when they were some distance away. Once again, her command was obeyed. She gasped as the animal, taking off as though the very devil himself were after them, thundered powerfully beneath her. It was both frightening and thrilling, and she could do little more than hold tight while being borne farther and farther into the mysterious, enveloping cover of the trees.

She tossed a quick look heavenward. The sky was ablaze with the twinkle of a thousand stars, but she had no idea how to make use of them to find her bearings. *Which way was Sydney?*

The longer she rode, the more uneasy she became. She recalled Jonathan's warning about trying to make it to Sydney on her own, recalled as well his promise to find and punish her if she tried to escape. A sudden shiver ran the length of her spine. She tugged on the reins in an effort to convince the horse to slow his frantic pace a bit, but he seemed intent upon running until he could run no more. A very real fear began to wrap about her heart. . . .

Moments later, horse and rider burst from the trees into a clearing. Again, Alex tried desperately to halt the animal's wild flight. She succeeded—all too well.

The horse, responding to the sawing of the reins, suddenly stopped dead in his tracks and reared up on his hind legs. A sharp, breathless cry broke from Alex's lips as she found herself pitched backward. Losing her grip on the reins, she tumbled to the ground. She landed heavily in the grass, its thickness cushioning her fall. Still, the breath was knocked from her body, and she lay stunned while the animal galloped away into the night.

The sound of approaching hoofbeats rose in the air. Before Alex quite knew what was happening, another rider emerged into the clearing. He abruptly reined his horse to a halt, swung down, and dropped to his knees beside her.

"Alex!" She heard Jonathan call her name. His voice was edged with worry, and she would have been shocked to glimpse the fierce light of emotion in his eyes. "Alexandra, can you hear me?" He did not wait for an answer before running his hands over her shoulders, arms, and legs in a swift but thorough examination. "Are you hurt?" he demanded, cradling her against him.

"No, I—I don't think so," she stammered weakly. She peered up at him in the darkness. Resting within the warm circle of his arms, she did not yet realize that her skirt was tangled up about her thighs. Nor was she aware of the fact that her sleeve was torn and her face dirty, her bodice twisted crookedly across her breasts. She knew only that she had been afraid, and was afraid no more.

"Blast it, woman! What the hell did you think you were doing?" he ground out.

"What?" she gasped, startled at the sudden change.

"Whatever else I may have thought of you, *Lady Alex*, I did not think you a half-wit!"

"A half-wit?" Numbness gave way to indignation, which in turn provided her with all the strength she needed. Pushing away in a burst of fury, she climbed unsteadily to her feet at last. Her head spun, but she refused to surrender to weakness as a grim-faced Jonathan drew himself upright before her. "I was following the only course of action open to me."

"You little fool, you might have been killed!" His hands shot out to capture her shoulders in a hard, punishing grip. "If I hadn't come after you—"

"Let go of me!" she cried. She struggled to be free, her own hands coming up to push at his chest, but he seized her wrists and relentlessly forced her arms behind her back. He yanked her close.

"Have you no idea what could happen to you out here?" he demanded, his tone both harsh and reproachful.

"My thoughts were more aligned with what could happen to me back *there*!" she retorted, with a nod over her left shoulder. Her sense of direction was still woefully inadequate, but her meaning was well taken. "Indeed, I was willing to risk unknown dangers for those that did not require any stretch of the imagination!"

"What are you talking about?"

"You know perfectly well what I'm talking about!" Glaring up at him in the moonlight, she was too angry to be alarmed by her present circumstances. "You, sir,

with your assurances of chivalrous treatment— If ever I
was a half-wit, it was when I made the decision to go
with you!"

"Would you truly rather I had left you in that
prison?"

"Yes! If I had but known then what I know now—"

"And what is that?" He cut her off, his voice deceptively even.

"Exactly what I suspected from the very beginning. I
do not for one minute believe you installed me in the
room next to yours for the sake of my own welfare.
Even in England, Captain Hazard, such 'arrangements'
are not entirely unheard of!" She tilted her head farther
back, her eyes magnificently ablaze when she proclaimed with considerable feeling, "I will not be your
paramour!"

"I don't recall having asked."

She gasped as though she had been struck. Observing
the faint, mocking smile on his face, she grew even
more enraged. She renewed her struggles with a vengeance.

"Let me go, you scoundrel!"

Jonathan gathered her closer, then groaned inwardly
as her soft, tempting curves wriggled against his hardness. His smoldering gaze raked over the stormy beauty
of her countenance, dropped to where her breasts were
threatening to spill out of the low-cut bodice of her
gown, and traveled back up to her face.

The look in his eyes struck a chord of fear in Alex's
heart. Too late, she realized the peril she had brought
upon herself. Paling, she abruptly ceased her struggles.

But the spark of desire had already been ignited.
With a muttered oath, Jonathan lowered his head and
did what he had been longing to do since he had first
set eyes upon her. His mouth crashed down upon hers,

his arms tightening about her until she could scarcely breathe.

She moaned low in her throat—whether in protest or pleasure, she could not have said. Her eyes swept closed, her senses reeling beneath the sweet mastery of his assault. She had been kissed before, of course, but never like this. *Never like this.*

His lips were warm and strong, demanding a response. She found herself swaying against him, only to suffer a sharp intake of breath when the kiss suddenly deepened. His hot, velvety tongue thrust between her parted lips. Another moan rose in her throat as he boldly, hungrily explored the moist cavern of her mouth.

Of their own accord, her hands crept up to his shoulders. She trembled in the possessive ardor of his embrace, acutely conscious of his hard-muscled warmth against her. Her lips moved beneath his, while a new, unfamiliar longing flared to life deep within her. She had no time to think, no time to consider the possible dangers associated with being all alone with a man in the moonlit darkness. . . .

The kiss ended as suddenly as it had begun.

Alex's eyelids fluttered open. Flushed and breathless, she stared up at Jonathan in dazed bewilderment.

"No more, by heaven!" he ground out, his hands curling about her upper arms to hold her firmly away from him.

The inordinately savage gleam in his eyes prompted her to gasp anew. Why should he be angry? she wondered, shocked by his reaction. The kiss had been none of her doing. Finding no words, she could only stare mutely up at him while his voice, whipcord sharp, sliced across her in the stillness of the night.

"You're an even better actress than I gave you credit

for, yet still not good enough!" His expression grew even more thunderous, his fingers digging into her flesh. His gaze flickered hotly downward to the delectable curve of her breasts. "I cannot help but wonder how many other men you've tempted to madness, how many other poor fools you've deceived with your 'innocence.' You may have the face of an angel, but you've the charms of a strumpet, and I'll be damned if I'll let myself be taken in!"

"Why, how dare you!" she finally choked out. Her cheeks burned with righteous fury, her eyes kindling with blue-green fire. "I have never set out to deceive anyone, and I can assure you, sir, that the very last thing I want is to tempt *you*. Now take your hands off me!"

"With pleasure!" He released her at last and strode away to where his horse waited. Glaring murderously at the broad target of his back, Alex blinked back sudden tears and adjusted her bodice. She winced as a pain shot through her hip—she was sure she'd find an ugly bruise there tomorrow—but she decided that she'd be hanged before she would let Jonathan Hazard know of her injury.

"Since you have formed such an ill opinion of me, you may as well allow me to go to Sydney," she insisted, watching as he angrily gathered up the reins. The warmth of his lips still lingered upon hers, and she flushed with embarrassment at the memory of her own brazen response.

"You'll stay at Boree." He led the horse to where she waited.

"I cannot stay! Not after tonight. Not after you—"

"What happened tonight is best forgotten," he decreed tersely. His rugged features were inscrutable now, his piercing gaze hooded as he paused before her. There was no indication of the battle he still waged with himself. "But if you ever again try to escape," he warned, "I'll not be so merciful."

"Is this what you call mercy?" she challenged in furious disbelief. She folded her arms tightly beneath her breasts and glared up at him, unmindful of the fact that her actions only served to make her look all the more desirable. "Refusing to hear the truth, condemning me to seven long years of slavery, and then—then forcing your attentions on me? It is a peculiarly *American* brand of mercy, I suppose, and one that I find loathsome!"

"You were judged guilty a long time before now. I did not impose your sentence." Unable to prevent his eyes from straying again to the full, creamy swell of her breasts, he offered up yet another silent curse. "As for the last—it was a kiss, nothing more. And you were far from unwilling."

"That is not true!" she was almost too quick to deny. Much affronted, she opened her mouth to say more. But she never got the chance.

"Silence, Lady Alex, or you *will* feel the brunt of my wrath." He seized her roughly about the waist and tossed her on the horse's back. Mounting behind her, he clamped an arm about her waist and pulled her back against him. She crimsoned as her hips came into shockingly intimate contact with the lean hardness of his thighs, and she was certain she heard him draw in a sharp, rasping breath.

He reined about and set a course for home. Alex tried to remain stiff and unyielding, but she found herself increasingly tempted to lean against him while the two of them rode back through the forest. The trees were filled with a quiet thumping and rustling, sounds made by the koalas and possums and other nocturnal creatures as they foraged for food. Bats flew in the moon's soft glow above. The unseen dingo chased its prey along the banks of the nearby river. There was a strange peacefulness about the land, an age-old order to its wild and untamed beauty.

But there was neither peace nor order in Alex. Releasing a highly troubled sigh, she glanced down at the powerful arm about her waist. She could feel the tenseness in Jonathan's body, could feel the strong and steady beating of his heart whenever her back brushed against his chest. *It was a kiss, nothing more,* he had said. But was that true? she asked herself, remembering the sweetly compelling fire of his lips upon hers. Heaven forbid, had she not felt a passionate stirring of her own blood?

A sudden movement in the undergrowth caused her throat to constrict in alarm. Her wide, searching gaze lit upon one of the odd-looking animals she had observed on her trip upriver from Sydney. It was very large, bearing a faint resemblance to an oversized, long-tailed rabbit.

"Kangaroo," Jonathan murmured close to her ear.

His voice, rich and vibrant and so unequivocally male, sent a shiver dancing down her spine. She sucked in a ragged breath and tossed a look full of confusion up toward the starry panorama of the sky.

Jonathan was equally perplexed by what had passed between them that night. He wasn't a man given to either remorse or uncertainty. And yet he was feeling a healthy dose of both emotions at present.

His eyes glowed with a fierce light once more as they moved back to the woman in his arms. She was a vixen, he told himself severely. A beautiful, redheaded Jezebel who was probably well accustomed to using her body to get what she wanted. He cursed himself for a fool. He was no randy, inexperienced young stripling to be caught in a woman's trap. He had seen far too much of the world to display so little reason.

His mouth tightened into a thin line of fury at the memory of his own folly. He had lost his head; he would not make that mistake again. From that night onward, his behavior toward her would be as it should be, master to servant. He would damn well keep his distance. *No matter how great the temptation to do otherwise.*

When they arrived back at the plantation, he guided the horse into the stable, dismounted, and in stony-faced silence pulled Alex down as well. She was surprised to discover that the recalcitrant horse she had borrowed earlier had found his own way back. Sparing the animal a brief, accusatory look, she rounded on Jonathan.

"My feelings have not changed, Captain Hazard!" she declared, eyeing him narrowly in the darkness. "I cannot remain here—"

"You can and will." His tone, low and holding an undercurrent of barely controlled violence, made it clear he would brook no further resistance. Turning his back on her, he quickly lit a lamp, then slipped the bridles off both animals and began rubbing them down with a handful of straw.

Alex frowned resentfully, but said nothing while she stood nearby and watched him. Noting how the lamplight emphasized the strands of gold in his dark hair, she allowed her fiery gaze to move lower—across the broad, sinewy expanse of his back and shoulders, visible beneath the clinging fabric of his white linen shirt, and lower still ... to where every inch of his hard-muscled buttocks and legs were outlined by fitted breeches as he bent to his task. He was truly, wickedly attractive, she mused with a sudden breathlessness. Indeed, he would put the other men of her acquaintance to shame. Her cheeks grew warm at the memory of what it had felt like to be locked within the powerful circle of his arms, to be kissed with such hot-blooded fervor. . . .

Jonathan finished with the horses and caught up the lamp. When he turned to face Alex, she flushed guiltily. But she concealed it with a show of angry bravado.

"How is it you managed to follow me?" she demanded.

"You should have exercised a bit more caution," he replied, his mouth twitching. "My sense of hearing is not quite as dull as you would wish." His anger had diminished by now, and he was beginning to see the humor in the whole affair. "You were not so difficult to track. And it might interest you to know that you were headed back toward Parramatta."

"Parramatta?" Her gaze widened, then fell beneath the penetrating steadiness of his. "I—I *shall* make it to Sydney eventually, Captain Hazard." Her words were somewhat lacking in conviction, even to her own ears.

"Eventually, perhaps." He was satisfied when her eyes flew back up to his face. It required an iron will to keep from sweeping her close again, for she looked at once seductive and vulnerable with her torn, dirty gown and tousled cap of flame-colored curls. "But for now, you'll abandon all thought of escape and make yourself useful here."

"Useful?" she challenged, her voice edged with suspicion again.

"I thought we had come to an understanding in that regard, Miss Sinclair." His own manner had become distant, and there was no hint of warmth in his deep green eyes. "You'll look after my house—nothing more."

Taking her arm, he led her from the stable. She considered resisting, but she was honestly too tired to fight anymore at the moment. The day had been both long and exhausting, and the prospect of sleeping in the canopied four-poster upstairs was not at all unpleasant . . . just so long as she did so with the doors securely bolted on the inside.

Chapter 5

Alex awoke the next morning to the faint, oddly comforting sound of someone chopping wood in the near distance. Stretching languidly beneath the covers, she opened her eyes and knew a moment's panic when she didn't recognize her surroundings. Her silken brow cleared in the next instant as realization dawned. Of course, she recalled as she relaxed back against the pillow, she was at the plantation. Jonathan Hazard's plantation.

Releasing a sigh, she finally pulled herself upright in the bed. Her soft, sleep-drugged gaze traveled first to the window, then to the connecting doorway. The man had kept his word—she had passed the night undisturbed.

Mildly surprised at how deep her slumber had been, she tossed back the covers and swung her legs over the edge of the feather mattress. The white cotton nightgown she was wearing was much too large; its voluminous folds virtually swallowed her whole. But she was grateful for the loan of it just the same. The thought of sleeping naked was enough to make her blush, doubly so when she added the consideration of the bold American's proximity.

Gracefully brushing a hand through the short, luxuriant thickness of her hair, she detected the appetizing aromas of coffee and bacon wafting up from the kitchen below. She could not help but smile at the thought of Tilly. Once again, it seemed, the woman had come to her rescue.

Another sigh escaped her lips. In spite of her reluctance to play the part of Jonathan Hazard's servant, she felt honor-bound to help the kind, good-natured Tilly. And she would much rather work than sit idly about, watching the hours crawl by at a snail's pace.

She glanced down at the borrowed dress she had flung across the foot of the bed the night before. It was marked by grass stains and streaks of dirt, and was also in sad need of repair. Her eyes clouded at the disquieting memories the sight of it evoked. She moved an unconscious hand to the bruise on her hip, but it was the sudden, wickedly pleasurable warmth spreading throughout her body that served as the most vivid reminder of the previous night's "adventure."

Determinedly pushing all thought of it to the back of her mind, she stood and padded barefoot across the room to the washstand. She performed her morning toilette with a quick thoroughness, then donned a plain white chemise, an equally unadorned pair of drawers, and black cotton stockings. Lastly came the gown she had been given at Parramatta. It was ugly, true enough, yet far more serviceable than the other.

After tying on her sturdy boots and giving her hair a dozen strokes with a hairbrush retrieved from the dressing table, she moved across to the door. She slipped the bolt free—and was amazed to find that the key in the outer lock had already been turned. Had her "employer" smugly assumed she would make no further attempts at escape?

Her brows knit together into a frown, but she was still resolved not to dwell on what had occurred be-

tween them. Sailing forth from the room, she headed
downstairs to the kitchen. Her gaze was drawn to the
portraits lining the walls along the staircase. Two of
them were likenesses of attractive, golden-haired
women, one placidly maternal and the other much
younger, with a mischievous twinkle in her eye. Next to
their portraits was one of a man who looked to be an
older version of Jonathan.

She paused to survey the painting more closely. Yes,
she told herself, there were the same strong, chiseled
features, the same piercing green eyes and dark brown
hair. The man must be his father, or perhaps even his
grandfather. Whatever the case, it seemed that the Hazard men were all handsome devils. *Especially the one
who held her fate in his hands.*

Frowning again, she gave herself a mental shake and
continued on her way. Just as she had expected, Tilly
was bustling about in the kitchen. There was no sign of
either Jonathan or Finn Muldoon.

"Good morning to you, miss," said Tilly, beaming
her an infectious smile.

"Good morning." Alex returned the greeting with
genuine warmth. "I'm sorry I slept so late. I should
have—"

"No need for that. It was to be expected, seeing as
how last night was your first here. The captain's already
eaten, and Muldoon as well." She lifted the pot of coffee from the stove and asked, "Would you be hungry?
We've a fine breakfast this morning."

"It smells heavenly. And yes, I am hungry, thank
you."

"Good. If you'll but sit down, I'll be fetching you a
plate."

"You're the one who should be sitting," Alex insisted, hastening forward to gently but firmly take the

coffeepot from her. "And I am perfectly capable of waiting on myself." A soft smile of irony tugged at her lips. She had always been waited on by others in the past; while not exactly helpless, she *had* been much indulged.

Tilly complied without argument, taking a seat in one of the chairs beside the worktable. Alex poured them both a cup of coffee, then filled two plates with generous portions of bacon, eggs, and freshly baked biscuits. She sat opposite the other woman and proceeded to eat more heartily than she had done in a long time. The food was simple yet tasty, and she couldn't remember having enjoyed a meal more. The food aboard ship had been absolutely dismal, the meals at the Factory little better.

"Coleen and Agatha will be coming to help with the cleaning today," Tilly announced, smiling at her appetite. " 'Tis their habit to come Tuesday and Friday, regular as clockwork. Both have babes in arms, but the captain pays them well. And their husbands be that proud of their working in the main house."

"How many people live here at the plantation?"

"Oh, I'd say fifty or more, all told. Mind you, we've plenty of children to go around," she noted, with a soft laugh. Her eyes shone earnestly when she asserted, "The captain is a good and kind master, miss. Others would not be so. He gives all a fair chance, he does. And it is rare to see him lose his temper."

"I wonder how it is that an American came to settle in a faraway British colony," Alex mused aloud, staring toward the dark, steaming liquid in her cup. She was dismayed to realize how fascinating she found the subject of Jonathan Hazard.

"He was a ship's captain," said Tilly. "Muldoon served him even then. But I can't say what it is brought him here. He's a private man, for all his good-hearted ways."

"I—I find it strange that he has not yet married." Alex cursed the dull flush that crept up to her face.

"I've said the same to my Seth. Every freewoman in New South Wales—them not already spoken for, that is—would count herself a queen if he would but cast his eyes her way. It matters not that he's an American. 'Tis rumored that Governor Macquarie himself be trying to get him wed. To a proper English lady, I'll wager," she speculated, a rare frown of disapprobation creasing her brow. "One with a rich family and her nose always in the air."

"Am I the only convict Captain Hazard has brought here?" Alex questioned, trying to ignore the irritation she felt at the thought of the governor's matchmaking efforts. Why in heaven's name should it matter to her if the man took himself a wife, highborn or otherwise?

"There be a few others, field hands mostly, but none of them women," replied Tilly. She pushed her plate away and asked on sudden impulse, "Why did you tell Muldoon you were a true lady?" Her eyes immediately filled with contrition when she observed Alex's discomfort. "I'm sorry, miss, I should not have—"

"It's quite all right, Tilly," Alex assured her, with a rather weak smile. She hesitated a moment, then explained with carefully chosen words, "I told you yesterday that my story was an incredible one. I have not yet found anyone to believe it. Still, I offered Mr. Muldoon the truth." She watched as Tilly pondered her declaration for several long seconds before meeting her gaze again.

"If that be so, then mayhap I could help in some way."

"Not unless you're willing to assist me with an escape," Alex remarked. Her voice held little hope.

"No, miss. I—I couldn't do that," Tilly said, looking pained.

"I surmised as much. But perhaps you *could* help me get word to the governor."

"The governor, miss?" Her eyes grew round as saucers.

"He's the only one with the power to grant me a ticket-of-leave," Alex pointed out. She reached across the table and covered the other woman's hands with the warmth of her own. "Please, Tilly. All I am asking is the opportunity to send a letter. Captain Hazard need never know."

"I can't do it!" Tilly exclaimed. She pulled her hands away and got up from the table, shaking her head. "Please, miss. Don't ask me to go against the captain."

"You wouldn't be going against him," protested Alex, hastily rising as well. Her own eyes were bright with heartfelt entreaty. Although she had not intended to appeal to Tilly for help, she found herself doing so nevertheless. The unbidden memory of Jonathan Hazard's embrace, and her own pleasure in it, made the need for action even more imperative. *It was a kiss, nothing more.* An inner voice taunted her with his words, then asked whom she feared the most—him, or herself?

"He need never know!" she reiterated, her color high once more. "What possible harm can it do? Once the governor learns of my plight, he is sure to see that I am restored to my family."

"Then you must speak to the captain," Tilly advised in a calm, rational tone now. "He is a friend to the governor, and—"

"He will not listen to me." Alex sighed dispiritedly.

"Time and again, I have endeavored to convince him of my innocence, but he refuses to hear the truth."

"I'm sorry, miss. Truly I am," murmured Tilly. It was clear that she did not know what to believe. She turned and crossed to the back door, her steps slightly hurried as she went. "I've got to tend to my boys. Coleen and Agatha should be here soon. They're a good sort, they are, and will do whatever chores you ask of them."

Alex merely nodded in response. After Tilly had gone, she sank back down into the chair and buried her face in her hands. She became lost in her thoughts, so much so that she sprang to her feet in startlement when the door swung open a short time later.

" 'Mornin'," said a plump, apple-cheeked young blonde who swept inside with her long red skirts swaying and a basket of fruit over one arm.

"We're to help you in the house today, Miss Sinclair," the blonde's companion announced. She was the older of the two, and a good deal slimmer, her plain muslin dress hanging loosely about her bony frame. "I'm Agatha Willoughby, and this is Coleen O'Toole."

"How do you do?" Alex replied politely. "Mrs. Howarth told me to expect you. I—I'm afraid I am not yet familiar with the household routine."

"We'll show you how all is done, Miss Sinclair," Agatha reassured her, with a shy, tentative smile.

"You *do* have the look of a lord's darlin'," Coleen blurted out, subjecting Alex to a quick, critical assessment.

"I beg your pardon?" Alex countered in bewilderment.

"Muldoon said we weren't to make mention of that," Agatha whispered an admonishment.

"Finn Muldoon is far too full of himself," Coleen opined, thoroughly unrepentant. She ambled forward and set the basket on the worktable, then lifted her chin and told Alex, "We've none of us your fancy airs, Miss Sinclair, and I'm thinkin' you'll be that much happier here if you remember you're no better."

"Coleen!" snapped Agatha.

"Countin' yourself so fine will make things hard for you, 'tis certain," Coleen continued, persistent in warning Alex.

"I shall keep that in mind," Alex replied, meeting the Irishwoman's gaze in a silent understanding.

She had encountered other women like Coleen these past several months, women who resented the fact that she was different. In truth, she mused with an inward sigh, she couldn't entirely blame them. Though they would not believe her a true aristocrat, she at least behaved and sounded like one. They seemed to view her as a representation of the upper classes—the very ones who continued to turn a blind eye to the cruelty of shipping the less fortunate to Australia.

"And I am no man's 'darling,' Miss O'Toole," she quickly added, her mouth curving briefly upward.

" 'Tis *Mrs.* O'Toole," the blonde corrected loftily. "Sure it is, the captain will have no unmarried females about. Save for the housekeeper. We've often wondered—"

"Coleen and I will get started upstairs, Miss Sinclair," Agatha saw fit to intervene. She was appalled at her friend's impertinence—and wasted no more time before grabbing Coleen by the arm and virtually dragging her from the room.

Alex turned and directed a calculating look toward the back door. For a fleeting moment, she toyed with the notion of simply walking outside and continuing on until she reached the river. She knew, however, that she wouldn't get far before someone caught sight of her.

Judging from the sounds drifting in through the sun-glazed windows, the plantation was a beehive of activity at that hour of the day. Men were tending to the animals and the crops and the numerous, everyday chores that kept them occupied until nightfall. Women were washing and mending clothes, cleaning and cooking, and caring for their lively and ever-increasing broods. Boree was like a tiny kingdom, she mused—with Jonathan Hazard as its sole sovereign.

Her blue-green gaze sparked with resentment as it made a broad, encompassing sweep of the room in which she stood. Once again, it occurred to her that she could simply refuse to perform her assigned duties. But she told herself that the gesture would appear both childish and unforgivably small-minded. It wasn't Jonathan Hazard's good opinion she sought, of course. No indeed. Yet she had little doubt that he would somehow force her to do the work. He could be quite intimidating . . . and persuasive.

The morning wore on. After tidying the kitchen, Alex went to join the other two women upstairs. She found Coleen in the bedroom—Jonathan's bedroom—that adjoined her own. Her heart pounded erratically as she stepped through the doorway, for it struck her that she was intruding upon his private domain. Though he was absent, she could sense his presence at every turn.

"The captain's a fair tall one, he is," remarked Coleen, smoothing the wrinkles from the freshly laundered sheets she had just tucked into place on the bed. Her manner was a bit more respectful now, thanks to Agatha's stern reminder that no matter what they thought of Miss Sinclair's tip-top ways, she was still in charge of the household and could dismiss them if she was of a mind to do so.

"Did you ever see such a monstrous thing?" Coleen asked, with a sly grin. Her nod indicated the bed.

"No," Alex murmured. She swallowed hard, her cheeks coloring faintly while she surveyed the massive four-poster dominating the room. It was considerably larger than the one in which she had slept. Carved from solid oak, it towered so far above the floor that anyone without benefit of its owner's superior height would find it necessary to use a footstool to reach the mattress. The posts were a good six inches in diameter, the canopy of a heavy, wine-colored brocade, and the headboard nearly as tall as the ceiling. It wasn't at all difficult to envision the handsome, virile master of the plantation stretching out upon its more than adequate length.

Her blush deepening, she swallowed again and tried desperately to ignore the way her whole body trembled.

"Had it made special, he did," Coleen disclosed, tossing a down-filled satin comforter atop the sheets. "Shipped all the way from America. The rest of the things as well."

Alex forced her eyes away from the bed and took note of the wardrobe, chest, and other furnishings. Everything bespoke an undeniable masculinity.

"You can start on the room next door down if you like," the blonde suddenly directed as she plumped the pillows. "Agatha's gone to fetch more linens." She paused in her task to fix Alex with an impudent, knowing look. "But then, 'tis *your* room joined to the captain's, isn't it?"

"The choice of accommodations was not of my own making," Alex insisted coolly.

"Be that as it may, you cannot help but feel it an honor to be set above," said Coleen, well aware of the risk she was taking, yet prompted to take it all the same.

There had been a time, not long after her own arrival at the plantation, when she would have gladly traded her honorable situation as the wife of Paddy O'Toole for the dishonorable one as the mistress of Captain Hazard. That was before she'd had a babe and settled in, but the memory of his firm, angry rejection still stung her pride.

"An honor?" Alex echoed, frowning in puzzlement. "How so, Mrs. O'Toole?"

"Come now. We're both of us women. Why not admit you were chosen for your pleasing looks?"

"What?"

"The captain's the same as any man," Coleen maintained, with a shrug. She gave a defiant toss of her head and folded her arms beneath her ample bosom. "Do you not think we're all of us saying the same—that you must have put a fire in his blood or else he'd not have brought you here? You act as if you've never dirtied your hands. You know nothing about keeping a house. Now why else do you suppose he'd have chosen you?"

"Why, that—that's a despicable accusation to make!" Alex sputtered, all the more defensive because the very same thing had occurred to her. "If you ever again have the audacity to—"

"What will you be doing? Have me put out? Or flogged?"

The Irishwoman's features grew even more rebellious as she abruptly spun about, loosened the laces on the front of her bodice, and yanked her gown down across her shoulders. Alex gasped when she saw the faded yet still highly visible lash marks crisscrossing the pale skin of her back.

"I've been whipped before, I have!" Coleen declared almost proudly. "And clapped into irons, and starved, and even worse!" She pulled her dress back into place and rounded on Alex again. "There's little you could do to me that hasn't been done before!"

"Good heavens, do you mean to tell me you were mistreated by Captain Hazard?" gasped Alex, horrified at the thought.

"Don't be daft," the blonde charged scornfully. "It wasn't him, if you must know. No, nor anyone else at Boree. But the pain of it's not to be forgotten."

"I—I'm sorry," Alex stammered, looking away while her heart stirred with mingled outrage and pity for what the woman had suffered.

"Why should you care? You've had an easy time of it, haven't you?"

"I cannot deny that." She met Coleen's belligerent gaze once more and solemnly asserted, "But things have changed. And in spite of what you believe, it was never my intention to be 'set above' by Captain Hazard. I accepted his offer because it was the only chance I had to regain my freedom. Or at least, I thought it was," she added, with another frown.

"Then you're not the captain's woman?" Coleen demanded, obviously still skeptical.

"I am not." *The captain's woman.* Why on earth should the sound of it provoke such a tumult within her?

"If that's the truth, then you'll have a hard time living it down all the same."

"It is my hope that I will not find it necessary to do so."

"And what is it you're meaning by that?" Coleen asked, her eyes narrowing with suspicion once more as she watched Alex move back to the doorway.

"Only that my future plans hold no place for Captain Jonathan Hazard." With that cryptic statement, she left Coleen alone and headed into her own bedroom. Agatha joined her there a few minutes later, proving to be a much more cheerful companion as the two of them continued with the housekeeping chores.

When the hour of noon approached, Alex sought a well-earned respite from her labors. Agatha and Coleen had already taken themselves off to their own houses, and Tilly had not yet arrived to help her with the meal. Drawing off the apron she had earlier found in the kitchen, she tossed it across the foot of the banister and wandered outside to the front veranda.

She had enjoyed far too little fresh air and sunshine since her imprisonment. There had certainly been an ample supply of it before she had reached Australia. Weather permitting, most days on board the ship had been spent above decks, washing and mending, taking a turn along the rail, or simply reveling in the all too brief freedom that was such a stark contrast to the cramped darkness below.

Her eyes sparkled with ironic humor as she strolled across to one of the columns and idly curled an arm about its slender, whitewashed breadth. Aunt Beatrice would scarcely recognize her now. All those years spent avoiding the sun, bleaching away freckles with buttermilk, and never venturing outside without virtue of a hat and gloves . . . There had been no buttermilk available to her these eight months past, no hats and gloves, and in truth, no inclination to bother about such trivial matters. While her skin was still smooth and unblemished, it had taken on a soft golden hue that would have been considered quite unfashionable back in London.

"Good day to you, Miss Sinclair."

Drawn from her reverie, she turned her head and saw Finn Muldoon sauntering toward her. He was an odd little man, she reflected, but not at all unlikable. She recalled what Tilly had told her about him. Now that she knew he had served Jonathan Hazard for a number of years, their relationship wasn't such a mystery any longer.

"Good day, Mr. Muldoon." Lowering her hand to her side, she straightened and watched as he stopped to peer up at her from the foot of the steps.

"Would you be wanting a look around?" he offered, with his trademark grin. Dressed in a pair of white canvas trousers and a short blue jacket, he looked as if he were still ready to pass along the order to weigh anchor.

"That would be very nice, thank you, but I'm afraid I am waiting for Tilly," she answered, her gaze moving past him to search the nearby row of cottages for any sign of her good-natured instructor.

"She'll be coming a bit late today," the Irishman told her. "Sent a message, she did, saying you were to do as you pleased for a bit."

"But what about your dinner?"

"The captain's not yet ready for a meal. As for myself," he proclaimed, climbing up to gallantly offer her his arm, "I'd be a cross-eyed loon for certain if I missed the chance to parade about in the company of a beautiful woman."

Her mouth curved upward in wry amusement. Sparing only a perfunctory glance back at the house, she accepted his arm and accompanied him down the steps. They set off across the yard, with the sunlight filtering down upon them through the trees and the warm, aromatic breeze caressing their faces.

"We've a fine place here, Miss Sinclair," Muldoon remarked, sweeping his hand outward in a grand gesture. "The finest anywhere, to my way of thinking."

"Including Ireland, Mr. Muldoon?" she challenged, with a faint smile.

"Never be asking a true son of Eire such a question," he cautioned in mock soberness.

"What does the name Boree mean?" she suddenly thought to inquire. Her gaze was bright with interest as it traveled about the grounds, which were virtually deserted now due to the midday break. Everything looked at once natural and well ordered. It was indeed a fine place, she mused, then felt a traitor to herself for having judged it so.

" 'Tis an aborigine word—'the enduring one.' The captain chose it for good luck."

"I've not yet seen any of the aborigines. We were told of them, of course, during the voyage."

"And what is it you were told?"

"That they are a strange, secretive people who practice sorcery and worship the dead," she replied, with an involuntary shudder.

"Sorcery?" He smiled and shook his head. "Not in the way you'd be thinking. They're deeply religious, they are, and hold that magic is in the land itself. 'Tis said they believe the stars above are but a road along which the ghosts of the dead traveled. The past is sacred to them, you see." His smile faded, his eyes filling with regret when he told her, "The sad fact is, you'll be seeing few enough of them . . . because they've been pushed out of the way."

"By men such as Captain Hazard?" There was a note of indictment in her voice.

"It happened long before the captain set his mind to leaving the sea," Muldoon gently disputed. "If you're after blaming anyone, you'd best look all the way back to Captain Phillip with his first settlement on these shores. 'Twas England herself tried to 'civilize' the natives. She brought the smallpox as well as the greed."

Alex frowned and looked away, unable to think of a

response. They lapsed into silence for a few moments after that. Muldoon started regaling her with stories about the difficult first days of the plantation as he escorted her past the barns and the stable, on past the homey little cottages to a vast, emerald green field dotted with plump white sheep. She felt another sharp pang of homesickness as she gripped the upper rail of the fence and allowed her gaze to move slowly over the field. The scene could easily belong in the very heart of England.

"The finest wool in all the world," said Muldoon, his tone brimming with pride. He lifted a foot to the bottom rail and folded his arms leisurely across the top one. "We've a wagon full waiting to head down to Sydney at first light tomorrow. Merino it is, first raised by John MacArthur nigh on to thirty years ago at Parramatta. But then, you'd be knowing that already, wouldn't you, Miss Sinclair?"

"No, Mr. Muldoon, I would not," she confessed, her eyes clouding at the mention of Parramatta. "I knew next to nothing about Australia before I left England, and I learned little more on the journey here." The ship's surgeon had generously allowed her the loan of what few books he had brought with him on the voyage, but they had been volumes of either English history or medical instruction.

"Did you not weave the cloth while at the Factory?"

"No. I—I was locked away in a cell most of the time. It was by prior arrangement, so I was told." She started to explain in detail, but decided against it. With a sigh of weary resignation, she told him, "The whole story is one of betrayal and injustice, and I'm quite sure you would find it as implausible as everyone else has done. Suffice it to say that had it not been for Captain Hazard, I might well have spent a good many weeks or months in that prison." Perhaps even forever, she thought, then mentally scolded herself for having so little faith. Eventually her uncle would find her. He would find her and take her back to England, and she could forget everything that had happened since that awful day in London. *Everything?* an inner voice mocked. Her fingers tightened about the rail.

"So you're beholden to the captain," the old seaman beside her murmured.

"Not in the way others here seem to believe," she was quick to deny. Her eyes were full of fire when she turned to him and avowed, "I am no trollop, Mr. Muldoon!"

"I would never have thought it to be so," he declared in all honesty. Flashing her a conciliatory smile, he met her fiery turquoise gaze with his lively pale blue one and said, "You are a lady, true and proper, and I'll be rearranging the face of any man who says different." His words had the desired effect of calming Alex's temper.

"You, sir, are a silver-tongued rogue," she pronounced, a soft laugh escaping her lips.

"Sure, and haven't I been called worse?"

Having reached a better understanding of each other, they started back toward the house. Muldoon left her at the front veranda with the announced intention of finding his master. She gathered up her skirts and headed inside, certain that Tilly would have arrived by that time.

"Tilly, I—" she began as she swung open the door to the kitchen. She broke off with a gasp when she found not the expected Tilly, but a deceptively impassive Jonathan.

"Tilly's not here yet." He stated the obvious. His green eyes darkened to jade at the sight of her, but he offered no hint of warmth as he folded his arms across his chest and stared at her from the other side of the worktable.

"What is it you want, Captain Hazard?" she demanded, with a valiant attempt at composure.

A soft blush stained her cheeks, while inwardly she groaned in dismay as the memory of his kiss filled her mind. It didn't help matters any that he looked so attractive at the moment—in an earthy, hot-blooded way. His dark hair waved rakishly across his forehead, his shirt was unbuttoned halfway down to where it was tucked into his breeches, while a thin sheen of perspiration glowed upon the taut, bronzed skin revealed by his open collar and rolled-up sleeves. He might have been mistaken for a common field hand. But no, she thought as her breath caught in her throat, there was nothing *common* about him.

"A meal would be nice," he drawled, his deep-timbred voice resonating throughout the room.

"Would it?" She drew herself up proudly, defiantly erect, and informed him, "I'm afraid you'll have to wait until Mrs. Howarth arrives. You could, of course, entrust your fate to me in that regard, though I'm sure you would be reluctant to do so. After all, I might very well poison your food if given half the chance." Her color deepened when he allowed a smile of pure amusement to touch his lips.

"I'll be more careful in the future," he promised, then quickly sobered again. "The truth is, I came to tell you that I'll be away this evening."

"Away?" she echoed.

"I will not return until tomorrow." He did not elaborate any further, except to say, "I'm leaving Muldoon in charge. You're to stay in your room once darkness falls."

"Am I to be kept a prisoner above every night?" Her eyes flashed with indignation at the thought.

"Until you can be trusted."

"Then you had best clap me in irons and be done with it, for I will never surrender to you!"

"You will," he decreed in a tone laced with steel. "Here and now." His eyes held a dangerous gleam, and his features were grim as he moved slowly about the worktable to advance upon her. She instinctively retreated, her own gaze wide with that strange combination of fear and excitement she had felt the night before. "My patience is wearing thin, Miss Sinclair."

"As is mine!" she retorted bravely, then gasped when her back came up against the immovable barrier of the wall.

"You accepted my offer. And by heaven, you'll live up to your part of the bargain."

"We made no bargain between us!" Her pulse gave a wild leap as he came to a halt immediately before her. She turned to flee, but he lifted a hand to the wall, blocking her avenue of escape with his arm. Her eyes flew up to his face.

"Do you not yet realize that this is the safest place for you?" he demanded, sorely tempted to shake her for emphasis, yet afraid of what else he might end up doing if he dared to touch her. "Damn it, woman, the whole of Australia is full of men completely lacking in principle or—" He broke off with another muttered curse, then sought to rein in his temper while pointing out in a quiet, measured tone, "You could well find yourself the captive of some black-hearted bastard who wouldn't think twice before tossing your skirts above your head!"

Shocked, Alex crimsoned from head to toe. But she quickly recovered, her own temper flaring to match his.

"And why should you be so concerned with my wel-

fare?" she countered. "You don't know me! You don't
know anything about me!"

"I know all I need to know. And like it or not, I am
responsible for you now."

"How very noble!" She angrily crossed her arms beneath her breasts and tilted her head back to fix him
with a hot, furious glare. "When I agreed to go with
you, I had no idea I would be trading one prison for another."

"I never misled you." His smoldering gaze raked
over the delicate, becomingly flushed contours of her
face. "No, nor promised you anything other than fair
treatment."

"You may keep your promises, Captain Hazard. Yes,
and you may keep your noble intentions, and your
cooking lessons, and—and your fine bed!" She regretted the words as soon as they were out of her mouth.
Mortified, she watched as a slow, mocking smile spread
across his ruggedly handsome countenance.

"I find the direction of your mind quite fascinating,
Lady Alex."

"You didn't choose me for my *mind*, Captain Hazard,
and we both know it!" she recklessly shot back. She attempted to push past him, but he raised his hands to her
shoulders. It was a mistake.

Alex caught her breath upon a gasp and looked up at
him again. His eyes burned down into hers. For several
long moments, time stood still.

And then, reason gave way to temptation once more.
Throwing all caution to the winds, Jonathan ground out
an oath and swept her masterfully against him. She
gave a breathless cry of startled protest, raising her
hands to push at his chest, but he would not be denied.
His powerful arms tightened about her supple, wrig-
gling curves like a vise. His mouth descended upon hers

with such captivating fierceness that her legs threatened to give way beneath her.

Merciful heaven, not again! she thought, defiance and desire battling within her. Her head spun dizzily. That same warmth she had felt once before returned to spread outward from the vicinity of her abdomen as he kissed her deeply, passionately. She was all too conscious of the feel of his virile body against her curves, of his manly scent and the heat surging through every inch of his tall, hard-muscled frame.

Her hands trembled as they crept up to his shoulders. Her lips parted beneath the ardent, demanding pressure of his, and she moaned softly when his tongue set up a hungry exploration of her mouth. She was given no time to think, no time to remember the guilt and humiliation she had felt after the previous kiss they had shared. The current embrace was all flash and fire. *And the consequences be damned.*

Another low moan rose in her throat when one of his hands stroked impatiently downward. His strong fingers closed upon the well-rounded curve of her bottom with bold familiarity, urging her even closer. Her face flamed as she felt the undeniable evidence of his arousal against her belly, and she gasped anew when he lifted her higher in his arms and allowed his hot, branding lips to trail downward along the silken column of her neck to where her pulse beat at an alarming rate of speed at the base of her throat. His mouth moved lower still, roaming across the tops of her breasts as the full, creamy flesh swelled above the modestly scooped neckline of her bodice. She gasped again and again, certain that her blood had turned to liquid fire in her veins.

Swaying against him in unspoken surrender, she entwined her arms about the corded muscles of his neck. Her eyes swept closed once more, her head falling back while the world receded and the newly awakened yearning held her enthralled. It was madness, sheer, intoxicating madness, yet she could find neither the strength nor the inclination to put a stop to it. . . .

The sound of approaching footsteps outside the door brought them both crashing back to reality. Alex struggled to regain control of her breathing as she was hastily, albeit reluctantly, set back on her feet and released. She raised one unsteady hand to the wall for support, while the other fluttered up to where her heart pounded so erratically within her breast. Her beautiful eyes were bright with mingled passion and bewilderment as they met the steady, deep green intensity of Jonathan's. He gave her one last penetrating look before turning to face the woman who had interrupted their fiery embrace.

"Oh, I—I didn't know you were here, Captain," Tilly stammered when she opened the door. Her surprised gaze shifted from Jonathan to Alex and back again. Though she could not help but notice Alex's high color, she did not remark upon it.

"I was just leaving," Jonathan announced.

"We'll be having your dinner ready soon," Tilly assured him.

"I'm not hungry." He declined with a faint smile. "And I've got business elsewhere." He looked toward Alex again, warning grimly, "You'll do as Muldoon says while I'm gone, understand?"

"Perfectly!" she retorted in a low, seething tone. Pained that he could treat her with so little regard after the intimacy they had just shared, she flung him a murderous look. Apparently unscathed, he turned on his booted heel and strode outside.

Once he had gone, Tilly closed the door and turned to smile apologetically at Alex.

"I would have come sooner, but my Jamie—he be the

eldest—took it in mind to chase after a lizard and got his finger cut for all his troubles. Nothing would do but that I cuddle him awhile. And then my youngest, Will, set up such a ballyhoo for his dinner that his poor father took himself back to work with nothing but a cold slice of bread to stick to his ribs. I do hope you've not been waiting too long, miss?" she asked as she tied on an apron.

"No," murmured Alex. "I've not been waiting too long." Shaking her head numbly, she wandered back to the worktable and sank down into a chair.

"I'm glad to hear of it. Anyway, I expect Muldoon will be wanting a hot meal, even if the captain's decided against it." She set about gathering the ingredients, her eyes full of silent, knowing compassion as they moved frequently to the younger woman. Not even a team of wild horses could drag out of her what she'd seen when she'd opened the door. No, and she wouldn't be telling her Seth, either, for wouldn't it be just like a man to jump to the worst conclusions?

Still shaken from her latest encounter with Jonathan, Alex sat in preoccupied silence for a few moments. She couldn't believe it had happened again. How could she have been so weak-spirited as to let him touch her that way? She flushed with embarrassment. God help her, she had actually *wanted* him to do it. She had wanted him to sweep her into his arms and kiss her until she forgot all else save him. The memory was even more shameful and disconcerting than the one she had been trying to forget all day long.

Panic rose within her. What would happen the next time? And the next? She was no baseborn little doxy to be toyed with. No, indeed. She was Lady Alexandra Sinclair. She didn't belong at Boree; she didn't belong in Australia at all. And she most assuredly didn't belong in the arms of an arrogant, green-eyed American who treated her with such a shocking lack of respect.

She had to get away. Now. Before it was too late.

Pulling herself up from the chair, she wandered past Tilly to take up a stance at the sink. She scarcely realized what she was doing as she began pumping water into a kettle. *We've a wagon full waiting to head down to Sydney at first light tomorrow.* Her hand stopped in midair, her eyes sparking with renewed determination when she suddenly remembered Finn Muldoon's words.

Of course—the wagon! she told herself. Fate had finally proven kind. It had given her the gift of Jonathan's absence as well as a means to get to Sydney. It was up to her to find a way to take advantage of the gift. And find it she would.

Chapter 6

Alex crept gingerly out into the darkened hallway. A smile of triumphant satisfaction tugged at the corners of her mouth when she spied the sleeping figure of her "guard" at the top of the staircase, but she cautioned herself against overconfidence. She still had to make her way out of the house and across the yard. And even if she succeeded in concealing herself in the wagon, her absence would eventually be discovered and a search called for. Sydney was a good many miles downriver; there was always the possibility that someone would find her before she reached the city. She knew she wouldn't be able to rest easy until she was finally standing before the governor. That *he* would believe her story, she was certain.

Closing her eyes for a moment, she offered up a silent prayer for both the strength and the courage to face whatever lay ahead. This time, she would not fail!

Amazingly, she marveled with a shake of her head, everything had proceeded according to plan thus far. Finn Muldoon had given his full cooperation when she had offered him wine with the evening meal and an ample supply of his master's best brandy afterward. Tilly had already gone home by that time, leaving the two of them alone in the house. They had enjoyed a pleasant conversation before Muldoon—apologizing for the need and obviously beginning to feel the combined effects of the wine and brandy—had locked her in for the night. Since she had secretly unlocked the connecting door between Jonathan's bedroom and her own, she had not protested his action—and had even graciously assured him that she understood he was only carrying out the orders he had been given.

She had remained awake throughout the night. And then, a short time ago, when the sky had glowed with the first faint stirrings of the dawn, she had hastened into Jonathan's room to make use of her prearranged exit. Her eyes had strayed nervously toward the massive oak bed, as though she half expected to hear its owner's deep-timbred voice reaching out to her in the darkness. A strange melancholy had gripped her heart when his image rose in her mind, but she had staunchly pushed it aside and slipped from the room.

She felt a sharp pang of remorse as she now moved slowly past Muldoon, whose resounding snores drifted up to her from where he lay sprawled, dead to the world, across a chair. It troubled her greatly to have played such a trick on him. Yet she'd had little choice. Surely he would forgive her when he discovered that she had been telling the truth all along, she thought with an inward sigh. He and Tilly had both been so kind.

Careful not to make any noise as she descended the stairs, Alex made straightaway for the kitchen and the back door. She caught up a small bundle of food before easing the door open and stepping outside. Just as she had done upstairs, she paused to close the door behind her. She was determined to leave no visible evidence of her departure. God willing, no one would even know she was gone until much later.

The air was cool and sweet at that early hour of the day, and she inhaled deeply before racing across the yard to the barn. The wagon was waiting exactly where she had last seen it. Her hands were shaking as she gathered her skirts above her knees, climbed up to where the soft wool had been piled higher than a man's head and covered with a canvas tarpaulin, then pressed herself flat so that she could burrow, feetfirst, beneath the aromatic, fleecy mass. Once in place, she pulled a thin covering of the wool over her head and settled down to wait.

It wasn't long before her ears detected the sound of voices. While she lay tense and motionless, scarcely daring to breathe, workers hitched up the team of horses and secured the tarpaulin with a crisscrossing of ropes. The driver climbed up to the wagon seat, and, after exchanging a few more words with the other men, finally snapped the reins together above the horses' heads and bellowed a command. The wagon lurched forward, the wheels bouncing and the wood creaking in protest as the driver set a southeasterly course beneath a clear, rose-hued sky.

Alex expelled her pent-up breath in a long, ragged sigh. She had done it! She was on her way to Sydney at last. She would never again have to face the sort of hardship and degradation she had endured these eight months past, never again have to bend herself to the will of another. And she would never again see Jonathan Hazard. *That* particular prospect should have filled her with intense pleasure. But inexplicably, it did not. . . .

The day's journey proved to be every bit as difficult—perhaps even more so—as she had feared. It was hot lying amid the wool, and the smell was suffocatingly strong. An hour or so after leaving the plantation, she opened the bundle she had brought with her. She drank deeply from the bottle of water, but she found that she had little appetite for the bread and cheese.

The constant swaying motion of the wagon served to make her feel nauseous. Still, she bore her discomfort in silence. She even dozed off for a while, only to awaken with a start when the wheels jolted over a particularly deep rut in the road. Pulling the wool away from her face, she drew in a long and grateful breath of fresh air. Her gaze traveled over the passing landscape, and she tossed a look above to note with some surprise that the sun was already blazing directly overhead.

Morning gave way to afternoon. Alex hastily concealed herself once more whenever she heard other wagons or horses approaching. Her constant companions, aside from the heat and motion, were the perennial croaking of the cicadas and the birdsongs drifting heavenward on the wind. Twice, the driver pulled the wagon to a halt in order to let the horses rest. She was especially careful to keep herself hidden at those times, all the while battling the powerful urge to flee her oppressive cocoon and set out on foot.

The trip seemed endless. She could not have said exactly how long she lay quiet and miserable in the wagon. Just when she was sure she could bear no more, she caught the distinct, salty smell of the sea. They were approaching their final destination!

She sprang into action at last. It was no easy task to scramble free of the mountain of wool and pull herself upright, but she determinedly did so. She hesitated only an instant before jumping from the slow-moving wagon. Landing in a patch of thick grass beside the road, she fell to her knees and cast a swift, worried glance toward the driver. Satisfied that he had not seen her, she quickly climbed to her feet and shook her skirts down into place. Her eyes sparkled with the assurance of victory when she observed the city rising before her in the near distance.

"Thank God," she whispered. Several conflicting emotions played across her face as she stood there in the wagon's wake, but the only one she would acknowledge was relief. Though feeling perilously light-headed from both hunger and fatigue, she gathered up her skirts and hurried toward the nearby forest. She would wait until the wagon was a good distance ahead, then continue along the road. With any luck, she would spend that night beneath the governor's roof. As a freewoman, not as a convict or a servant . . . not as Jonathan Hazard's plaything.

Sydney. The very birthplace of Australia was nestled between low, tree-darkened hills and the sea. Here, less than forty years ago, the first shiploads of convicts had literally carved a new life from the rocks. That early settlement of tents and log huts had evolved into a flourishing city (though small by English standards) where two-storied brick and stucco houses sat in neat rows with gardens and picket fences and other markings of domesticity.

Not that all was tranquil; to be expected, there was another side to Sydney as well. Down along the waterfront, the worst elements of the largely criminal population had given rise to brothels, taverns, gaming houses, and slums. Even with soldiers on constant patrol, it was next to impossible to keep the peace among people who felt they had been cast out of paradise to spend the rest of their lives in hell.

The heart of the settlement, of course, was the harbor. Guarded by spectacular cliffs, its glistening, deep blue waters were nearly always crawling with a wide variety of ships—sealers and whalers, merchantmen and military frigates, and the convict transports, which still arrived on a regular basis with their unwilling human cargo. The vessels would pass more than a dozen small islands on their way into port, islands that had, in the not so distant past, been sacred to the aborigines. On several of these jagged, desolate-looking keys, the most insubmissive of the convicts had once been kept in chains and placed on starvation rations. It was said that their ghosts tried to snatch present-day crewmen from the decks of passing ships.

But Alex cared nothing about ghosts, nor about the city's rich and colorful history. Her mind was set on a single purpose—to find the governor's house. She was oblivious to the many curious stares and admiring glances she attracted as she made her way through the noisy, bustling crowd on Market Street. The air was choked with the smell of fish and smoke and unwashed bodies. All about her, there was commotion. Fresh produce, clothing, household goods, and a wide variety of other items were being offered for sale in wooden stalls set up for that purpose. The voices of both buyers and sellers joined with the usual sounds of the city to create an uproar that intensified her growing trepidation.

Dear Lord, which way? she wondered, rudely jostled by the throng of marketgoers whenever she tried to move. Even if her sense of direction had been more reliable, she would have found little use for it. She had been in Sydney only once before, on the day she had been taken from the transport ship and hurriedly transferred to another boat for the trip upriver to Parramatta. As a result, none of the city's landmarks were familiar to her.

Her situation showed no immediate sign of improvement. She realized that she'd stand little chance of success without someone's help. Her wide, troubled gaze searched the crowd. Spying a gray-haired woman smiling affectionately down at a small boy in front of one of the stalls, she pushed through the crowd to her side.

"Please," she entreated, gaining the woman's attention with a gentle but insistent tug on her sleeve, "could you tell me where I may find Governor Macquarie's residence?"

"The governor?" The woman's eyes filled with obvious disapproval when they took in the sight of Alex's torn, dirty dress and tousled mass of curls. "What would you be wanting with a man such as him?"

"I must speak with him right away!"

"Oh, *must* you?" the woman scoffed. In contrast to the gentle smile it had formed only moments ago, her mouth now curled into a sneer. "Well, then, you'd best be getting yourself spruced up a bit if you're to take tea with Old Stringybark!"

"Please, you don't understand! I have to—"

"Away with you, or I'll call the watch!"

"No, wait!" Alex implored, but to no avail. She watched in helpless frustration as the woman seized the boy's hand and pulled him along with her to another stall.

Frowning, she turned and anxiously looked about for someone else to try. There were so many people. Surely one of them would have enough compassion to help her. She caught her lower lip between her teeth and cast another quick glance up at the sky. The sun had already started its descent toward the endless blue of the horizon. It would be dark soon. What would she do if night fell and she still had not achieved an interview with the governor? Panic threatened to strike again....

"Are you in trouble, girl?"

She spun around at the sound of a woman's voice behind her, only to discover a slender young blonde clad in a tight, slightly worn red gown that was cut a bit too low in the bodice. The woman's hair was tangled and falling down out of its pins, and her eyes were dull and red-rimmed, but she at least appeared willing to help.

"I—I am trying to find my way to the governor's residence," declared Alex, raising her voice to be heard above the surrounding din. She was nearly knocked off balance by a passerby carrying a basket laden with sponges. "Please, can you tell me how to get there?"

"It isn't far." Her gaze narrowed as it made a swift assessment of Alex's own less than elegant attire. A faint smile touched her lips before she offered, "I can show you the way soon enough."

"Thank you," Alex replied gratefully.

Her blue-green eyes were shining with hope as she followed the young woman past the remaining rows of open-air stalls. They soon emerged from the crowd. Without a word, the blonde turned at the end of the street and headed down a much narrower avenue leading toward the waterfront. The buildings began to take on a somewhat shabby, ramshackle appearance, and the people they passed looked to be a much coarser sort.

Alex felt a growing uneasiness as she glanced about. She quickened her pace in order to catch up with her taciturn guide.

"Are you certain this is the right way?" she asked.

"Certain enough," the woman replied, with a noncommittal shrug.

"But, I . . . Surely the governor's house is located a bit farther away from the wharves," she remarked, searching the other woman's face. It was oddly expressionless.

"We've a stop to make first."

"A stop?" Her brows drew together in a frown of bewilderment. "What are you talking about?"

"It won't take long," was all the woman would say.

Dissatisfied with her response, Alex wanted to interrogate her further. But they were by this time entering the infamous area known as "The Rocks"—and the sights she beheld were enough to make her forget, at least for the moment, the other questions that rose in her mind.

Ironically, this section of the waterfront was where the proposed colony of New South Wales had become a reality. The first store, hospital, prison, and barracks had been built along the shore; now, it was inarguably the most miserable site in all the city. Here, prostitutes eased the loneliness of sailors and often got their throats cut for their troubles, razor gangs preyed upon the weak and incautious, men were shanghaied to become unwilling, ill-treated members of ships' crews, and convicts of every age and description toiled in the bond stores and warehouses from dawn till dusk with very little hope of deliverance.

Alex's gaze widened with shocked dismay as she observed women posing half naked in the doorways. They laughed and called out suggestively vulgar invitations to the men who passed by. On one of the wharves opposite, two sailors were fighting over a keg of rum; on yet another, a ship was being loaded with the precious merino wool that would be taken back to England. The tall masts of windjammers bobbed to-and-fro in the harbor, while the long, gathering swells of the ocean crashed in waves that left white foam boiling and hissing on the sand.

In spite of the salt-tinged wind whipping across the docks, the smells were stronger and more offensive than ever before, noted Alex, wrinkling her nose in disgust. And although darkness had not yet fallen, the taverns were already overflowing with patrons intent upon drowning their sorrows in a tankard of ale. Some of these early revelers spilled out onto the cobbled streets, staggering drunkenly toward the various "houses of vice," which seemed to flourish in every port city throughout the world.

Alex had seen enough. More alarmed than she cared to admit, she seized the blonde's arm in a firm grasp and literally pulled her to a halt.

"I demand to know where we are going!"

"To the governor's house," the woman replied, jerking her arm free. There was a strange glint lurking in her eyes, and she offered Alex a smile that was disturbingly cryptic.

"I cannot believe the governor—" Alex started to protest, only to break off with a startled gasp when a passing man suddenly lunged for her.

"Come 'ere, girl!" he growled. His speech was slurred, his coarse features suffused with bright red color, and he smelled as though he had not bathed in weeks. Alex struggled to pry his greasy fingers from about her arm.

"Let go of me!" she commanded in furious indignation, pulling and twisting in his grasp.

"You're a flash piece of mutton, you are," he opined, with a malignant rumble of laughter. He grabbed her other wrist and yanked her up hard against him. While not a large man, he was nevertheless quite strong, his many years at sea gifting him with a wiriness far superior to most other men his size.

Alex gave a sharp cry of protest. Her angry, frightened gaze flew to her companion. But the woman offered no assistance; she merely stood watching with an odd look of detachment on her face.

"Help!" screamed Alex, her struggles intensifying as her malodorous captor sought to press a wet kiss upon her mouth. "Please, someone help me!"

"No use in that," the man jeered. "It's catch as catch can in this place." Once again, he tried to kiss her, but she jerked her head away in time to prevent it and cried out in another futile attempt to summon aid. She did not know that screams were an all too common occurrence here. Though she attracted several curious glances, and some smiles as well, no one was willing to interfere in what they judged to be a simple disagreement between a sailor and his chosen *fille de joie*. Even the few soldiers on patrol turned a deaf ear to her pleas.

Alex battled a fresh, powerful wave of nausea and landed a hard yet ineffective kick upon the man's shin. His grip tightened, his yellowed teeth flashing in a triumphant grin as she made a failed attempt to repeat the tactic. Then, suddenly recalling something her uncle had once taught her, she brought her knee smashing forcefully upward against his unprotected groin.

He gave a hoarse, staccato yelp of pain and doubled over. Alex finally managed to break free. Leaving her assailant cursing and on his knees in the street, she whirled about and began to run back along the wharves. The blonde gave chase.

"You're going the wrong way!" she shouted.

"You were not leading me to the governor's house at all, were you?" Alex accused, stopping so that she could confront the woman with her suspicions. "And why in heaven's name didn't you help me?"

"You needed no help," the woman stated matter-of-factly. "And I told you, we've a stop to make first." She smiled and pointed in the opposite direction. "It's but a stone's throw away now."

"Is it indeed?" Her turquoise eyes were blazing, her breasts rising and falling rapidly beneath her bodice as she fixed the blonde with a narrow, dubious look. The woman seemed far from trustworthy now, but what other choice did she have? She wasn't at all certain she could find her own way back to the more respectable part of the city, and there was always the possibility that she would end up both lost and alone when night came.

"It will be dark soon," the woman pointed out as though she'd read her mind. "You'll not want to be down here then. I can see that you get to the governor's in plenty of time beforehand."

Reluctantly Alex conceded the truth of her words. She nodded in silent agreement and accompanied the woman down the street once more. They passed the greatest proliferation of taverns without further incident, then headed into an alleyway just north of the shoreline avenue. The strains of fiddle music—a lively Irish jig— drifted out to them from the narrow rows of buildings there, with the added bonus of voices, male and female alike, raised in boisterous laughter.

"This is where I live," the blonde finally announced.

Alex looked up and saw that they were standing before a two-storied wooden structure in dire need of paint. A crudely lettered sign bearing the likeness of a chicken hung above the door. THE ROOST, it read. She frowned at the sight of it, her uneasiness returning.

"I shall wait for you here," she told her unnamed guide.

"There's no need. It will only take a moment's time."

"No." She shook her head and reiterated, "I prefer to wait outside."

"Please yourself then."

The woman raised a hand and knocked on the door, then allowed her mouth to curve into another wan smile when it was swung open to reveal a dark, barrel-chested man who stood nearly seven feet tall. The brawny giant stared wordlessly down at her, his hawkish gaze narrowing when it shifted to Alex.

"I've brought Flora a new girl," said the blonde. She gave a curt nod toward Alex. "She's a 'special,' she is. Talks like a real lady. I'd best be getting a pretty penny for this one."

Alex inhaled sharply, her eyes flying to the woman in stunned disbelief. *A new girl?* The awful truth began to dawn. Before she could utter either a question or a protest, however, the giant scooped her up in his arms and bore her inside the building.

"Put me down!" she demanded, kicking and squirming with fiery vehemence. But he was strong as an ox, his arms tightening about her until she struggled to draw breath.

"Take her upstairs," the other woman directed. "I'll fetch Flora myself."

"No!" Alex gasped, her eyes full of a desperate appeal as she looked to the blonde. "Please, you—you cannot do this!"

"You'll settle in soon enough," the woman assured her, with no hint of remorse. "We all do, you know."

"Settle in?" she echoed, the color draining from her face. "*No!* Let me go!" Panic-stricken, she screamed and fought with all her might, but could not prevent the man from carrying her swiftly up a darkened staircase to the second floor of the house. Her wide, horrified gaze searched frantically about for any sign of a possible rescuer. There was none.

The sickening aromas of incense, rotting food, and unsanitary toilet facilities tainted the air, while the faint sounds of moans and curses drifted out from behind the half dozen closed doors they passed. Her captor headed toward an open doorway at the far end of the dimly lit corridor. The small room they entered was bathed in the soft golden light of a whale-oil lamp. There was no

window, and the only furniture consisted of an iron bed-
stead, a chair, and a washstand.

The mute giant dropped his furiously defiant burden
on the bed. Another sharp gasp broke from Alex's lips
when she landed atop the stained and frayed quilt covering the hard lumpiness of a mattress. While she
scrambled into a sitting position, the man left her alone
in the room, closing the door on his way out.

Alex was on her feet in an instant, flying to the door
and pulling on the knob. But it was too late. The key
had already been turned in the outer lock.

"You cannot do this!" she cried once more, raising
her hands to beat on the door. "I am here against my
will! Please, you must let me go!"

The only response her desperate pleas elicited came
from within the room next door, where a woman bellowed to her to "keep quiet or else feel the lash on your
back." Alex heaved a ragged sigh and felt hot, bitter
tears stinging against her eyelids. Choking back the sob
that welled up deep in her throat, she felt her legs buckling beneath her. She slid down to the floor and leaned
her head and shoulder wearily against the splintered
door while her eyes swept closed.

Held captive in a brothel. It was beyond belief! How
could she have been so stupid, so utterly careless and
naive? She should have known better than to trust a
stranger, woman or not. She should have known better!

"Dear God, what am I going to do?" she cried, her
voice nothing more than a hoarse, tremulous whisper in
the lamplit darkness of the room. She dared not think
about what would happen if she failed to escape this latest form of imprisonment.

Jonathan Hazard's face suddenly swam before her
eyes. Her throat constricted at the vision, her heart
yearning for the feel of his strong arms about her. He

had warned her. He had told her of the dangers she would be facing if she were fool enough to set out on her own. But she had refused to listen. Heaven help her, she had confused proud defiance with stubborn recklessness. She would give anything, anything in the world, if only she were back at the plantation instead of this vile, degenerate place, waiting for something too terrible to imagine.

She opened her eyes again. Ignoring the tremor that shook her, she dashed impatiently at the tears coursing down the flushed smoothness of her cheeks. There was no time to be wasted on either self-pity or regrets—*or* on longings she could not understand.

She climbed to her feet and allowed her gaze, brimming with renewed determination, to make a swift, encompassing sweep of the room. By all that was holy, she was Lady Alexandra Sinclair! She had not persevered through all the trials and tribulations of the past eight months just to have defeat forced upon her now, when victory lay within reach at long last. There had to be a way out!

Her eyes shifted back to the lamp burning on the chair beside the bed, then lit with triumph. That was it! She would lie in wait until the door opened again, then use the lamp as a weapon against the silent guard or whoever else stepped inside the room. Once the intruder had been knocked senseless, she would race back down the stairs and out the front door of the house, never looking back—and never again placing her life in the hands of a stranger. Jonathan Hazard had been a stranger, she reminded herself with an inward frown. Yet he was different . . . so very, very different.

Swallowing a sudden lump in her throat, she started forward to fetch the lamp. But before she could reach it, the door swung open without warning. She inhaled upon a loud gasp, her pulse leaping in fearful startlement as she spun about.

A large-boned woman, perhaps forty years of age, stood framed in the doorway with the giant looming directly behind her. She was wearing a tight, low-cut gown of amber satin. Her hair, a brassy color that could not possibly be her own, was piled high atop her head, and her face had been powdered and rouged to such an extent that her blue eyes appeared strangely opaque.

"I'm Flora," she announced, surveying Alex with a derisive little smile. "What do you call yourself, girl?"

"I am Lady Alexandra Sinclair, and you have no right to keep me here! Either release me now, or—"

"Sally said you was a 'special,' " murmured Flora. Her smiled broadened with satisfaction, while her gaze darkened with avarice. "We'll fix you up a bit, and get you a fancy gown. I'll wager them poor bastards out there'll be linin' up day and night once word gets out we've such a fine new girl. And a redhead at that."

"You cannot keep me here!" Alex declared hotly, her anger overpowering her fear. "What you are attempting to do is against the law, and I shall see you punished for your treachery if you do not allow me to leave this very moment!"

"You need a lesson in manners, girl," said Flora, smiling again. She gave a curt nod over her shoulder. "There's a gent downstairs, a regular, who'd pay well for the privilege of bein' the first."

"No!" Alex breathed, shaking her head in denial. She made a desperate attempt to flee the room, bolting for the doorway, only to cry out shrilly when the giant caught her up and bore her back to the bed. Although she fought him like a veritable tigress, he flung her down upon the mattress and moved back to resume his place behind the brothel's proprietress.

"Off with the dress," Flora directed her in a cold voice.

"Go to the devil!" Alex shot back. She sprang from the bed again and rounded on the woman with her magnificent eyes defiantly ablaze. "I shall *never* surrender to this—this black-hearted villainy!"

"The major'll have it off of you soon enough," Flora predicted, with a soft and scornful laugh. Turning away, she ambled back out into the corridor. Her burly, hawk-eyed companion subjected Alex to a menacing look before closing the door.

Alex quickly snatched up the lamp and flew back across the room. Positioning herself with defensive readiness beside the door, she leaned close to the wall in order to listen for the next set of approaching footsteps.

The wait was an excruciatingly long one. Her whole body tensed in alarm when she finally heard someone coming. She blew out the flame, raised the lamp high, and held her breath.

The key was turned in the lock, the door eased slowly open. Light from another lamp in the hallway spilled into the room. At the first glimpse of a man's head, Alex brought the heavy, makeshift weapon in her hands smashing downward.

But her intended target was too quick for her. Avoiding the blow that might well have parted his skull, he knocked the lamp aside and flung the door wide. His hand shot out to close about Alex's wrist as she tried to dart past him. He yanked her from the shadows.

"I've Flora to thank for the warning," he said, his tone one of mocking amusement. He was an attractive man, of medium build, with sandy brown hair cut short in the military fashion and a noticeable air of superiority about him. And he was wearing the uniform of an officer in the New South Wales Regiment.

"Let me go!" She struck out at him with her free hand, but he seized both of her arms and held her squirming body before him in the lamplight. His steely gaze filled with a hot, lustful appreciation of her charms.

"Damn, but you're even more beautiful than Flora led me to believe!"

"You don't understand!" she exclaimed. Abruptly ceasing her struggles, she raised her eyes to his face and tried to make him see reason. "I do not belong here! I am not one of Flora's—"

"Ah, but you are now, my sweet."

He pulled her roughly out into the hallway with him, caught up the lamp hanging from a hook on the wall, and thrust her back into the room. While she stumbled against the chair, he slammed the door shut and set the lamp on the dusty, bare wooden floor.

"You are an officer in His Majesty's service," Alex pointed out, whirling to face him again. "You have a code of honor to uphold, a duty to your king and country."

"I owe allegiance to no one save myself whenever I am at my leisure." His hands moved up to liberate the brass buttons on the front of his long-tailed coat.

"At least consider what I have to say." She drew herself haughtily erect and told him with as much composure as she could manage under the circumstances, "I am Lady Alexandra Sinclair. My uncle is Lord Henry Cavendish. If you will but assist me in reaching the governor, I—"

"I'm afraid the governor's wife would not approve," he quipped dryly. With an almost predatory smile, he began advancing on her. She backed away, her wide, luminous eyes darting feverishly about in search of other possible means of defense.

"Please, you must listen to me! I am telling you the truth! And even if I were not, you have no right to—to do *this*!"

"I paid for the right. And I can assure you that I mean to get my money's worth."

Another strangled cry escaped her lips when he lunged for her. She found herself toppled backward onto the bed. The major seized her wrists and forced them above her head, then placed his own body atop hers. She turned her head to one side when he attempted to kiss her, but she was powerless to prevent him from pressing his mouth to her neck.

"No!" she screamed, writhing violently beneath him. "Please, stop!"

"You'll be begging me to continue before this night is through," he boasted. He moved a hand downward to tug impatiently at her skirts. She balled her own hand into a fist and landed a punishing blow to the side of his head, then tried to jerk her knee upward. Her attacker swore and grabbed her wrist again, his fingers tightening with brutal force about her flesh. He brought his face close to hers, and she blanched at the vengeful, malevolent glint in his eyes. "I'll make you pay for that, you little whore!"

"I am not a whore!" Alex said, her voice rising in panic.

She felt bile choke her throat. Fear and repulsion threatened to make her faint. *Dear God, this can't be happening!* she told herself, her blood pounding in her ears while she arched her back in a futile attempt to push the major off her. She closed her eyes tightly and offered up a silent prayer for deliverance. She couldn't bear the thought of this man or any other taking by force what was hers alone to give. . . .

Suddenly the door crashed open.

The major ground out an oath and sprang from the bed. His aristocratic features were flushed with anger when he spun abruptly about to berate whoever had dared to intrude upon his well-rewarded privacy.

"What the bloody hell—?" he snarled. He never got the chance to finish the sentence.

Chapter 7

Alex quickly struggled into a sitting position on the rumpled covers of the bed, her mouth forming a silent O as she witnessed her attacker crumpling to the floor.

Incredulous, she looked at the man who stood ready to deliver yet another well-placed blow to the major's chin. His handsome face wore an expression that could best be described as murderous, while his deep green eyes held an absolutely savage gleam.

"Captain Hazard!" she said, with wonder. Her heart stirred wildly at the sight of him, her whole body flooding with the most profound joy and relief she had ever known. Just for a moment, Jonathan's gaze met hers. What passed between them then would never be forgotten.

"Damn your eyes, Hazard!" the major ground out, staggering to his feet now. He rubbed at his bruised jaw and confronted Jonathan with a vengeful scowl. "The woman is mine! I paid Flora—"

"One more word, Major Beaton," Jonathan threatened in a tone that was dangerously low and level, "and I'll give myself the pleasure of killing you!"

The other man paled visibly. Although he continued to glare, he had enough sense to keep his mouth shut. Capt. Jonathan Hazard was not a man to be provoked—at least not without serious—perhaps even deadly—consequences. More than one poor fool had discovered the ferocity of the American's temper these two years past.

Beaton watched in furious, tight-lipped silence as Alex scrambled from the bed and impulsively cast herself upon her rescuer's broad chest.

"Thank God you've come," she proclaimed. Severely shaken by her ordeal, she closed her eyes and heaved a shuddering sigh when his arms came up to encircle her with their possessive, hard-muscled warmth.

"Are you all right?" he asked, his own voice raw with emotion.

"Yes."

She stirred, tilting her head back to look up at him. Her eyes were glistening with unshed tears, and her delicate features reflected such anguish that he felt his heart twist achingly. At the same time, his blood boiled with white-hot rage. He shifted his smoldering gaze back to the man who had dared to touch her. Battling the urge to beat him senseless, he took a single, menacing step toward him.

"I had no idea she was spoken for," Major Beaton hastened to explain. He backed fearfully away from Jonathan's wrath, his words breaking from his lips in a nervous rush. "I swear to you, I was told she was mine for the taking. You can ask Flora yourself if you do not believe me."

"By heaven, you red-coated bastard," Jonathan bit out. "I should wring your neck for what you've done!" He took another step.

"Please," Alex appealed tremulously, her hands grasping at his arm, "take me out of this horrible place." As much as she despised the major for what he had tried to do, she did not want to see him dead. And there was very little doubt in her mind that Jonathan

Hazard was entirely capable of killing him with his bare hands. "You—you were in time. He did nothing! *Nothing!*"

Jonathan looked down at her again. He could not remain unmoved when he glimpsed the distress in her sparkling turquoise gaze. Telling himself that she had been through enough, he reluctantly called a halt to his purposeful advance. In a manner that was at once strong and gentle, he took her arm and led her from the room.

Behind them, the major made his way over to the bed and sank heavily down upon it. He swore revenge. And he vowed to have the woman whose sweet, tantalizing charms he had so briefly tasted. . . .

The brawny giant was waiting for Alex and Jonathan at the foot of the stairs. He moved to block their path, his dark eyes locking in silent combat with the piercing green of Jonathan's.

"Step aside," ordered Jonathan. The other man stood his ground. "Step aside, or—"

"Where the devil do you think you're goin' with my new girl?" Flora demanded as she bustled forward to confront them. Alex caught her breath and pressed instinctively closer to Jonathan, who slipped an arm about her waist and moved his other hand beneath his coat to the small, silver-handled pistol he had tucked into the waistband of his breeches.

"This young woman is not one of your employees," he uttered tersely.

"And who the bloody hell are you to be tellin' me—?"

"My name is Hazard. Captain Jonathan Hazard. And I intend to see that you are prosecuted to the full extent of the law for the crime of kidnapping."

"Kidnapping? Here now; you got no call to threaten *me!*" Flora exclaimed defensively. "Why, I was just givin' the girl a place to stay. Come in off the streets, she did, and lookin' like a rag-tailed bunter as you can well see."

"Then you'll not object to our leaving," parried Jonathan. His fingers curled about the handle of the gun, while his gaze flickered warily back to the man who appeared ready to launch an attack. Alex swayed against him, her legs feeling perilously weak for a moment until she rallied and stood firm, waiting to see what would happen next.

Following several long, tense seconds, Flora capitulated, though she did so with a decidedly ill grace.

"Take the little bitch. Take her and good riddance! But don't think you can be comin' back here with the watch—I pay good money for protection, I do!" She gave a curt, angry nod to the burly guard. With one last mute glower, he finally moved out of the way.

Alex felt light-headed with relief once more as Jonathan led her from the house. Surprised to find that darkness had already fallen, she took a deep breath and peered heavenward to watch a thin circle of clouds wander across the moonlit brilliance of the sky. A sudden, involuntary shiver ran down her spine when a gust of cool wind tugged at her skirts, but she reveled in the feel of it. *The nightmare was over.*

She stole a glance up at her silent, grim-faced escort. His arm was still securely about her waist. She was grateful for his support, and even more grateful for the fact that, once again, he had rescued her from adversity. Truly, she told herself in wonderment, it was a miracle. Jonathan Hazard had declared himself her guardian— guardian *angel* was more like it.

A scruffy-looking young man was waiting nearby with Jonathan's horse. He took the coin Jonathan tossed him and sped away to exchange it for an hour's worth of strong spirits. Lifting Alex to the animal's back, Jonathan swung up behind her and gathered up the reins. Alex leaned gratefully back against him as he reined about.

"How did you manage to find me?" she asked. They had already reached the main waterfront boulevard, lit now with streetlamps and fairly bursting with the raucous sights, sounds, and smells the night always brought with it. "How could you—?"

"Later," he decreed, his face inscrutable.

Reluctant to press the issue at the moment, she fell obediently silent while they rode through the crowd of merrymakers. No man accosted her this time; no man would have dared after catching a glimpse of her protector. At the next cross street, Jonathan guided the horse up the hill. They soon emerged into a noticeably more respectable area of the city, one where the well-tended houses sat in neat rows and the pleasant scents of flowers and woodsmoke filled the air.

After traveling a short distance farther, Jonathan reined the horse to a halt and dismounted. He pulled Alex down as well and led her up a narrow, flower-lined path toward a charming house of yellow brick. A sign proclaiming it to be THE CORNWALL INN hung from the whitewashed veranda, which ran the length of the building's second story.

"Why are we stopping here?" Alex queried, a frown of puzzlement creasing her brow.

"The inn is owned by a friend of mine," said Jonathan. "A man by the name of James Tanner. We'll be staying here for the night."

"But, I—I thought we would be returning to the plantation."

"It's too late for that now. We'll head back in the morning." He finally drew his arm from about her waist, but cupped a hand beneath her elbow as they climbed the front steps. A balding, bespectacled man wearing a crisp white shirt and gray wool breeches met them at the door. He smiled warmly at Jonathan.

"So, you've found her," the man remarked in satisfaction. He swung the door wide and offered a hearty welcome to them both. "You must be tired, Miss Sinclair. I'll have hot water for a bath sent up right away. And you, Jonathan, are no doubt in need of the same," he added, clapping him affectionately on the back. "You've been too long in the saddle this day, that much is for certain! Never fear about your horse—I'll look after it. Ellen's readied your rooms, and we'll be having your supper on the table soon enough."

Alex offered their genial host a weak smile. Curious as to how he had already gained knowledge of her name, she made a mental note to ask Jonathan about it—and a good many other things—once she had rested a bit. For now, she was perfectly willing to let herself be ushered upstairs to a room where a fire blazed its comforting warmth and a large metal bathtub waited to be filled.

"I've given Captain Hazard the room next to yours, Miss Sinclair," James Tanner told her as she preceded him inside the small yet prettily decorated bedchamber. "If there's anything you require, anything at all, you've only to let me know."

"Thank you," murmured Alex. Her eyes moved instinctively back to Jonathan, who stood towering above the older man at his side. He said nothing, but a brief smile touched his lips before he and his friend left her alone.

She heaved an audible sigh once they were gone. Feeling quite drained, both physically and emotionally, she wandered across to a floral-upholstered chaise and sank down upon it. Her mind replayed the exhausting events of the day—in particular those of the past hour—and she felt tears of release gathering in her eyes. She buried her face in her hands and let them come. . . .

Within the space of one short hour, she felt remarkably better. She had eaten the biscuits and drunk the tea James Tanner's wife, Ellen, had brought up—"to tide you over until supper," the quiet, kindly woman had explained. She had scrubbed herself from head to toe in the bathtub, allowed the hot, soapy water to ease the lingering tension from her muscles, and then dressed in the fresh undergarments and gown she had found waiting for her on the bed. Surprised at how well the borrowed clothing fit, she turned to face her reflection in the tall, cherry-framed mirror beside the fireplace.

The gown was by far the prettiest she had worn since leaving London. Of white striped muslin with a printed floral pattern in lilac bordering the hem, it featured a very high waist, a very low, rounded neckline, and short puffed sleeves. She had added a tucker of ruffled white lawn to the décolletage, so that it was a trifle less daring. The fine silk drawers and matching chemise she wore underneath felt heavenly next to her skin, as did the delicate, cream-colored stockings secured with pale blue satin garters. Completing the ensemble was a pair of flat-heeled kid slippers, fastened by ribbons crossed over the foot and round the ankle, and a shawl of brilliant green wool.

Her hair, still damp in spite of her efforts to towel it dry, curled riotously about her face. She frowned at the sight of it, then found herself wondering if Jonathan Hazard thought her lack of long curls made her appear less feminine. Perhaps he would prefer that it were waist-length; perhaps he would prefer that it were honey gold or black as midnight instead of the color of warm chestnuts.

"Fool," she muttered, with another sharp, self-deprecating frown at her reflection. It was ridiculous to be concerned with such trivial matters, especially at a time when her life was so desperately unsettled. She had committed the unforgivable sin of running away, she had very nearly been ravished, and now she was facing a night alone (well, *virtually* alone) with the man who was both her champion and her tormentor. Why in heaven's name should she care whether or not she possessed his good opinion?

"Miss Sinclair?"

She started guiltily at the sound of his voice. Coloring, she whirled away from the mirror and turned her wide, luminous gaze upon the door.

"Yes?" she called back.

"Our supper awaits."

"I—I'm not hungry." Cursing herself for a coward, she folded her arms tightly beneath her breasts and tried, without a great measure of success, to ignore the tumultuous beating of her heart.

"Nonsense," said Jonathan.

She blinked in astonishment when he opened the door and stepped inside. He, too, had bathed and changed, and now wore a dark blue waistcoat over his white linen shirt and beige doeskin breeches. His black knee boots shone from the cleaning they had been given, while his thick, dark brown hair waved damply across his forehead. He looked quite handsome and dashing—indeed, thought Alex, every inch a vibrant, hot-blooded American male.

She swallowed hard, her blush deepening as his eyes traveled over her with slow, boldly possessive intimacy. It was apparent that he, too, liked what he saw. Particularly when his burning gaze lingered on the exposed upper curve of her breasts.

"Would you risk offending our hosts?" he challenged, his tone low and full of wry amusement. He gave her a smile that was positively disarming.

Her mouth fell open, for she was caught off-guard by his indulgence. She had expected him to be angry, to scold and threaten, or even worse. What trick was he playing? she asked herself.

"I—I gave you no leave to enter," she stammered in a muddle of emotions.

"True enough," he conceded, with even more startling equanimity as he moved closer. "But I wanted to make sure you were not ill."

"No," she murmured, her gaze falling beneath the steadiness of his. "I am not ill." She unfolded her arms and turned away, her cheeks warming anew as she murmured impulsively, "Truly, Captain Hazard. I don't know how I can ever thank you for coming to my rescue. If you had not—"

"But I did." His features had grown quite solemn now, and his voice held a discernible edge. "My only regret is that I did not find you sooner."

"I consider it a miracle that you were able to do so at all." She spun about to face him again, the dancing flames of the fire reflected in her beautiful eyes. The many questions she had been saving finally tumbled out in a breathless rush. "How *did* you know where to search? Why, I might have been anywhere! What led you to that particular establishment? And how could you have learned of my disappearance and then traveled to Sydney so quickly? It was scarcely dawn when I left the plantation—"

"Concealed in a wagon loaded with wool," he finished for her. The merest ghost of a smile touched his lips at the sight of her well-deserved uneasiness, but he could take no pleasure in it. "When I arrived home shortly after noon, I was met with the news of your escape. And of the suspected means by which you had achieved it. I rode back to Sydney in all haste."

"But, how did you know to look for me in . . . ?" Her voice trailed away as she shuddered, a shadow of remembrance crossing her face.

Jonathan resisted the sudden, powerful urge to draw her close. A wave of protectiveness welled up deep within him again, as did a renewed burst of vengeful fury toward the man who had caused her pain. He was not through with Major Beaton, No, by heaven, he told himself, the cowardly blackguard would pay for what he had done.

"Once I had satisfied myself that you were not at the governor's house," he continued, "I immediately set a course for the waterfront. It's no secret that young women are lured there with promises of sanctuary. My instincts told me that the same fate had befallen you. The Roost is but one of many places I intended to search. It might well have taken me longer if not for a timely stroke of good fortune."

"A stroke of good fortune?"

"You were seen by an acquaintance of mine." His eyes darkened when he recalled how he'd felt when Jeremiah Barclay had provided him with the clue to her whereabouts. Fate had at least been kind enough to let Jeremiah venture outside one of his favorite haunts in time to observe Alex and the other woman hurrying past; thank God the old sea dog had not been too drunk to remember what he'd seen. "His description of you was remarkably accurate. And he recognized your companion. This isn't the first time she has played her tricks on Flora's behalf."

"I see." Alex drew in a ragged breath and moved slowly past him to take up a stance before the fireplace. "And Major Beaton? How is it you are acquainted with such a man?"

"Sydney is not a large city." Offering no further comment on the subject, he watched intently while she folded her arms beneath her breasts once more. The firelight played across her face, setting her delicate, heart-shaped features aglow and accentuating the perfection of her figure.

"What about Mr. Tanner?" she then asked. "How did he know my name?"

"I stopped here first, to enlist his son's help. Daniel works in one of the warehouses. He knows the waterfront quite well."

"I am surprised, Captain, that you did not inform the authorities," she commented dryly. It was obvious that both her strength and her spirit were returning full force. "I am, after all, an escaped convict, and—"

"Do you really think I'd be fool enough to trust the members of the regiment with a woman such as you?" He shook his head and gave her a crooked half smile. "I must admit, it would have done my pride little good to have it known that I was outfoxed by one of my own servants. And a woman at that. Besides, involving the soldiers would have done nothing more than delay the search. They're not exactly welcomed with open arms among the city's more 'colorful' inhabitants."

"No, I—I suppose not," she stammered lamely. She returned her bright, troubled gaze to the fire before demanding, "What do you intend to do with me now?"

"I intend to escort you down to supper."

"And then will you take me to see Governor Macquarie?"

"I dined with him last night. I'm not anxious to repeat the visit so soon."

"Did you tell him about me?" she asked, her eyes lighting with hopefulness as they flew back to his face.

"No."

"But, why not?"

"What is there to tell?" He leisurely closed the distance between them again, his own gaze warming while his mouth curved upward with a hint of mockery. "That I have taken on the responsibility of a convict who claims to be of noble birth? That my new housekeeper is a willful, flame-haired little vixen with a skill for dramatics and a penchant for misadventure? No, I would have been thought the worst kind of fool had I spoken of it. And your story would have been met with nothing but laughter." He would not admit, even to himself, that there was yet another reason. *A far more significant one.*

"If you truly think my story false, if you believe I am both a thief and a—a woman of easy virtue, then why, sir, should you have cared if Major Beaton had had his way with me?" she demanded. Dismayed to feel the hot color flaming in her cheeks, she lifted her head proudly and flung him a narrow, accusatory look. "Why did you threaten to kill him?"

"Whatever she may be," Jonathan replied in a cold, clear tone, "no woman deserves to be treated so brutally."

"So will you therefore appoint yourself 'guardian' to all the other women suffering a like fate on the waterfront? Will you also rescue *them*? Indeed, will you give them shelter and allow them the use of such borrowed finery?" she concluded, emphasizing this last by abruptly tangling a hand in the gathered fullness of the gown she was wearing.

"The others are not in my care. And the clothing is not borrowed."

"What?"

"I bought the things for you yesterday," he revealed, his green eyes darkening to jade as they raked appreciably over her once more. "I'm glad to see I got my money's worth."

"But, why—why did you do such a thing?" Her own eyes grew round as saucers; she caught her breath on a soft gasp when he drew even closer.

"Because, my dear Miss Sinclair, I could not abide the sight of that blasted prison gown any longer."

"I was unaware, Captain Hazard, that my appearance was so important to you."

"It's only natural that it should be, since I will be looking at you every day for the next seven years," he asserted, with one sardonically raised eyebrow.

"Not if my efforts to escape ever meet with success," she retorted. A faint, unintelligible cry broke from her lips when his hands shot out to close upon her arms.

"Damn it, woman! Haven't you learned your lesson *yet*?" he ground out. His gaze seared relentlessly down into the glorious, blue-green fire of hers, and a thunderous scowl furrowed his brow when he asked, "What the devil is it going to take for you to realize that there is no escape?"

"I told you once before that I would never willingly subject myself to the bonds of slavery!" She brought her hands up to push at his chest, but he held fast.

"I thought you had suffered enough to make you see reason. Apparently, I was wrong."

"Take your hands off me!" she ordered, her voice rising. She glared up at him in reproachful fury. "You have no right to touch me, no right at all! Would you prove yourself the same as Major Beaton?" She was immediately filled with remorse for having voiced what she knew to be an unfair comparison, but it was too late.

For Jonathan, her words had much the same effect as a slap across the face.

His temper flared, but he kept it in check. The merest suggestion of a smile played about his lips as he released her. For several long moments, they stared at each other like two combatants in an undeclared but no less genuine war. The only sounds to be heard in the room were the soft hissing of the fire and the ticking of the clock on the wooden mantelpiece above. The air was rife with a tension so thick it might well have been visible.

Alex waited, wide-eyed and breathless, for Jonathan's response. When he did speak, she was plagued by a sudden, inexplicable ache in her heart.

"*Touché*, Lady Alex," he drawled. His expression grew distant. Without another word, he turned on his booted heel and crossed to the doorway in three long, angry strides. He was already pulling the door closed behind him when Alex made what would soon prove to be a fateful mistake.

"I shall not return to the plantation with you," she vowed rashly. "I am not going to leave Sydney until I have spoken with the governor!"

Jonathan stopped dead in his tracks. He pivoted slowly about. His eyes burned across into hers, while a single, telltale muscle twitched in the clean-shaven ruggedness of his cheek.

"You will do as I say," he decreed. His tone was one of deadly calm.

"I shall enlist Mr. Tanner's help, or perhaps even his wife's," said Alex, warming to the idea. If she had known him better, she would have taken heed of the look in his eyes and ceased her mutinous outburst before it was too late. "*They*, at least, seem to possess a certain amount of decency. I'm quite sure—"

"You'll not involve them in your half-witted little schemes."

"Will I not?" She gave a defiant toss of her head and declared loftily, "While I am grateful to you for your assistance this night, Captain, my determination remains as strong as ever. And neither you nor anyone else can prevent me from achieving my goal of freedom."

"Regardless of the dangers?"

"I shall face them willingly!"

Try as he would, Jonathan could not remain unaffected by the challenge. He had intended to treat her with kindness and patience, to summon forth an added measure of self-control in his dealings with her. But the memory of her lying beneath Major Beaton still burned in his mind. The possibility of another such occurrence was enough to make him see red.

It was the last straw. His conscience waged a swift, fierce battle with his more earthy impulses—and lost.

Alex's eyes flew wide open again, her throat tightening in alarm as she watched him storm back into the room and slam the door. She gathered up her skirts and raced impulsively toward the window, but he caught her about the waist and yanked her back against him.

"By heaven, you belong to me now, do you understand?" he gritted out close to her ear. His voice, low and husky and brimming with barely controlled anger, sent a shiver dancing down her spine. She gasped when he forced her abruptly about to face him. "*You're mine!*"

She had no time to argue, no time to scream or struggle or even finish drawing in a deep, shuddering breath.

He swept her close, his strong arms encircling her while his mouth swooped down to capture hers.

Once again, she felt as though she had been touched by fire. It *was* a fire, of course, a wild, intoxicating blaze of mutual passion that would not be denied. She squirmed against him, but her objection was at best halfhearted. Her arms displayed a life of their own as they first raised in opposition, then entwined themselves about his neck in unspoken surrender.

He kissed her hungrily, deeply, his lips warm and strong and demanding, while his hot, velvety tongue thrust provocatively at hers. Her head spun, her legs grew weak. She was certain she would have fallen if not for his arms about her.

He swept her higher in his embrace. Dimly aware of her feet leaving the floor, she kissed him back with such sweet, innocent ardor that he groaned inwardly. His arms tightened about her with fierce possessiveness. The kiss grew even more compelling, the passion that had been simmering between them from the very first now flaring hotly and vibrantly into its own.

Jonathan suddenly scooped her up in his arms and carried her to the chaise. He sat down upon it, cradling her on his lap while his mouth scorched a fiery path downward, along the silken column of her neck, to where her breasts swelled above the low-cut bodice of her gown. She gasped when he impatiently tugged the white lawn tucker free, thereby exposing a delicate portion of her full, creamy bosom. Her eyelids fluttered open; warm color flooded her cheeks at the first touch of his lips upon the upper curve of her breasts.

"Jonathan!" she said breathlessly. Her eyes swept closed once more while her hands curled convulsively upon his broad shoulders. A low moan rose in her throat, and her hips squirmed restlessly atop his lean, hard-muscled thighs as his mouth roamed across the ripe, satiny flesh. Her head fell back, while her breath became nothing but a series of soft gasps.

With one arm holding her securely about the waist, Jonathan smoothed his other hand down along her spine. He swept her skirts upward before she could stop him (*if* she had been of a mind to do so), then trailed his fingers up along her shapely leg and over her hip. His hand closed about the saucy curve of her bottom, which was covered only by the delicate white silk of her drawers. He explored her well-rounded derriere with a boldness that prompted her blush to deepen and sent another delicious shiver down her spine.

He pulled her even closer, to where his aroused manhood throbbed with near torturous intensity. His lips continued their feverish, tantalizing assault upon her breasts while she instinctively arched her back. In that small part of her brain still capable of rational thought, she told herself that his kisses and caresses were nothing at all like Major Beaton's—whereas the major's had been cruel and repulsive, Jonathan Hazard's were pleasurable beyond belief.

Through a haze of passion, she realized that no other man had ever made her feel this way . . . no other man had dared to touch her as this one was doing. It was wicked, it was wrong. *It was heavenly.*

Jonathan's voice of reason also made a last valiant effort to be heard. But desire was raging through him, thundering in his loins like a veritable powder keg of sensation waiting to explode. He wanted Alex more than he'd ever wanted any woman. From the first time he had set eyes on her at Parramatta, she had filled his senses and haunted his dreams and set his blood afire. It was more than just her beauty—it was her spirit and her courage, her damnably enchanting, ladylike demeanor. She was at once infuriating and irresistible. And God help him, he longed to possess her, body and soul. *She was his.*

His hand moved purposefully around to the juncture of her thighs as his mouth returned to capture hers. Before she could guess his intent, his fingers delved within the edges of her open-leg drawers. She gasped against his mouth, her eyes flying wide open when he touched the silky triangle of auburn curls between her slender thighs. His warm, skillful fingers parted the delicate folds of pink flesh to claim the tiny bud of femininity.

Alex tensed in alarm. The caress was too intimate, too bold . . . too sinfully inflaming. She grew afraid, both of her own secret desires and Jonathan's more obvious ones. The spell was broken at last.

"No!" she cried hoarsely, tearing her lips from his. She pushed at his arms and struggled to rise, but he would not release her. "Please, let me go!"

"Blast it, Alexandra!" he ground out. His green eyes smoldered down into the stormy, turquoise luminescence of hers. "What the devil—?"

"You *are* no different from the major!" she said, more out of fear than anything else.

Jonathan's handsome features became a grim mask of fury. Anger and frustration burned within him. Torn between the urge to turn her across his knee—and the much more tempting impulse to finish what he'd started—he wisely chose to do neither.

Alex found herself released and set on her feet with nothing resembling gentleness. Flushed and breathless, she jerked her skirts down into place while Jonathan scowled darkly and tried, without success, to prevent his eyes from straying to the rapid rise and fall of her breasts. He offered up a silent, blistering oath and headed for the doorway again.

"We're expected downstairs," he proclaimed in a low, piercing tone as he yanked the door open.

"I'm not hungry!" she reiterated. How on earth could she sit down to a meal with him after what had just happened? She crimsoned at the memory of what he had done . . . of her own willing participation in the embrace. And as usual, she hid her embarrassment and confusion behind a show of proud defiance. "I want nothing more than to be left alone!"

"You'll come with me now, *Lady Alex*, or I'll damn well carry you."

It was no idle threat. She sensed in him a violence that was perilously near the surface. Flinging him a resentful glare, she bent and retrieved the piece of white lawn he had snatched from her décolletage, tucked it back into place, and swept angrily forward.

"Very well, Captain," she said. She drew to an abrupt halt a short distance away from where he stood watching her every move. Blissfully unaware of the fact that he was finding it so very difficult to keep his hands off her, she told him, "I shall accompany you to supper tonight. I shall return to the plantation with you tomorrow. But I'll be *hanged* if I'll ever again let you touch me! As God is my witness, I—"

"Your point is well taken." He cut her off brusquely, his eyes glittering harshly. Alex's eyes shot blue-green sparks at him again, but she said nothing more before marching past him and out into the hallway.

Supper proved to be a brief, though perfectly dismal, affair. Alex was at least thankful for the fact that their hosts put in frequent appearances during the meal, for she was in no mood to make idle conversation with Jonathan. He sat across from her and seemed every bit as anxious as she to avoid talking. But his penetrating, unmerciful gaze was constantly upon her; she would have been panic-stricken had she known the direction of his thoughts.

Seeking refuge in the privacy of her room afterward, she hastily bolted the door and leaned back against it. She could hear Jonathan moving about in the bedchamber next to hers, but she endeavored to pay no attention to the sounds as she undressed and climbed between the fresh, lavender-scented covers of the bed. The fire was nothing but a glowing pile of embers now, the room bathed in the pale moonlight filtering through the lace curtains at the window. The clock ticked comfortingly in the silence.

Alex released a long, uneven sigh. Her gaze wandered traitorously toward the wall that separated her room from Jonathan's. There was no connecting door. Still, she felt far less than secure.

Jonathan Hazard was an enigma, an absolute mystery, she mused with a frown of discontent. How was it possible that a man could be so heroic one moment and so roguish the next? There was simply no understanding the man. *And no resisting him, either.* The truth of that particular thought was something she preferred not to face. Yet her heart was not deceived. . . .

Blushing at her own shamelessness again, she frowned and rolled abruptly onto her side. She punched at the unresisting softness of her pillow. Her eyes swept closed, but sleep eluded her as the night deepened.

On the other side of the wall, Jonathan was equally restless. He stood at the window, his arms folded across his chest and a somber expression on his face. His magnificent emerald gaze was fastened on the dark, glistening waters of the harbor in the near distance, but his mind was filled with thoughts of the beautiful, redheaded "lady" in the room next door.

It was long past midnight before he finally took himself to bed. And even then, the dawning realization of his true feelings would allow him no peace.

Chapter 8

They headed back to the plantation the next morning.

For Alex, the long night had been filled with troubling dreams in which she was being menaced by a dark, faceless adversary. Her deliverance had arrived in the form of a rakishly handsome knight—a tall one with green eyes, of course—who had first vanquished the evil foe, then caught her up before him on a magnificent white charger. Without uttering a single word, he had spirited her away to a turreted castle rising like some magical paradise in the mist-cloaked night.

What had happened after that was not so well remembered as the rest. She could recall only hazy, fleeting images of a softly blazing fire, a glass of sweet wine that warmed her down to her very toes, and a kiss so rapturously compelling that she felt all her inhibitions melting away. . . .

It was a dream best forgotten. Berating her imagination for such absurdly romantic notions, she colored and shifted in the saddle. Her beautiful eyes were underscored by faint shadows, and she was plagued by a nagging sense of disappointment as she rode alongside Jonathan. She told herself it was because her quest to see the governor had met with failure, because fate kept dangling the promise of freedom before her only to cruelly snatch it away again. For now, at least, she didn't even want to think about another attempt at escape; yesterday's events had taught her more than she had bargained for.

Perhaps it was time, she conceded with an inward sigh, to offer both her mind and her body a well-earned respite. There were certainly worse things than spending a few days at a place such as Boree.

Glancing surreptitiously at her traveling companion, she saw that his face still wore an expression that could best be described as guarded. He had scarcely spoken at breakfast, and it wasn't until they were taking their leave of the Tanners that he had finally come near her. Her stomach had performed a strange flip-flop when he had seized her about the waist and tossed her atop the horse James Tanner had loaned them.

Heaven help her, she must be incredibly wicked to be so affected by the man's slightest touch. *It had been anything but slight last night,* an inner voice reminded her. True enough, she thought as she bit at her lower lip, it had been hot and masterful and more intoxicating than any wine. And surely, she was little better than a "painted woman" for having welcomed it.

Her hips squirmed uncomfortably about in the saddle again, and she rearranged her skirts about her legs in a futile attempt to cover her ankles. The pale blue muslin gown she was wearing—yet another gift from Jonathan—was simple yet impeccably tailored. With its empire-waisted bodice, modestly scooped neckline, and short puffed sleeves, it was both cool and becoming. She had been tempted to inquire, acidly, how he had gained such an impressive knowledge of women's attire. She had also wondered (though never out loud) how he had been able to insure such a remarkably good fit. When she had protested that neither of the two new gowns she had been given were suitable for riding, she had been met with the rather irritating news that her old gown had been burned.

"We'll rest here," said Jonathan, his deep-timbred voice startling her from her reverie.

They had followed the road into the cool shade of a forest. A narrow stream trickled along a rock-strewn path through the fragrant tangle of underbrush, where various tiny creatures moved stealthily about. Overhead, the sky was heavy with thick, ominous gray clouds that promised the rarity of summer rain.

"How much farther is it to the plantation?" Alex queried as she drew her own horse to a halt beside Jonathan's.

"An hour's ride. Perhaps more," he amended, tossing a quick glance heavenward.

He dismounted and turned to pull her down as well, but she hastily swung her leg over the saddle horn and slid to the ground on the opposite side. Wincing at the sudden, sharp pain in her backside, she took a wobbly step forward and tried to hide her embarrassing discomfort by smoothing some of the creases from her skirts. She bristled when she looked up and glimpsed the unholy light of amusement in Jonathan's eyes.

"Might I ask what you find so humorous, Captain?"

"It's no more than you deserve," he replied, his gaze flickering briefly downward. They both knew what he meant.

She watched in resentful silence as he gathered up the reins of both horses and led the animals to the stream. Her stomach growled in protest at the lack of food. She had eaten a breakfast of fresh fruit and hot buttered scones, but that was hours ago. At least her appetite was returning, she mused with a faint smile of irony. If only her emotions, and her scruples, could grasp normalcy once more.

"Mrs. Tanner sent a packet of food if you're hungry," Jonathan told her. His ability to read her mind never failed to disturb her.

"I'm not, thank you," she was quick to deny, then cursed her own stubbornness. She wandered over to the stream and carefully dropped to her knees upon the grassy bank to drink. Leaning down, she cupped a hand and dipped it beneath the water's surface. She raised it to her mouth.

"What was it you stole?" Jonathan startled her by demanding.

"I—I beg your pardon?" she stammered breathlessly. She turned her head to find him regarding her with a strange intensity as he approached the spot where she knelt.

"You were transported for thievery." He stopped close beside her, his eyes raking over her upturned countenance. "What did you steal?"

"Nothing! I told you before, I was falsely accused and convicted." Scrambling to her feet, she planted her hands on her hips and lifted her chin to confront him dauntlessly. "And I was under the distinct impression, sir, that you did not want to know anything about my past!"

"I didn't," he allowed, with the ghost of a smile. "But that was before you decided to lead me on a merry chase all over New South Wales."

"I fail to see why that should change anything!"

"Nevertheless, things *have* changed," he declared cryptically. "More than you realize."

Alex opened her mouth to offer a reply, but no words would come. She closed her mouth again and was alarmed to feel herself growing warm beneath his steady, penetrating gaze. As always, she was acutely conscious of his nearness, of his strength and his masculinity and the heat emanating from his hard-muscled body. But there was something different about him this time—something that both frightened and excited her. Something that made her heart stir wildly, almost painfully, within her breast.

"I find that I am hungry after all," she finally murmured, turning away in confusion. As she did so, the heel of her left boot slipped on a rock. An audible gasp of alarm escaped her lips when she felt herself tumbling backward. In one lightning-quick motion, Jonathan slipped an arm about her waist and pulled her up against him.

"Careful, Miss Sinclair," he advised softly. His eyes glowed with a potent combination of amusement and desire as they traveled over her. "Were you to get wet, the remainder of our journey would prove even more uncomfortable."

"Please, let me go," she demanded in a weak, tremulous voice. Her hands pushed ineffectually at his chest.

"You haven't by any chance got a husband or two back in London, have you?"

"What?" Her own eyes widened with stunned amazement before she denied indignantly, "I— Of course not! I have never been married!"

"Nor kept by some titled young fop with more money than brains?" All traces of humor suddenly vanished. His gaze darkened, his blood firing with jealous fury at the thought of any other man holding her as he was doing now . . . of any other man drinking deeply of her sweet lips and stroking the soft, well-rounded suppleness of her curves. The vision that rose, unbidden, in his mind was sheer torture.

"Kept?" Alex frowned up at him in bewilderment, only to crimson in the next instant when his meaning sank in. "You have no right—" she started to protest, pushing at him in earnest now.

"I have every right." His arm tightened possessively about her while his other hand shot upward to cup her chin. She trembled at the fierce, thunderous look on his face. "You know it as well as I do."

"I haven't the faintest idea what you're talking about!" she gasped out, her eyes sparkling up into his. Her knees felt weak, her breathing was terribly erratic, and she had the distinct impression that she was about to be kissed. Her fingers curled upon his broad shoulders. Her lips parted in an invitation that was not entirely subconscious.

"Damn you, Lady Alex," Jonathan swore in a voice that was little more than a husky whisper. "Damn us both."

She was shocked—and chargrined—when he abruptly spun her away from the water's edge and released her. Her bright, perplexed gaze followed him as he strode back to where the horses nibbled leisurely at the thick grass. He caught up the reins and led the animals forward. She struggled to regain her composure, all the while wondering why he had not taken advantage of the moment . . . and why she had wanted him to so very much.

"Let's go," he directed her tersely. "You've cost me enough time as it is."

"*I've* cost you—?" She broke off, her eyes filling with blue-green fire. "You did not have to come after me! As a matter of fact, Captain Hazard, it would have been far better if you—"

"If I had let Major Beaton or some other man bid you a proper welcome to The Roost?" he supplied in a low, bitter tone. His own gaze smoldered as he drew to a halt before her.

"There would have been no danger of that happening if you had only agreed to take me to see the governor in the first place!" she retorted, two bright spots of angry color riding high on her cheeks.

"So help me, woman," he ground out, "if you mention the governor again, I'll give myself the pleasure of beating you!" He knew he would never do so, but the little wildcat had the accursed ability to provoke him to violence quicker than anyone he'd ever known.

"It comes as no surprise that you would resort to such threats. You are, after all, an *American*!" Alex countered dramatically. "How could I expect you to behave with anything other than the barbarism and savagery exhibited by your fellow colonials?"

"We've not been 'colonials' from the time we sent your fellow Englishmen running back to good King George with their tails tucked between their legs." His mouth twitched with mocking humor.

"If you're so ready to boast of your country's victories, then why have you chosen to settle in Australia?" She folded her arms beneath the fullness of her breasts and cast him a haughty, challenging look. "It is, after all, a British outpost. Why are you not back in America where you belong?"

"I belong here." His expression grew tight-lipped once more, his eyes gleaming dully as he reached for her. He had intended to lift her up on the horse's back, but she retreated a step in order to avoid his grasp.

"Perhaps so, but *I* do not!"

He seized her about the waist and pulled her toward him until their bodies were very nearly touching. They were both aware of the electricity between them, of the heat and passion that had blazed to life the first time their eyes had met across the dark, musty confines of the prison cell. Neither of them had ever known such a powerful attraction. It was surprising and unnerving, exciting and captivating. *It was inevitable.*

"I say you're wrong," Jonathan murmured in a low, splendidly vibrant tone. His emerald gaze held no anger now, only a tenderness and warmth that made her pulse leap. "I think you were led here the same as I was."

"I—I don't know what you mean."

"Don't you?" He drew her closer, his strong arms slowly, masterfully, encircling her. She shivered when her breasts came into contact with his chest. "When I was younger, I scoffed at the notion of destiny. But the years have taught me otherwise."

"Please," she pleaded, though she could not have named the exact purpose of her entreaty. Her hands gripped the sinewy hardness of his upper arms; she tilted her head back to feel herself branded by the look in his eyes.

"You're mine, Alexandra."

"No!" She shook her head and tried desperately to make him see reason. "This is not—"

"I was reluctant to face it as well," he confided, with a faint smile of irony. "But there's no denying it any longer. Not after last night."

"Please, don't." She was truly alarmed now, frightened of both him and herself. "Let me go!"

"Never."

Her eyes flew wide open. She struggled, but it was far too late for that. A cry of mingled protest and pleasure rose in her throat as Jonathan's mouth descended upon hers. He kissed her long and hard, his lips and tongue fairly ravishing the softness of hers. She swayed against him and lifted her arms to his neck. Her heart pounded in tempestuous unison with his as passion took flight. She felt an acute sense of loss, of disappointment and frustration, when he suddenly raised his head.

"By damn, you'd tempt a saint," he murmured huskily. "And God knows, I am no saint."

Flushed and breathless, Alex could only stare up at him in bemusement. She waited expectantly for him to kiss her again, but he did not. His hands slid back down to her waist, and he spun her about, lifting her onto the saddle at last.

"If we don't leave now, we may well get caught in the storm." It was with no small amount of reluctance that he released her and moved around to his own horse. He swung agilely up into the saddle. "I've witnessed more than my share of gully washers in the past two years."

"Gully washers?" she echoed. Glancing overhead, she saw that the clouds appeared more foreboding than ever. The air was heavy with the fresh scent of rain now, and the wind was beginning to tear and flail at the leaves. She had scarcely noticed the changes.

"With any luck, we'll make it back before the worst of it breaks." He reined about and led the way back to the road. "Stay close."

Still reeling from the kiss, as well as the bold declaration of ownership that had preceded it, Alex touched her heels to the horse's flanks and rode after him. The storm within her was a fitting match for the one threatening to send a deluge upon the earth at any moment.

They did not, unfortunately, reach the plantation in time. The heavens opened up less than half an hour after they emerged from the forest. Lightning streaked prophetically across the sky, thunder answered with its rumbling intonation, and rain lashed at the sun-baked ground with a fury that was at once merciless and benevolent.

Alex bent her head against the downpour. Jonathan had flung a canvas slicker across her shoulders, but it offered scant protection from the rain. She rode onward, trying to keep pace with him, yet falling behind just the same. He came back for her. Seizing control of her reins, he led her horse behind his while she tightened her grip on the saddle horn and prayed they would find shelter soon. The cold raindrops stung her face; her body tensed with apprehension whenever a new clap of thunder shook the earth. Still, she had only to look at Jonathan to gather courage again. His presence made her feel safe. She realized that it had been that way from the very beginning.

The storm was still raging when they finally crossed the boundaries of Boree. Jonathan drew the horses to a halt in front of the house. Finn Muldoon and one of the other men materialized to look after the weary animals. Alex offered no objections when Jonathan pulled her from the saddle and carried her inside the house. He did not put her down until they were upstairs in her bed-chamber, where a fire had already been lit in anticipation of their return. A lamp burned on the table beside the bed, its soft golden glow adding to the room's welcome.

"You'll need to get out of these clothes right away," Jonathan pronounced, setting her on her feet. She nodded in agreement, smoothed a wayward lock of wet hair from her cheek, then glanced down to observe the puddle of water forming about her boots.

"The carpet will be ruined!" she noted breathlessly. Her eyes flew back up to Jonathan's face when she heard his soft, mellow chuckle.

"You look like a half-drowned kitten." His eyes twinkled affectionately. He was even more drenched than she, his dark hair curling across his forehead, his shirt and breeches plastered to his virile, lithely muscled body. He reached up to peel the slicker from about her shoulders. Her muslin gown clung damply to her curves, a fact he did not fail to notice. He tossed the slicker to the floor and told her, "I regret the discomforts of the journey. But there was no place to stop—"

"Perhaps, Captain Hazard, you arranged this as yet another illustration of the many dangers awaiting me should I ever try to escape again," she remarked saucily. Her knees grew weak when his mouth curved into a slow, disarming smile.

"You've a sharp tongue, Lady Alex. And the spirit to go with it." His fathomless, deep green gaze traveled warmly over her face. She could have sworn he meant to touch her, but he did not. Frowning, she watched as he turned and sauntered back to the doorway. "I'll see that you get hot water for a bath."

"I am perfectly capable of fetching it myself," she retorted, then mused with an inward smile of irony that the old Lady Alexandra Sinclair would never have thought of performing such a menial task.

"Nevertheless, you're to stay here and get undressed," ordered Jonathan. He felt his loins tighten at the sudden, hotly pleasurable image his words evoked. Resisting the urge to offer his assistance (the prospect of playing lady's maid had never been so appealing), he left and closed the door behind him.

He would have been delighted if he had known that Alex's thoughts had taken a similarly wicked turn. Blushing, she gave a soft groan and moved to stand before the fire. Her hands shook as she unlaced her boots and tugged them off. She set them aside and hastened to unfasten her gown. It fell into a wet, sadly wrinkled heap about her ankles—and was soon followed by her drawers, stockings, and chemise. Shivering in spite of the nearby flames, she quickly wrapped a light wool blanket about her naked body and sank down to the braided rug in front of the hearth.

Her eyes moved willfully toward the connecting door. Although her ears detected no sounds in the other room, she could not help feeling uneasy. And vulnerable.

You're mine, Alexandra. Her trepidation increased tenfold as those particular words returned to haunt her. Jonathan had uttered them last night, and again today, she recalled. But what, exactly, had he meant by them? Were they simply a pointed reminder of the servant/master relationship? Or did their significance extend far beyond that?

A good deal wiser than the pampered young miss who would have grown indignant over an emboldened suitor's chaste kiss, she was inclined to suspect the latter. Jonathan Hazard had made no secret of his desire. His kisses were becoming more frequent, and more dangerously compelling. Although loath to admit it, she could no longer deny that she found him irresistible in the extreme. The very thought of his embrace was enough to fill her with both shame and longing—in truth, too much of one and not enough of the other.

"Dear Lord, what am I going to do?" she whispered, her eyes wandering back to the fire. Seven years, she thought in dismay. Seven long years of living under the same roof, sleeping in the room next to his, and forever worrying about their mutual, shockingly powerful attraction. It was an impossible situation.

Another tremor, one that had nothing to do with the cold, shook her as she transferred her pensive gaze to the window. Rain pelted the glass and drummed on the roof overhead, while the winds continued to rake and howl ferociously across the countryside. It was the middle of the day, yet the sky was quite dark, lit only by the occasional, jagged flash of lightning.

A knock sounded at the door. Alex inhaled sharply. Turning her head, she called out an invitation to enter. She was expecting to see either Tilly or Agatha, or perhaps even Coleen. But it was Finn Muldoon who opened the door and strode inside with a large wooden bucket of steaming hot water in one hand. He carried a bucket of cold in the other.

"Mr. Muldoon!" gasped Alex. Her face flaming, she wrapped the blanket more securely about her and sprang to her feet. "I—I was not expecting *you*."

"Sure then, Miss Sinclair, I've no wish to be disturbing you," he apologized, with a respectful nod and an ear-splitting grin. "But the captain took himself off to the stable and left the kettles boiling on the stove. I thought you'd be feeling the need of a bath after the soaking you took this day."

"Yes, I was indeed. Thank you very much." Though still embarrassed, she smiled and watched as he disappeared behind the screen to empty the buckets into the tub.

"We're that glad to have you back, Miss Sinclair," the old Irishman declared. "And to see you've come to no harm. Sydney's a wicked place, it is."

"I'm afraid you're right about that," she murmured, her eyes clouding at the memory of the previous day's events.

"You'll be staying put now, I suppose." He emerged again and gave her a look that was kindly, almost paternal. "The captain was fit to be tied when he found out you'd gone."

"He was merely angry that I had run away."

"It was more than that," insisted Muldoon. He crossed back to the doorway, but paused before leaving.

"I've never yet known the captain to go tearing off like a blessed lunatic. Saints be certain, if he'd not found you—" He left the sentence unfinished and shook his head before exhorting with genuine concern, "You'd best have a care. There're many without the captain's good will. Serve your time here at Boree, where you're safe." He turned away again.

"Mr. Muldoon?" Alex detained him on sudden impulse.

"Yes, miss?"

"I—I'm sorry I took advantage of your fondness for liquor the other night."

"That's all right, miss," he replied, his usual good humor returning. His eyes virtually danced as they met hers. "No harm done. Save for the tongue-lashing still to come from the captain, that is. I expect I'll be feeling the sting of his words before the night is through. Still, I've felt them before, and I've not yet suffered lasting pain." Chuckling, he headed out into the hallway with the empty buckets.

Alex's features relaxed into another smile as he closed the door. She hesitated only briefly before padding forward to throw the bolt into place. That done, she hurried across to the screen and flung the blanket aside, then lowered her body into the bathtub. A sigh of contentment escaped her lips as the water's soothing warmth engulfed her. She closed her eyes and leaned back against the tub, losing herself in her thoughts while listening to the storm's unabating fury.

She did not hear the door to the adjoining room open. Nor did she become aware of someone's approach until it was too late. . . .

"Alexandra?"

The voice was Jonathan's. And it was coming from the other side of the screen.

Her eyes flew wide open as she stifled a cry and sat bolt upright in the tub. Water splashed over the sides, but that was the least of her worries. Instinctively rising to her feet, she snatched up the length of toweling beside the tub and draped it about her glistening, naked curves.

"How dare you!" she said, trembling with shocked outrage. She glared murderously at the screen, envisioning the man who stood hidden from view. "Get out of here at once!"

"I brought you some dry clothes."

"A likely story."

"One that's simple enough to validate," he parried. His blood ran hot at the thought of what lay behind the screen. It was all he could do to refrain from flinging the blasted thing aside and feasting his eyes upon her naked body— No, by heaven, he wouldn't be satisfied with merely looking. *Soon,* he promised himself, though it was scant consolation at the moment.

"You might have knocked, Captain Hazard, before—"

"I might have. But I knew you were in no position to answer." He set the bundle of clothing on the bed and tried, unsuccessfully, to force his burning gaze away from the screen. The temptation was fierce, painful, making his teeth clench and his features grow taut with the effort it was costing him.

"Will you please get out?" Alex demanded once more. A strange, mischievous excitement filled her. She blushed fiercely from head to toe, her breath catching in her throat as she waited for him to leave. *Or to stay.*

Several long, highly charged seconds passed. Another rumble of thunder shook the house. This time, Jonathan's self-control triumphed. Wishing he weren't so damned noble, he turned and strode back to his own bedroom, closing the door softly behind him.

Alex released her pent-up breath in a loud sigh of relief. Several conflicting emotions played across her face as she climbed slowly from the tub. Perplexed and shaken by what had happened—and by what *might* have happened—she crimsoned again and scurried across to lock the door. She was partially to blame, of course; she had unlocked it the night of her escape. How could she have forgotten to check it?

Jonathan Hazard had proven himself to be a gentleman after all, she reflected dazedly, her eyes clouding with even more confusion when she caught sight of the clothes he had placed on the bed. He certainly could have taken advantage of the situation. What would her response have been if he had come around that screen and swept her into his arms?

An accursed warmth spread slowly, deliciously, throughout her body. God help her, she was no better off than before. And what was worse, she wasn't at all certain she *wanted* to be.

Chapter 9

They settled into a truce, albeit a precarious one, for the next several days.

Alex performed her duties as housekeeper with increasing skill and alacrity. Tilly, Coleen, and Agatha were always willing to help, but it became a matter of pride for her to be able to handle more and more of the tasks on her own. Polishing furniture, changing bed linens, baking bread—she never would have thought it possible that she could willingly immerse herself in the role of servant.

Memories of her former life rose in her mind with less frequency now. She told herself it was only because she was simply too busy or too tired for nostalgia, which in itself would serve little purpose other than to make her heavyhearted. Nevertheless, she still felt an occasional pang of homesickness. And she still thought of escape, though the prospect of taking flight seemed less appealing than before. Her close call with disaster had left her wary; she had no intention of repeating the mistakes she had made. The next time she set out to find the governor, she would be better prepared.

Until that time arrived, however, she would follow through on her plan to make the best of things at Boree. Her spirits could certainly use a renewal. Eight long months of struggle, of fear and anger and even self-pity, had taken their toll. Perhaps, she mused distractedly, that was why Jonathan Hazard had been able to create such havoc with her emotions.

He was rarely at the main house of late. He disappeared after breakfast each morning and did not return until darkness had fallen. It was perfectly clear to her (and to everyone else) that he was avoiding her. Finn Muldoon put in a regular appearance at all three meals, but usually met her with the news that the captain would not be coming. She wondered if he was taking his meals elsewhere. The thought that he might be enjoying someone else's culinary expertise—and company—provoked an undeniable blaze of jealousy within her. Coleen had told her there were no unmarried women at the plantation. Was the arrogant rogue dallying with the wife of one of his own workers? she considered briefly, then admitted that it seemed unlikely. Whatever else he might be, he did not strike her as a man who would take pleasure in cuckolding another.

She managed to catch a glimpse of him every now and then as she wandered freely about the grounds. Sometimes Muldoon accompanied her on her late afternoon walks, sometimes she and Tilly would stroll beneath the cool shade of the trees, but she was also content to explore the plantation alone. She was slowly becoming acquainted with the other women, who often as not greeted her with a polite "good day, miss" and a tentative smile. The children were especially friendly now that she was no longer a stranger to them. They certainly harbored no particular suspicion or judgment concerning her position in the main house.

Wherever she went, her eyes never failed to search for Jonathan. She was completely bewildered by his sudden about-face. He was aloof and reticent whenever they chanced to meet, his visage inscrutable and his

piercing, gold-flecked emerald gaze offering no hint of
the warmth and passion it had once held. It was as if he
had suddenly become another person—a somber, unapproachable stranger who regretted their brief intimacy.

The nights were even more disquieting than the days.
She would lie troubled and wakeful beneath the canopy
of her bed and listen to the faint sounds of his movements in the next room. Hot color would fly to her
cheeks as she envisioned him undressing and climbing
into the massive four-poster he'd had shipped halfway
around the world. When all was quiet, she would release a long, ragged sigh and try to ignore the way her
whole body trembled.

She could remember every word he had spoken, every kiss and caress he had bestowed upon her. It was
painfully clear to her now that they had meant nothing.
He had said that she belonged to him, that he would
never let her go. Why had he changed his mind? Perhaps he was angry with her for running away to Sydney. Perhaps his desire for her had diminished to such
an extent that he no longer cared to pursue seduction.
He might well have decided that a convict was unwor-
thy of his attentions.

Whatever the reason, she should be glad of it. Indeed,
she should be profoundly relieved and grateful that he
treated her with such indifference.

Why then did her heart ache so?

It never occurred to her that Jonathan Hazard might
have a secret, well-contemplated purpose for keeping
his distance. Nor did she suspect that, on the other side
of the wall, his body burned for her each and every
night.

It was inevitable that something would happen. The
tension between them was building to a fever pitch.
And although neither was quite yet ready to acknowl-

edge it, the solution to their dilemma had always been within easy reach.

One evening, nearly a week after her return to the plantation, Alex stood alone in the kitchen and glanced pensively toward the window. Twilight was just beginning to settle upon the land. She had finished her chores for the day: the last meal had been cooked and served; the dishes had been washed; and both Coleen and Agatha had been sent home with plenty of food for their families. Once again, the handsome young master of Boree had neglected to bring himself to supper.

Frowning to herself in displeasure, she untied the strings of her apron, drew it off, and tossed it atop the worktable. She crossed to the back door, having impulsively decided to forego her usual custom of spending the remainder of the evening upstairs in her room, reading or sewing or belatedly composing a letter to her uncle. There was a strange restlessness within her, and more than a touch of loneliness to go with it. Heaving a sigh, she opened the door and stepped outside.

The setting sun had turned the sky into a blaze of color. The air was cool now, the gentle breeze carrying with it the familiar aromas of woodsmoke and honeysuckle. Already visible, the moon offered up the promise of a soft summer night. The plaintive howl of a dingo rose somewhere in the distance, while close by, the sheep and cattle stilled their unhurried wanderings in the fields.

Alex inhaled deeply and folded her arms across the bodice of her new work dress. Tilly had helped her make it, using a bolt of fabric they had discovered in one of the upstairs closets. Of light beige wool, the gown was far more practical than the ones Jonathan had given her, though admittedly not as becoming. The color was drab, the styling far too simple to be consid-

ered fashionable, yet it allowed her freedom of movement and was surprisingly cool.

With no particular destination in mind, she set off at
a leisurely pace across the yard. Her turquoise gaze
swept her surroundings with idle interest. A brief, wistful smile touched her lips when she looked toward the
row of cottages and heard the faint sound of children's
laughter. There were families there, she thought, people
who loved one another . . . men and women who shared
both the joys and the sorrows of a life carved out of a
faraway wilderness.

She had no one. Tossing a pained glance heavenward,
she closed her eyes and felt a lump rise in her throat.
She cursed the sudden urge to run back inside and shut
herself away in her room. Opening her eyes again, she
turned her steps toward the larger of the two barns.
Night was fast approaching, but she paid it no mind as
she went along. Her absence from the house would not
be noticed. Jonathan Hazard scarcely even knew she
was alive anymore.

She pulled the double doors open and slipped inside
the barn's cool, musty darkness. Having been there before, she recalled that a lamp hung from a post a few
feet away. She hastened forward to light it, then carried
it in one hand as she moved back to the tall wooden
doors. Leaving them only slightly ajar, she turned and
surveyed the interior of the barn.

The air was perfumed with the heavy, distinctive
smell of the wool piled nearly as high as the rafters in
one corner. Finn Muldoon had told her that it was good
business practice to hold some of it back until the demand in England brought higher prices. Thus, in spite
of the fact that the sheep had been shorn of their precious coats some weeks earlier, the barn still provided
storage for what had become the plantation's main

source of income. Food crops and cattle were necessary pursuits, but it was the merino wool that would insure a bright future for Boree.

Holding the lamp high, Alex strolled to the mountain of fleece and impulsively sank down into its aromatic softness. She set the lamp at her feet, lay back, and crossed her arms beneath her head while briefly contemplating the shadows given life by the oil lamp's steady flame. Her eyes swept closed. The image of a tall, green-eyed American forcefully insinuated itself into the chaos of her mind.

"Jonathan," she murmured. Only dimly aware of the fact that she had spoken his name aloud, she heaved a disconsolate sigh and wriggled farther down into the wool. "Dear Lord, what am I going to do?"

At that same moment, Jonathan was striding across the yard on his way to the house. He drew to a halt, his brows knitting together in a mild frown of bemusement when he spied the sliver of pale golden light escaping from the barn. Work had finished for the day. The men had gone home to their families, and Muldoon had announced his intention of riding over to one of the neighboring plantations to pay a long-delayed visit to a friend. Who the devil would be wandering about at such a late hour—and why?

Tugging off his hat, he slapped it negligently against his thigh and set a course for the barn. His eyes strayed back toward the house as he went. Oddly enough, there were no lights burning upstairs. He wondered if Alex had already retired for the night. As always, the thought of her lying in bed, her eyes closed and her sweet curves clad in nothing but a thin white nightgown, caused him to groan inwardly and battle a sudden, white-hot surge of desire.

By damn, he couldn't go on this way much longer.

His patience, his self-control, and his determination to put honor above passion, had been tested very nearly beyond endurance.

He had vowed to give both of them time. He had wanted to examine his own feelings, to find out if they were indeed as strong and long-lasting as he had begun to suspect. And he had wanted to make certain Alex's response to his kisses had been prompted by some true emotion as well. She seemed so innocent; it was increasingly difficult for him to believe that she was either a thief or an experienced enchantress. Still, it no longer really mattered. Whatever she had once been, she was his now. And sooner or later, he would make her admit it.

Reluctantly forcing his attention back to the barn, he approached the doors and eased them wider. He peered inside. His searching gaze darkened when it fell upon Alex.

He told himself to turn and walk away, to once again obey his nobler instincts instead of the wild, heart-stirring hunger she had set to raging within him. But there was nothing on earth that could make him leave.

He walked slowly toward her. His boots made no discernible sound upon the hay-strewn dirt floor. The lamplight played across his face and sent the dark figure of his shadow upon the wall, but Alex could take no warning from it. Her eyes were still closed, her mind still deep in thought.

Jonathan ceased his purposeful advance. He stood towering directly over her now. His penetrating green eyes smoldered as they traveled the length of her body. Unaware of his bold and appreciative scrutiny, she stretched her arms above her head and leisurely crossed one booted foot over the other. She caught her lower lip between her teeth for a moment, her expression one of secret yearning.

"Jonathan," she whispered again.

The sound of his name upon her lips was like setting fire to a powder keg.

Grinding out a curse, he dropped to his knees in the soft wool and reached for her. Her eyes flew wide open, and she gave a breathless cry of startlement at the first touch of his hands upon her.

"Captain Hazard!" she gasped. Incredulous and alarmed, and strangely excited, she found herself caught up against him. "What are you—?"

His lips came crashing down upon the parted softness of hers in a fierce, hotly demanding kiss that sent her pulse leaping. Solely on reflex, she raised her hands to push at his chest, but he would not be denied. A low moan rose in her throat as she squirmed within his masterful embrace. Disregarding her futile, halfhearted protests, he bore her down to the cushioning fleece with him. He landed on his back, his powerful arms holding her captive atop him. She brought one knee up toward his manhood in a last desperate attempt to put a stop to the madness. He swiftly rolled so that she was beneath him. His mouth welcomed her sharp gasp as his virile, hard-muscled frame pressed her trembling curves down into the wool.

Feeling as though she had become lost in one of her wicked dreams, Alex was unable to prevent her arms from entwining themselves about his neck. She began kissing him back, her tongue meeting every provocative thrust and swirl of his while her lips offered a sweet surrender. Flash and fire ... It had always been this way between them. And God help her, *she wanted it so*.

Her heart thrilled to his rough wooing, for it proved that he was far from indifferent. His ardor had not cooled after all. Indeed, she mused through a rapturous haze, if his present actions were any indication, he wanted her more than ever.

She grew frightened at the thought, yet she raised no convincing objections when he moved a hand up to the rounded neckline of her bodice. He tugged so hard on it that the buttons running down the back of the dress gave way. With dizzying swiftness, he swept both the bodice and her chemise downward, baring her breasts. She gasped again to feel a rush of cool air on her naked skin.

He gave her no time to think. His mouth left hers to roam feverishly, lovingly, across her face, then trailed a fiery path downward along her neck to her full, creamy breasts. She suffered a sharp intake of breath when his mouth closed about one of the rose-tipped peaks. His lips suckled greedily, his hot, velvety tongue swirling with provocative haste about the delicate nipple.

"Jonathan!" Alex cried his name once more. It was neither a plea for mercy nor a demand for retreat. Liquid fire coursed through her veins, and she arched her back instinctively beneath him, her fingers curling upon his broad shoulders while he continued his exquisite assault upon her breasts. His hand came up to join with his mouth, exploring and teasing and inflaming. She struggled for breath, her head tossing restlessly to-and-fro atop the soft cushion of wool.

His other hand tangled within her skirts and raked them upward. Another loud gasp escaped her lips when his fingers closed upon her thinly covered bottom. He grasped boldly, possessively, at the delectable roundness before his hand swept around to delve within the opening of her drawers. She uttered a strangled cry of protest then, but his lips returned to capture hers.

A moan rose in her throat, and her eyelids fluttered

swiftly open when he touched the silky triangle of auburn curls between her thighs. His warm, skillful fingers parted the folds of moist pink flesh. Though she began squirming in earnest now, she could not prevent him from claiming the treasure he sought.

Alex stiffened. A deep tremor of passion shook her as he began a gentle yet urgent stroking. She was certain lightning streaked through her body, certain she would be scorched. Her own desire frightened her every bit as much as his. She was an innocent, true enough, yet she knew what inevitable course their passions would follow. . . .

She could not let it happen. Everything else she had once held dear had been taken from her. This was the only thing she had left, the only thing she could give freely. How could she bestow it upon a man who cared nothing for her?

A sudden, sharp pain sliced through her heart. As much as she wanted this sweet madness to continue, as much as she yearned for Jonathan Hazard's kisses and caresses, she could not risk a lifetime of regret for a single night's pleasure. She was little better than a slave to him, a possession to be used and cast aside. The mere thought of it was enough to bring her crashing back to reality.

Abruptly turning her head, she pushed at his chest and tried to close her thighs against the sinful temptation of his fingers.

"Please, stop," she entreated, her voice choked with emotion.

"By heaven, woman! What game is this?" he ground out. His eyes were filled with a near savage gleam, his handsome face thunderous as he glowered down at her.

"It is no game. Now let me go!" She struck out at

him, but he seized her wrists in an iron grip and yanked her arms above her head.

"Perhaps you think to bargain for your freedom, is that it?" Desire still blazed through him, his manhood throbbing painfully. His furious, burning gaze raked over her flushed countenance, then dropped lower to the heaving fullness of her naked breasts. He muttered an oath and fought against the urge to take her anyway. Though he had never yet forced a woman, *this* woman made him want to consign reason and integrity to the devil. "Was it your plan to offer your body in exchange for your ticket-of-leave?" he said accusingly, his tone low and simmering with barely controlled violence.

"No!" she cried out. Crimsoning beneath his wrathful scrutiny, she felt hot, bitter tears spring to her eyes. "No, I—I want no bargain with you." She writhed and twisted in his grasp, trying desperately to escape. "Let me go!"

Jonathan swore again. He knew that he could not force her. He knew that she would hate him, and herself, if he finished what he'd started. And yet, *he had to have her*.

The solution rose with startling clarity in his mind. He was reluctant to accept it at first, fully aware that there could be no turning back. But his heart stirred at the prospect. In truth, it was the only way.

Alex was stunned when he suddenly released her and drew his tall frame upright. She blinked up at him for several long seconds before scrambling to her feet as well. Her hands shook as they hastily clutched the gown to her bosom. She stood wide-eyed and breathless before him in the lamplight. Feathery bits of wool clung to her hair, and her ripe breasts were still half exposed in spite of her efforts to shield them from his gaze.

For Jonathan, the sight of her adorable dishabille made his decision all the more certain.

"I've a bargain of my own to offer you, Alexandra Sinclair," he announced quietly.

"I told you, I—" she started to protest.

"Even you can no longer deny what is between us." His green eyes glowed warmly down into the luminous depths of hers. The ghost of a smile played about his lips. "It's time to face the truth. And pay the piper."

"I don't know what you're talking about." Though her mind screamed at her to flee, her body refused to obey. And why the blazes did she feel the traitorous impulse to sway closer? Jonathan's next words came to her as if from a great distance away.

"I'm talking about marriage."

"What?" She could not have heard him correctly.

"We're going to be married," he decreed. "As soon as possible."

"You—you cannot be serious!" she stammered. Her eyes grew round as saucers within the delicate oval of her face, while her legs threatened to give way beneath her.

"Never more so," he assured her.

"But, this is impossible!" She shook her head in disbelief. "How can you want me for your wife? We have known each other such a short time, and I am your housekeeper!"

"I'll hire another."

"You have always believed the worst of me," she reminded him, still reeling at his incredible proposal. "To you, I am nothing but a common thief, a transported convict who is bound to you for seven years. Why on earth would you want to give me your name?"

"Why do you think?" he challenged softly. He took a step toward her, his gaze smoldering anew. "I want you more than I've ever wanted any woman. And your passion runs as hot as my own."

"No!" It lacked conviction, even to her own ears.

"You're mine, Alexandra."

"*Yours* indeed," she replied scornfully. Another fiery blush crept up to her face when she charged, "You only want me in your bed!"

"I'll not deny it. But it goes beyond that. I could have taken you tonight and left us both none the wiser for it."

"Then why didn't you?" she retorted, lifting a hand to dash angrily at the single tear that coursed down the flushed smoothness of her cheek.

"Because, damn it, I want more than that!" She gasped when his hands suddenly shot out to close about her bare shoulders. Trembling, she tilted her head back and gazed up at him with a mixture of confusion, dismay, and a pleasure so intense that it alarmed her. "I want all of you!" he told her, his features dangerously grim.

"That, sir, is something I'll never give to any man!" she countered.

"You'll give it to *this* man," he vowed. He yanked her up hard against him, his fingers digging into her soft flesh. "Body and soul, you belong to me!"

"You don't own me, Jonathan Hazard. I may be little more than chattel in your eyes, but that still doesn't mean you have the right to—"

"I have every right. And by all that is holy, you *will* be my wife!"

"Would you truly enter into such a marriage?" she demanded, trying her best to ignore the wild pounding of her own heart. "I am, after all, a convict."

"And I am an American." His mouth twitched, and there was a roguish light of amusement lurking in his gaze now. "We're well matched, wouldn't you say?"

"This is madness," she said between ragged breaths. *Dear God, the man had taken complete leave of his senses!* Either that, or it was he who was playing some sort of cruel game.

"Call it what you will, the fact remains that we were meant to be together."

"I cannot marry you."

"You can and will!"

"No! Good heavens, I—I don't even know you!" She felt panic rising within her, but she couldn't have said whether it stemmed from his vow to possess her, or her own inclination to let him.

"We've a lifetime to become acquainted." His hands slid downward along her arms, finally coming to rest upon her slender waist. He gazed deeply into her eyes. "Is the prospect of marriage to me really so distasteful, Alexandra? Just as you did that day I found you at Parramatta, you'd do well to consider your options. As my wife, you'll no longer have a sentence hanging over your head. You'll be mistress of Boree. Neither I, nor anyone else, will hold your past transgressions against you."

"I have no past transgressions!" she exclaimed in a weak, tremulous voice. "And I don't understand any of this."

"Then don't try. Just say yes."

"How can I? How can I possibly consent to such a cold-blooded arrangement?"

"Cold-blooded?" he challenged, with a soft, mocking smile. Then he revealed, "Your consent isn't necessary."

"What do you mean?"

"I mean, my dearest Lady Alex, that you have no choice in the matter. In truth, I hold your life in my hands. I can sign your papers of indenture over to whomever I please. And I can marry you off. To my-self, if I so choose."

"Would you take an unwilling bride?" she demanded, lifting her head in proud, angry defiance. The gesture belied the sweet warmth spreading throughout every inch of her body.

"You won't be unwilling," he promised.

Before she could ask him the significance of those words, he decided to prove his point in a manner that would leave little doubt in either of their minds. He lowered his head, his mouth descending upon hers in a kiss that, although a good deal gentler than its predecessors, made her shudder with a renewal of passion. She was so affected that she very nearly bared her breasts again as her hands moved with a will of their own toward his neck, but she managed to snatch the fabric up in time to prevent that particular disaster. When he finally raised his head once more, she opened her eyes and saw that his were brimming with an irresistible combination of tenderness, resolve, and desire.

"You're mine, Alexandra," he repeated. His deep-timbred voice sent a chill down her spine.

She stared breathlessly up at him. Her emotions were in an absolute uproar; she no longer knew what to feel or believe. With another unintelligible cry, she pulled away from him at last and fled to the doorway.

Jonathan made no attempt to stop her. He watched, silent and deceptively impassive, as she disappeared into the darkness outside. And then, his mouth curved into a faint smile of satisfaction.

Chapter 10

Alex slept little that night. And when she finally ventured downstairs the next morning, it was only to discover Jonathan waiting for her in the dining room.

"You're late, Miss Sinclair," he noted wryly.

She drew up short, her eyes widening and rosy color burning in her cheeks at the sight of him. He sat in his usual place at the head of the table—or rather, what had *been* his usual place until recently. This was the first time he had stayed for breakfast in almost a week.

Seeing him again brought memories of the previous night's madness flooding back to her mind with a vengeance. She was, however, determined to behave as though it had never happened. He was no doubt regretting his impulsive, and highly preposterous, proposal of marriage. Now that they were facing each other in the cold light of day, reason would surely prevail.

"What are you doing here?" she demanded, with a valiant attempt at composure.

"Waiting for my breakfast. And for you."

She was dismayed to feel her heart flutter. Acutely conscious of his eyes upon her (she had the distinct impression that he was undressing her in his mind), she folded her arms beneath her breasts and battled the sudden, cowardly impulse to flee. She was wearing the pale blue muslin gown he had given her. The buttons of her work dress would have to be sewn on again—if she could find them, that is. The thought of returning to the barn made her groan inwardly.

"Where is Mr. Muldoon?" she asked, a telltale quiver in her voice.

"Out."

He slowly drew himself up from the chair now. The sunlight filling the room lit gold in his dark hair. Alex caught her breath on an audible gasp and hastily uncrossed her arms. With a will of their own, her eyes traveled the whole length of his virile, hard-muscled body before returning to his face. Her apprehension increased when she saw that he was smiling. The smile was soft, almost predatory, and served to dash her hopes that he had changed his mind. Judging from the look in *his* eyes, the cold light of day was of no help whatsoever.

"I—I will see to your breakfast." She hurried toward the kitchen doorway, but he moved to block her path.

"Alexandra." He spoke her name as though it were an endearment. Her pulse leapt, and her gaze was clouded with confusion when it flew up to meet his. Although he did not touch her, she felt branded all the same.

"Please, Captain Hazard. I have work to do."

"I was 'Jonathan' last night," he was ungallant enough to remind her.

"I would prefer that we forgot about that—that unfortunate incident." Her color deepened, and her eyes fell. "The memory of it is humiliating in the extreme, and I'm quite sure your suggestion was prompted by nothing more than—"

"It was no suggestion," he disputed quietly. He longed to sweep her close, to taste the sweetness of her lips again, but he feared he would not be able to stop with one kiss. Not after last night. No, by heaven, not after the hours he had spent lying in his bed with his body on fire and his damnable sense of honor telling him he couldn't surrender to the urge to take her before the wedding. The problem, and well he knew it, was that the little vixen had captured his heart. So he was behaving as a gentleman in spite of himself, he reflected ironically. *But not for long.*

"Whatever it was," said Alex, "I think it would be best if I were to leave the plantation!"

"Never." There was no amusement in his gaze now, and his rugged features appeared very grim.

"You said you could sign my papers of indenture over to someone else," she said feelingly. "Well then, do so. Or else let me go to Sydney."

"I thought we had settled that."

"We have settled nothing." She released a long, eloquent sigh of exasperation and abruptly presented her back to him. "It is impossible for me to remain here any longer. God help me, I admit that the physical attraction between us is too strong to ignore. I admit that I have been shamefully weak spirited. But I have no intention of marrying you. Even if your proposal were genuine, I could not accept it. We are but strangers, and I don't belong here."

"You belong wherever I am," Jonathan declared, his green eyes darkening as they swept hungrily over her.

"No, I do not," she was too quick to deny. Her throat tightened painfully, and she was bewildered by the sharp, twisting ache in her heart. "I am Lady Alexandra Sinclair. I belong in England, not in Australia." She whirled to face him again. "Besides, what is between us is nothing upon which to base a marriage!"

"Is it not?" he challenged in a low, vibrant tone.

"No!" she flung back, her own voice rising perilously. "It isn't as though you held any true affection—"

"Would it make any difference if I did?"

"What?" she gasped.

"Would it make any difference if I were to tell you that I loved you?"

"Why, I— How could it?" She frowned and shook her head. "I would not believe you! How could you care for me and yet force me to your will?"

"Believe whatever you please," he told her solemnly. "But know that I mean to have you."

"You cannot marry a woman simply because you want her in your bed." She stepped impulsively closer, unaware that in so doing she provided him with a tempting view of the ripe, swelling curve of her breasts. "There has to be true regard, even if there is no passion. Perhaps in America marriage is entered into lightly and whimsically, but in England we consider the bonds of matrimony to be sacred."

"We've plenty of passion."

"Dash it all! Haven't you been listening?"

"I have indeed. But we are neither in America nor England." It was all he could do to refrain from crushing her to him then and there. "Australia has of necessity formed its own rules."

"And what is that supposed to mean?"

"Merely that, come Saturday, we will be wed." Obviously considering the argument at an end, he lifted his hat to his head and sauntered away into the kitchen.

Alex stared after him in shocked disbelief. She made her way over to the chair he had just vacated, sank down, and lifted a hand to where her heart beat so erratically within her breast. *Saturday*. Dear Lord, that was only two days away! What was she going to do?

There was always the possibility of another attempt

at escape, she thought in growing desperation. She could try fleeing on horseback again. She could even set a course for Parramatta instead of Sydney and plead with someone there to help her. But in truth, she had little doubt that Jonathan Hazard would find her.

She rose to her feet and began pacing distractedly to-and-fro beside the table. It seemed that her only hope at this point was to continue trying to make him see reason, to convince him that their marriage would be a terrible mistake. It was unlikely that anyone else at the plantation would seek to dissuade him from his purpose. Even Tilly, who had become a close friend, would not dare to interfere. And although Finn Muldoon had been kindness itself to her, it was difficult to imagine him counseling his master on such a personal matter. No, she concluded with a ragged intake of breath, she could rely on no one save herself.

You belong wherever I am. Wondering why those words did not fill her with fear and loathing (quite the contrary), she pivoted about and swept into the kitchen. Jonathan was gone. Without his breakfast. And without once touching her . . .

The next forty-eight hours flew by with merciless haste. By the time Saturday dawned, Alex was beginning to panic. She had tried everything. Seeking Jonathan out at every opportunity, she had voiced her objections to their union and pleaded with him to abandon his ill-conceived plan. She had stormed and fretted and defied. She had even resorted to tears on one occasion. But all her efforts had proven useless. His response had remained the same—she would be his wife.

He had offered her no specifics. And strangely enough, no one else had mentioned the wedding. They all behaved as if they were completely ignorant of it. She wondered if they *were*, if perhaps Jonathan had for some unknown reason decided to keep the proposed nuptials a secret. It only added to her disquietude.

Her nerves were strung tight as a bowstring all morning long. She was glad to be alone in the house—Tilly, Coleen, and Agatha were spending the day off with their families. Most of the workers had taken the wagons and journeyed to Parramatta to visit the stores and taverns. The few that remained at Boree were content to use the leisure time to rest or catch up on their household chores.

Although she had dressed and gone downstairs earlier than usual, she had not encountered Jonathan. Nor had she seen him the night before. It might well be that he was avoiding her again. She toyed with the idea of going in search of him, but decided against it. She had tempted fate enough.

The morning wore on. Alex subjected the house to a barrage of cleaning, desperately trying to turn her mind away from the day's significance. When noon came, she was at her post in the kitchen. But the meal she cooked went unappreciated, for neither Jonathan nor Finn Muldoon showed up to eat it. Her own appetite had long since fled. She took the food and headed for Tilly's cottage, only to discover that her friend was among those who had journeyed into Parramatta.

She glanced anxiously about as she returned to the house, half expecting to see Jonathan. There was no sign of him. It occurred to her, in a passing moment of weakness, that she could once again take advantage of his absence—as well as the absence of nearly everyone else—to make good on her escape. She even went so far as to hurry over to the stable and peer inside. Much to her surprise, she discovered that all of the horses were gone.

Her eyes blazed, for she had little doubt that Jonathan

had taken pains to insure her compliance. Muttering a highly unladylike oath, she stormed back to the house and resumed her tasks with even more all-consuming vigor than before.

Almost before she realized it, the sun was sinking below the horizon. And still, Jonathan had not come for her. He had apparently taken heed of her protests after all, she concluded. Night had fallen . . . and nothing had happened. The awful uncertainty was over. She could breathe a sigh of relief at last. *There would be no wedding.*

With an inexplicably heavy heart, she climbed the stairs and shut herself away in her room. She unfastened her gown and allowed it to fall in a heap about her ankles. She had bathed earlier in the day—and now desired nothing more than to crawl into bed and try to sort out her own feelings. They were more chaotic than ever, she mused ruefully, and like as not to stay that way so long as Jonathan Hazard was in her life.

Stripping off her chemise, drawers, stockings, and boots, she donned the new, white lawn nightgown she had finished hemming the day before. It fit her considerably better than the old one, and was quite becoming with its scooped neckline and very short sleeves. But she cared nothing about her appearance at the moment. Heaving another sigh, she turned and padded barefoot toward the bed. She reached for the coverlet to draw it back.

A loud, insistent knock sounded at the door behind her.

She started in alarm and spun about, her eyes very round and her heart pounding wildly. Certain that it was Jonathan who demanded entrance (who else would dare to disturb her at such an inappropriately late hour?), she was at first reluctant to answer. He had probably come to offer her an explanation—one she wasn't at all sure she wanted to hear.

"Yes?" she finally called out.

"I'd like a word with you." His familiar, splendidly resonant voice had no trouble making itself heard through the door.

"I'm terribly sorry, Captain Hazard." Her tone was cool, betraying none of the turmoil within her. "But I have no wish to talk to you."

"Open the door, Alexandra."

"Go away!"

"Open the door, or I'll break it down."

She gasped sharply. It was difficult to tell if he was serious or not—but if he was, there was little doubt in her mind that he would make good on the threat. The benefit of the doubt was best given, she realized. She could well imagine what might happen if he came crashing inside with his temper inflamed.

Her eyes kindled before turning toward her nightgown. She frowned and hastened to catch up the primrose cotton wrapper lying across the foot of the bed. Tossing it about her shoulders, she had just finished belting it on when she reached the door. She freed the bolt, wrenched the door open, and glared reproachfully up at Jonathan.

"Could this not have waited until tomorrow, Captain?" she demanded, with angry hauteur. A blush stained her cheeks as his gaze flickered intimately over her.

"Come with me."

"I—I beg your pardon?" she stammered. Without warning, he took her arm in a firm grip and forced her out into the hallway. "What do you think you're doing? Where are we going?"

"To a wedding."

"A wedding?" she echoed weakly. "Whose wedding?"

"Ours."

"*What?*"

"The parson's waiting downstairs," he informed her, with maddening calm, as he pulled her along with him.

"You cannot be serious!" she charged, too shocked at the moment to offer more than a token resistance.

"Haven't you yet learned not to doubt me?" His eyes were brimming with wry amusement—and something else she would prefer not to acknowledge. "I apologize for the lateness of the hour, my dearest Lady Alex, but I was unavoidably detained. There was another marriage ceremony to be performed first—an event long overdue, judging from the bride's profile. Reverend Stockbridge was more than happy to accompany me here. He had, I think, despaired of my ever entering into a state of wedded bliss." They had reached the staircase by this time, and began descending the carpeted steps at a slow, measured pace.

"You truly expect me to marry you *now*?" Alex exclaimed breathlessly. "For heaven's sake, I—I am wearing my nightclothes. And anyway, I don't *want* to be your wife!" Belatedly drawing to a stop, she raised her hand in a futile attempt to pry his fingers loose from her arm. Another gasp broke from her lips when he suddenly brought her up hard against him. He kissed her, thoroughly and passionately, then raised his head to give her a smile of such disarming warmth that she feared her legs would buckle.

"You'll marry me," he decreed.

Alex felt as though she were caught in a whirlwind. Still struggling, she was nonetheless pulled quickly down the stairs and into the pretty, lamplit parlor. Her fiery turquoise gaze fell upon the young man who rose,

Bible in hand, from the floral chintz-covered sofa. Looking every inch a member of the clergy in his somber black coat and matched breeches, he smiled benevolently at the sight of her and made her a slight bow.

"I am honored to make your acquaintance, Miss Sinclair. I am the Reverend Stockbridge, vicar of St. John's Church in Parramatta." If he considered it odd that her wedding attire should consist of a nightgown and wrapper, he was too much of a gentleman to mention it. Besides, this wasn't the first time he had seen a barefoot bride.

"Please, Reverend Stockbridge. This is all a terrible mistake!" she pronounced, her eyes full of a desperate appeal.

"Is it indeed?" he murmured, with a slight frown. He looked toward Jonathan, who clamped an arm possessively about Alex's shoulders.

"I've told you the circumstances."

"Ah, yes," said the parson, his brow clearing with remembrance. "The circumstances."

"What are you talking about?" demanded Alex. Her gaze narrowed as it shot back to Jonathan. "What did you tell him?"

"The truth." He nodded curtly at the other man. "It's getting late, Reverend."

"I quite understand, Captain. You've secured a witness?"

"I have." He tossed a glance back toward the doorway. Obeying his silent command, Finn Muldoon suddenly materialized. He entered the room with a sheepish grin. Like his master, he was still clad in his riding clothes.

"Mr. Muldoon!" cried Alex. Realizing that he was her last hope, she frantically entreated, "I beg of you, please try and make him see reason." There was no doubt which *him* she referred to.

"The captain's that determined, miss," the old Irishman answered regretfully. His pale blue eyes were full of sympathy as he moved forward to take his place behind the bride and groom.

"I am unwilling for this marriage to take place!" Alex declared in a flash of spirit, only to suffer a sharp intake of breath when Jonathan's arm tightened like a vise about her.

"Shall we begin?" said the parson. He opened his Bible, in the center of which lay his well-used ceremonial book.

"How *can* you, sir, a man of God, participate in such a travesty?" a still recalcitrant Alex saw fit to accuse him. "Does it not matter to you that I—?"

"Captain Hazard does you great honor, Miss Sinclair," he advised her. His manner was intended to be paternal, though he was only five years her elder. "Truly, my child. You should get down on your knees and thank the Lord that such a man has chosen you to be his helpmate in life."

"We'll give thanks together," Jonathan promised, roguish humor lurking in his emerald gaze. "Each and every night."

Alex flushed hotly. She made another attempt to squirm free, but he held fast. Though reluctant to face the inevitable, she decided to do what she could to salvage her dignity. Thus, she remained stiff and unyielding in his grasp while the parson began reading from his book. When it came time, Jonathan repeated his vows in a strong, clear voice. Alex's response was one of proud, furious silence. It did not matter. Her consent was assumed by all three men present, and the nuptials continued.

Three minutes. It took only three minutes for her to become Jonathan Hazard's wife. Her eyes widened with stunned disbelief as the parson, concluding with the familiar exhortation about a death-parting union, smiled and gave his permission (unnecessarily) for Jonathan to kiss the bride.

And then his arms were gathering her close, his lips descending upon hers in a kiss that warned of the night ahead. When he finally released her, she was light-headed and pink-cheeked again. The parson took her hand, clasping it with both of his own.

"Would that the wedding had taken place in God's house," he remarked, with a faint sigh. "But I fear your husband was in too much haste to make the proper arrangements. Well then, is that not often the case with people in love? I shall pray for your happiness." She stared mutely back at him, until he turned to offer Jonathan his felicitations. Finn Muldoon soon took his place.

"I wish the both of you well, miss—*Mistress Hazard*," he was quick to amend. After planting a hearty kiss upon her cheek, he took a respectful step backward, but couldn't resist another grin. "We'll soon get used to the name."

"What have I done, Mr. Muldoon?" she lamented in a pained whisper. She numbly shook her head. "What in heaven's name have I done?"

"You've gone and married yourself the best man as ever walked the earth," he reassured her solemnly.

"But, I—I didn't want this."

"Did you not?" His smile was both affectionate and knowing. "Sure as I'm standing here, mistress, I've never seen two people more suited to each other than you and the captain. And that's the gospel truth, it is."

"I fear I must be going now," Reverend Stockbridge announced to them all. "My own sweet wife awaits my return."

"I'll be riding along with you, Reverend," Finn Muldoon was quick to offer. "I've a mind to spend a night in town." He and Jonathan exchanged a look of mutual understanding before he accompanied the parson from the room.

Alex stood alone with her new husband. *Husband.* Dear God, she thought, this can't be happening. . . .

"The ring belonged to my grandmother," Jonathan told her quietly. She glanced down at the thin gold band he had slipped upon her finger. It felt strangely warm against her skin.

"I should not be wearing it," she murmured, a turbulent frown creasing her brow.

"Why not?"

"Because I am no happy, loving bride—and well you know it."

She forgot all about pride and dignity now. Her temper blazing, she impulsively twisted the ring off and threw it at him. He made no attempt to catch it, but regarded her with a steady, unnerving intensity. She swallowed hard, her throat constricting even more when the clock on the mantelpiece proclaimed the hour of nine. Each plangent chime seemed to be mocking her.

A heavily charged silence rose between them as they stared at each other. Alex folded her arms beneath her breasts and wondered distractedly how a man could manage to look both irresistible and menacing at the same time. Even in his dusty, white linen shirt and doeskin breeches, he was handsome. Devilishly so. *Husband.* The word burned within her mind once more, prompting her to shake her head in a vehement denial and break the silence at last.

"You may have forced me to wed you, Jonathan Hazard, but you cannot force me to—"

"We are man and wife," he reminded her, his tone

very low and level. He slowly advanced on her now. Panic shot through her.

"I will not be your wife," she cried hotly, backing away.

"You will," he vowed.

She turned to run, but it was much too late for that. He swept her up in his strong arms and bore her purposefully toward the staircase.

"No!" she screamed, kicking and squirming with all her might. "No, *damn you*! Put me down!" It was the first time she had ever employed those choice words, the sound of which made Jonathan's mouth twitch.

"Colorful language for a proper English lady, Mrs. Hazard," he drawled.

"Don't call me that!"

"You've tired of the charade then?"

"You know that's not what I meant." She struck out at his handsome head, then found herself tossed facedown across his shoulder. When she pummeled his back with her fists, he landed a hard, familiar swat upon the conveniently placed roundness of her backside. She gave a hoarse cry of outrage and fought all the more, while his arm tightened about her legs.

Her struggles, as always, proved futile. Within seconds, he had kicked open the door to his room, carried her inside, and deposited her none too gently atop the massive four-poster. She scrambled up to her knees on the feather mattress while he turned away to light the lamp and close the door.

"You cannot do this!"

"Do what?"

"You know perfectly well *what*!"

With its steady flame bathing the room in a soft golden glow, Jonathan carried the lamp forward and set it on the table beside the bed. Alex's eyes grew enormous when his hands lifted to the front of his shirt. One by one, he began liberating the buttons.

"Good heavens!" she gasped. "Surely you're not—?" She broke off abruptly, watching in mingled dread and fascination as he drew off his shirt. His skin gleamed bronze in the lamplight, his broad, powerfully muscled chest covered by a light coating of dark hair. His arms appeared entirely capable of crushing the life out of a man—or holding a woman close to his heart with unbelievable tenderness, she recalled dazedly.

She caught her lower lip between her teeth and struggled to regain control of her breathing. Without a word, yet with a faint, cryptic smile playing about his lips, her new husband took a seat on the edge of the bed and tugged off his boots and socks. When he drew his tall, magnificent frame upright again, his hands moved leisurely to unfasten his breeches. Alex came to life again at this point.

"No!" she choked out. She sprang from the bed and raced toward the doorway. He was upon her in an instant, scooping her masterfully up in his arms again.

"Have a care, Lady Alex, or I'll forget my vow to be a patient bridegroom," he warned, his voice laced with both passion and indulgent humor.

"Let me go!" She was startled when, instead of returning her to the bed, he set her on her feet before him. Before she could guess his intent, he tugged the belt of her wrapper loose and pushed the garment down her shoulders. "No, don't!" she choked out, tensing in very real alarm now. She sought to prevent his hands from their wicked purpose, but the wrapper was stripped from her body and flung aside. Clad only in her nightgown, she folded her arms across her thinly covered breasts. Sudden tears started to her eyes, prompted by equal parts of confusion and fear.

"You've no need to pretend such maidenly modesty with me," he told her.

"It is no pretense."

He frowned at the look of distress on her beautiful face. It occurred to him that perhaps she had been ill treated by someone even before that incident with Major Beaton. Hot, vengeful rage coursed through him at the thought, while at the same time his heart stirred with loving compassion.

"I will not hurt you, Alexandra," he promised softly.

She caught her breath on another gasp, her eyes flying up to meet his. What she saw reflected in their piercing, fathomless green depths made her own heart turn over in her breast.

"I do not . . . I have not . . ." Her voice trailed away. She felt her knees weakening, felt liquid warmth spreading through her whole body.

She did not protest when Jonathan swept her up once more and bore her slowly to the bed. He lowered her to the mattress. His viridescent gaze burned down into the shimmering blue-green of hers as he straightened and unfastened his breeches.

Surprisingly, Alex could not force herself to look away. She crimsoned when he stood before her in all his masculine glory. Her eyes grew very wide as they traveled over him—downward from his powerful upper torso to his trim waist and flat, rock-hard belly, across hips that were narrow and buttocks that were rounded to manly perfection, lower still to lean thighs and long, athletic legs. For only a moment, her gaze lingered on the spot where his manhood sprang from a cluster of tight dark curls.

She groaned inwardly and finally closed her eyes, her heart drumming in her ears while she reflected that he was without a doubt the most splendidly fashioned male she had ever seen. Her experience in such matters was, to be certain, quite limited, but she was confident of her opinion just the same.

Her confidence, however, did not extend to the "mysteries" of the marriage bed. Her eyes flew wide open again when she suddenly felt the hem of her nightgown being pulled upward. She came bolt upright beneath the canopy, her hands grasping at Jonathan's arm.

"Please, don't," she implored, though it sounded woefully unconvincing, even to her own ears.

"It's only right that a husband should look upon his wife."

"You mean his *slave*, do you not?" She regretted the words as soon as they were out of her mouth, but it was too late to take them back. Swinging her legs about, she attempted to escape from the other side of the bed. Jonathan was in no mood for yet another chase. His hands shot out to catch her about the waist before she had even reached the edge. A strangled cry broke from her lips when he pulled her back and lowered his own body atop hers.

His virile nakedness scorched her through the delicate fabric of her nightgown. She pushed frantically at his shoulders, but he seized her wrists and forced her arms above her head. His mouth curved into a brief, foreboding smile.

"You're a sharp-tongued wildcat, Mrs. Hazard," he murmured huskily. "It's time you were tamed." There was no anger in him, only love and passion and a long-simmering impatience to make her his own.

"Have you no decency at all?" she demanded, her breasts heaving beneath the gauzy, clinging cotton. Her eyes blazed wrathfully up into his. "It was beyond the realm that you refused to grant me the freedom that is mine by rights, but it is even more despicable that you should force me into marriage!" She drew in a deep, ragged breath before adding, "I was wed in my blasted *nightclothes*!"

"We'll have another wedding, a proper one," he promised solemnly, though his eyes held an unholy light of amusement. "You can wear all the finery you please. But in truth, I prefer you as you were tonight." His mouth descended upon hers at last. She moaned in protest and writhed beneath him, which only served to make her even more acutely conscious of his desire.

There was no playfulness in him now. His lips drank deeply, ardently, of hers, his tongue ravishing the moist cavern of her mouth and demanding a response she could not help giving. He released her wrists. One of his hands swept urgently downward to close upon her breast, while the other threaded within the silken, flame-colored curls at the back of her head. She moaned again, her own hands reaching across the bronzed hardness of his back. Resistance was driven from her mind with embarrassing ease; she surrendered to the kiss and forgot about all else save Jonathan and the sweet madness only he could create. . . .

The flames of passion burned hotter and hotter. With tempestuous haste, the nightgown was stripped from her body. She shivered when naked flesh met naked flesh, then shivered again as Jonathan's lips claimed the rose-tipped fullness of her breast. He drew the delicate peak into the searing warmth of his mouth, his tongue swirling and bathing and seducing while he suckled as greedily as any babe. Instinctively arching her back beneath him, Alex closed her eyes and grasped at his broad shoulders.

She felt well and truly branded by his touch, and her soft gasps and moans sent desire thundering fiercely, almost uncontrollably, through him. But he was determined to make her want him every bit as much as he wanted her ... determined to drive any lingering memories of past lovers from her mind forever. *By damn, she would know that she belonged to him alone!*

He lifted his body from hers. Her eyelids fluttered open; she gazed up at him in a mixture of chagrin and bewilderment. But he said nothing before suddenly turning her facedown upon the covers. She caught her breath, her arms clenching about the pillow when he lowered his head again and pressed a kiss to the nape of her neck. His lips wandered lightly, tantalizingly, across the silken curve of her shoulders and back, trailed downward along her spine, then set to roaming with bold intimacy over her saucy, well-rounded bottom.

Her face flamed. She stifled a breathless cry, her hips moving restlessly beneath his wicked caress. She could summon neither the will nor the strength to stop him, for though what he was doing was sinful and shocking, it was also highly pleasurable. He explored every delectable hill and valley, his teeth gently nipping and his tongue stroking hot and wet across the pale, creamy flesh.

With her whole body trembling and on fire, he rolled her to her back again and resumed his skillful, rapturous assault upon her breasts. His hand moved to the triangle of delicate auburn curls between her thighs. She tensed again when his warm, strong fingers deftly parted the moist silken folds and found the tiny, delicate bud of her femininity. There would be no denying him this time—not that she was in the least bit inclined to try. Her thighs parted wider of their own accord; her breath became nothing but a series of soft gasps as she felt her own expertly coaxed passions spiraling upward.

She was scarcely aware of Jonathan's mouth trailing down to her belly. A delicious tremor shook her when his tongue dipped within her navel. Her fingers tangled within the sun-streaked thickness of his hair, her lips yearning for the possession of his once more. But he was determined to prolong the sweetly savage torment until she begged for mercy. His mouth journeyed lower still. . . .

"Jonathan!"

Her eyes flew wide open. Telling herself that such a thing must surely be forbidden, she tugged on his hair and tried to make him stop. His hands curled firmly about her thighs, prying them open again. She squirmed and arched her back, which only served to bring her closer to the bold, conquering wildfire of his lips and tongue.

"Jonathan, please!" she choked out. Shame was soon vanquished by the desire streaking through her like lightning. A moan of pure pleasure rose in her throat, and her fingers threaded almost convulsively within his hair again. "Please!" Her head tossed on the pillow; she closed her eyes tightly against the most desperate longing she had ever known. She was certain she could bear no more!

"You're mine, Alexandra!" Jonathan decreed in a low, vibrant tone laced with passion. His fingers replaced his mouth as he slid upward on her body once again. "Say it!"

"No, I—I cannot," she whispered huskily, her hands grasping at his arms while her eyelids fluttered open. "Please, I—"

"By damn, I will hear you say it." His gaze smoldered relentlessly down into hers. *"Say it!"*

"I am yours!" The words came from deep within, breaking from her lips with a will of their own as her eyes swept closed again. "God help me, *I am yours!*"

Jonathan's mouth curved into a faint smile of triumph. His own desire was perilously near the outer limits of endurance, and he waited no longer before claiming what had in truth been his from the very beginning. With passion surging hotly through his body and his heart soaring, he slid one large hand beneath Alex's hips, lifted her slightly, and positioned his throbbing manhood at the entrance to her womanly passage. He eased himself forward. A groan rose in his throat at the honeyed welcome of her, and he thrust all the way into her at last. A sharp, breathless cry of pain escaped her lips as his hardness sheathed to the very hilt within her velvety warmth.

He frowned, his eyes darkening with surprise at the undeniable evidence of her virginity. *She had been innocent after all!* The discovery filled him with a mixture of remorse and exultance, but there was no time to think of it now. His hips began tutoring hers in the age-old rhythm of love, his thrusts swiftly, inevitably, deepening while she clung to him and felt the dull ache between her thighs giving way to unbelievable pleasure once more.

The fulfillment was both mutual and shattering. Alex cried out softly at the moment of completion. She felt as though she had been borne aloft to the very heavens, only to find herself drifting slowly back to earth. Jonathan tensed above her in the next instant. His liquid, life-giving heat poured forth, causing her to gasp anew.

In the aftermath of that first tempestuous union, Jonathan Hazard rolled to his back in the shadowy warmth of the bed and pulled his well-loved bride close.

She did not resist. Pliant and becomingly flushed, with the lingering glow of passion still shining in her eyes, she released a sigh of utter contentment. *You're mine, Alexandra.* He had proven the truth of those words. He had proven it well.

Chapter 11

"Why didn't you tell me?"

Alex stirred at the sound of his voice. The spell was broken. She frowned and heaved another sigh as she faced, with great reluctance, the consequences of her surrender. Confusion, anger, self-reproach, and the most intense feeling of satisfaction she had ever known warred together within her breast. What had happened was beyond belief. She would never have thought it possible that a mere physical act could be so incredibly soul-stirring. Then again, she recalled with an inward blush, there had been nothing *mere* about it.

"I—I don't know what you mean," she finally murmured. Her sense of modesty returning now, she instinctively tugged the rumpled covers across her body. She was frustrated in her efforts when Jonathan swept them away again. One of his hands came down to rest with warm possessiveness upon the naked curve of her hip, while the other smoothed tenderly along her arm.

"Why didn't you tell me you were still an innocent?" he said. His tone was at once affectionate and accusing.

"I certainly attempted to do so." She lifted her head from the loving cradle of his shoulder and cast him a narrow, highly indignant look. "But *you*, sir, refused to listen!"

"Guilty as charged," he admitted, a low chuckle rumbling up from deep within his chest. He pulled her back down. His features sobered when it suddenly occurred to him that perhaps she had spoken the truth about her identity as well. The possibility was one he would rather not consider at the moment. She was his wife. And by heaven, that was the only thing that mattered.

"I suppose you are congratulating yourself for ... well, for what you have done this night," she charged, with more than a touch of resentment.

"Have you any complaints, Mrs. Hazard?" he parried softly.

She blushed again and stiffened against him. Her fiery gaze strayed willfully downward to his powerful, lean-muscled thighs. And the significant darkness between. With an inward groan, she closed her eyes and drew in a shuddering breath.

Silence fell between them for several long moments. She lay still and pensive within his arms, her cheek resting upon his chest. She listened to the strong, steady pounding of his heart—and felt her own beating in unison. It seemed perfectly natural to be lying with their naked bodies entwined while the night deepened. But, how could it? she asked herself. Troubled by the sensations (all of them pleasurable) that rose within her, she shook her head as though she could somehow deny them.

"This is all a terrible mistake!" she reiterated, though with far less conviction than before.

"It was no mistake."

"How could it not be?"

She abruptly pushed up on one elbow and subjected him to yet another reproachful look. A wry smile touched his lips, for he could not help musing that the

look was "wifely" in the extreme. He had expected her
anger, of course. Yet he considered the sting of her temper a small price to pay for what he had gained in return. *I am yours.* The sweet memory of her surrender
was enough to fire his blood anew.

"You forced me to marry you!" she reminded him,
unaware of the temptation she presented with her eyes
ablaze and her bright curls wildly tousled. Her breasts
swept against his chest, taunting him with their full,
rose-tipped bounty. She was at the moment, however,
too caught up in righteous outrage to take warning from
the change in his expression. "Without so much as a by-
your-leave, Jonathan Hazard, I was wedded and bedded
and—"

"And will be so again," he vowed. He lifted a hand
to cup her chin, the look in his green eyes dangerously
compelling. "You are my wife now, Alexandra. And I
hold what is mine." She drew in her breath upon a
sharp gasp when his fingers trailed lightly downward to
the soft valley between her breasts. His gaze followed,
smoldering as it raked over her exposed curves. Her
skin shone all creamy and silken in the lamplight.
"You're even more beautiful than I expected."

"Don't!" she cried, dismayed at the sudden impulse
to melt against him. She pulled away and sat up, jerking
the covers partially over her at last. "What manner of
man are you? Why, for all I know, you might have done
the same to other women!"

"Done what?" he countered, with one mockingly
raised eyebrow. He rolled onto his side and drew himself up a bit, but made no attempt to shield his own nakedness. "Wedded them—or bedded them?"

"Both!" she shot back, trying in vain to keep her
gaze averted from his bronzed, undeniably masculine
form.

"I have never been married before. And you can rest assured that from this day forward, I will bed no other woman save you." Although his eyes gleamed with ironic humor, his words were spoken in earnest.

"You intend for *that* to set my mind at ease?" Before he could offer a reply, she frowned and moved to the edge of the mattress. Jonathan's hand immediately curled about her arm.

"The night is still young," he advised, his voice low and commanding.

"Will you not at least grant me a few moments' privacy?" she demanded tremulously. She was relieved when he let go of her arm and smiled.

"It would seem I owe you that much. But only for tonight. I want no barriers between us."

His words struck a chord of renewed trepidation in her heart. She slid from the bed and hastened to retrieve her wrapper. All too conscious of his bold, penetrating gaze upon her, she drew the garment on and swept—with as much dignity as she could summon under the circumstances—from the room.

Entering her own bedchamber, she closed the door and threw the bolt. She hurried across to the washstand, poured water from the pitcher into the bowl, and took up both the cloth and the cake of soap. Stripping off the wrapper, she began to scrub at her body, as if she could somehow erase the memory of Jonathan Hazard's touch. It was impossible, and she knew it. She truly *was* his wife now, in every sense of the word.

"Oh, Alex ... how could you?" she whispered brokenly, facing herself in the mirror. Her outward appearance had not undergone some miraculous transformation, but still, she would never be the same again. What would become of her now? she thought in rising panic. How would she ever be able to return to England?

Feeling the hot, accursed tears gathering in her eyes, she flung the cloth down into the bowl and donned the wrapper again. Her legs were trembling as she made her way over to the bed. She had just perched disconsolately upon the edge when she heard Jonathan's voice drifting to her from the other side of the connecting door.

"Alexandra?"

"Please, go away!" she called back, her own voice fraught with pain and confusion. Her life had been turned upside down; she wanted nothing more at the moment than to be left alone with her thoughts, no matter how upsetting they were.

But Jonathan was not of a mind to grant her wish.

"Open the door," he ordered calmly.

"I will not!" She shook her head in defiance, even though he could not witness her actions.

"Have we not already played this scene tonight?"

"Have you not already done enough?" she retorted.

"I'm warning you, Alexandra." His tone held a discernible edge now.

"Leave me in peace, damn you!" The malediction was beginning to rise to her lips with remarkable ease. "Do you not understand? I want no part of this marriage; I want no part of you!"

"You don't mean that."

"Yes, I do!" she insisted. She knew she was being irrational, yet she couldn't seem to help it. Dear God, why did she yearn for the touch of a man who had just ruined her every chance of happiness? It didn't make sense. Nothing made sense anymore. "You—you may have succeeded in *ravishing* me once," she stormed, still furiously battling the urge to cry, "but I'll be hanged before I'll ever let it happen again!"

There was a long silence after that. She held her breath and listened, but he offered no response. Mistakenly believing that the victory was hers, she heaved a sigh of relief and lay back upon the bed. She would not acknowledge the acute feelings of loss and disappointment that plagued her as she grasped one of the pillows and hugged it to her breast.

Suddenly the door crashed open.

Sitting bolt upright, Alex watched in fearful, wide-eyed disbelief as Jonathan strode toward her. He was clad in a loosely belted, dark blue dressing gown, his handsome face a grim mask of fury and his gaze holding the promise of a fitting retribution.

"There will be no locked doors between us, you little hellcat!" he ground out. A strangled cry broke from her lips when he caught her roughly up in his arms. He carried her back into his room, tossed her onto the bed, and imprisoned her body with his own. The fresh scent of soap hung about him, and his hair waved damply across his forehead, but it was the look in his eyes that commanded her attention—*and warned her that he would be master.*

"Surely you're not going to—?" She gasped, struggling beneath him. He held both of her wrists captive with one of his hands. His emerald gaze seared down into the stormy, blue-green fire of hers.

"I had planned for us to talk. But my plans have changed." His other hand swept downward to her breast.

"No!" She fought against him as best she could, but they both knew it was useless. Her emotions were thrown into utter chaos again, her heart stirring wildly.

"I—I hate you, Jonathan Hazard!" she hissed, with desperation.

"Hate me if you will," he replied in a deceptively even tone. "But know that you are mine!"

His lips captured hers. He untied the belt of his dressing gown, then jerked her wrapper open. His hand smoothed hotly, demandingly, over her body. She moaned and squirmed beneath him, half in protest and half in ecstasy. He suddenly rolled onto his back. Her eyes flew wide open as she felt her wrists being released, but there was no time to escape before he began teaching a second lesson in love.

He urged her farther upward, his mouth virtually devouring the well-placed ripeness of her breasts while he pushed the wrapper off her shoulders. His hands clamped about her buttocks, and she gasped against his mouth as she felt the burning hardness of his arousal beneath her thighs.

Desire sparked and blazed. It wasn't long before Alex was on the very brink of begging for release. This time, however, Jonathan demanded no such entreaty. While a delightful frown of bewilderment creased her brow, he lifted her by the hips and brought her down upon his rigid manhood. She blushed at the shocking intimacy of her position, but she was too caught up in the glorious whirl of passion to raise any objections. Her hands curled tightly upon his shoulders while she rode atop him, and she welcomed his thrusts with soft gasps and moans of pleasure. When their union reached its inevitable, earth-shattering conclusion, she cried out and collapsed upon his chest. Only then did he seek his own release.

Afterward, he cradled her against him again and smiled to himself at the certainty of a lifetime with his beautiful, hot-blooded bride. They drifted off to sleep at last, the steady beating of their two hearts slipping into that strange and mystical harmony that only the truest of lovers can ever know.

When Alex awoke the next morning, it was only to find her new husband gone. She turned her head on the pillow and glanced sleepily down at the empty place beside her. The mattress still bore the faint indentation of his body.

Hot color suddenly flamed in her cheeks. The memories of the previous night—*her wedding night*—flooded her mind and provoked a wild leaping of her pulse. Jonathan had made love to her a third and even a fourth time before the first gentle rays of the dawn had set the horizon aglow. The last "encounter," she recalled with a pleasurable shiver, had taken place after she had been awakened by the feel of her bridegroom's warm, seductive lips upon the back of her thigh. He had soon made it clear that he meant to kiss every square inch of her body. . . .

Tossing a helpless look up toward the canopy, she threw aside the covers and finally climbed from the bed. A faint, involuntary groan escaped her lips. Her body was plagued by an embarrassing soreness; she ached in places she hadn't even known to exist before now. *It should come as no real surprise,* her mind's inner voice gleefully put forth. She frowned and hastened to draw on her wrapper. Tying the belt, she wandered across to the window.

She tensed when she heard someone rap softly at the door. Wondering if it was Jonathan, though she couldn't imagine he would ever again bother to knock, she hesitated a moment before opening the door. It was Tilly who stood beaming her a warmly lit smile.

"Good morning to you, miss," she said. In her hands

was a silver tray laden with a pot of tea and a covered plate of food.

"Tilly!" Alex uttered in surprise. "Why, what are you—?" She broke off, coloring in mortification as it occurred to her what the other woman must be thinking. Her gaze fell toward her wrapper, and she searched for the right words with which to explain what was admittedly a scandalous-looking situation.

"I thought you might be wanting your breakfast up here this morning," Tilly announced, breezing inside with the tray and setting it on the marble-topped table near the wardrobe.

"You should not have troubled yourself," protested Alex, her gaze clouding with worry. "Especially in your delicate condition."

"Delicate?" The petite brunet gave a soft, pleasant trill of laughter. "Strong as a horse, I be, in spite of my size. Truth be told, I was scrubbing floors right up until the very day the boys were born, and like as not to do the same this time."

"Perhaps so, but I thought we had agreed that I was going to do the cooking from now on! You have your own family, after all, and—"

"You've not yet been a bride for a whole day's time." Tilly interrupted her kindly; her eyes were full of both sympathy and understanding. "You should feel no guilt for having still been abed, miss. Begging your pardon— *Mrs. Hazard*," she amended, with another quick smile.

"So, you—you know?" Alex stammered, feeling terribly uncomfortable in spite of Tilly's compassion.

"That I do. The captain told me first thing this morning. I expect as how he wanted to set my mind at ease when I asked if you were ill." The news of their marriage had not been so unexpected, Tilly mused silently. Anyone with eyes could see the two of them were headed for mischief. Praise God, it had come to marriage instead of the other. "The captain said you might be sleeping a bit yet, but since it was past noon already, I thought you'd be hungry."

"Past noon?" Alex echoed in further surprise. Her gaze made a quick, encompassing sweep of the sunlit room before falling again. "Has he told everyone else as well?"

"Most be in Parramatta still. 'Tis the custom to stay over Saturday night and then go to church Sunday morn. My Seth and I would have done the same, but I was feeling the need to be home." Moving forward, she searched Alex's face and probed gently, "Are you all right, mistress? If there be anything—"

"Oh, Tilly! I cannot believe what has happened!"

"Well, now. The wedding *was* a bit rushed," the other woman conceded, with a mild frown. "But what does time matter? Not a fig, really." She shook her head for emphasis. "Things be different here, not so proper and pretty as back in England. The captain was that determined to take you to wife, and it's no doubt pleased you are to have the matter settled between the two of you."

"Pleased?" She lifted a hand and ran it through her short, tousled curls. "For heaven's sake, I have known the man less than a fortnight. And if you must know, this marriage was *forced* upon me. I had no intention of becoming Jonathan Hazard's wife." She folded her arms beneath her breasts and began pacing distractedly to-and-fro. "I must get back to England."

"How can you say such a thing?" asked Tilly, visibly shocked. "For better or worse, mistress, you be wed to the captain now."

"It changes nothing." She ceased her pacing and curled an arm about the bedpost. Her head lifted in a show of proud determination that, whether she would yet admit it or not, had already been vanquished by a tall, green-eyed American. "My goal has always been to win my freedom, to convince the governor of my innocence and return to my aunt and uncle in London. As I told my *husband*, I do not belong here and never will!"

"I think, Alexandra, that you'd best be following your heart instead of your head," Tilly advised quietly. It was the first time she had ever called her by her Christian name. Alex's eyes grew very round, and she was dismayed to feel her cheeks burning again.

"I—I'm afraid I don't know what you mean."

"Do not, I pray you, mistress, make the mistake of pushing the captain too far." The warning was offered in earnest. "He's a good and fair-minded man, he is, but only a man for all that. He'll not take kindly to talk of leaving." She turned and ambled back to the door. Pausing briefly, she cast Alex a sad little smile that bespoke a wisdom far beyond her years. "You've done what many said would never happen—you've captured the captain's heart. He'll not be wanting it back. And unless I miss my guess, you'll not truly be wanting to give it up." With that, she was gone.

Alex wandered over to the table. Swallowing a sudden lump in her throat, she sank down into the large, wine-colored leather chair and absently poured herself a cup of tea. She contemplated all that Tilly had said, but could find no peace of mind as a result. Her gaze shifted to the tray again. Surprised at how famished she suddenly felt, she took the cover off the plate and proceeded to down every bite of the eggs, ham, and biscuits.

Later, after having treated herself to a sorely needed bath, she dressed and finally ventured downstairs. She strolled outside to the front porch, her eyes searching as they always did for any sign of Jonathan. Even though it was Sunday, she knew with a certainty that he would not be sitting idle somewhere. She had never known a man less suited to a life of leisure. He was so alive, so incredibly strong and vibrant and sure of himself—last night had offered substantial proof of that. . . .

Bemoaning the sudden, wicked turn of her thoughts, she felt guilty color wash over her as she moved across the porch and down the steps. The grounds were virtually deserted that afternoon; she remembered what Tilly had told her about the workers and their families staying on in Parramatta. She was glad of it, in a way. The last thing she wanted at the moment was to face a veritable barrage of questions and congratulations. No doubt some would believe she had schemed from the very beginning to become the mistress of Boree. Some, like Tilly, would accept the news matter-of-factly. And still others might be jealous that she, a convict with seven years' time still to serve, had obtained freedom so easily.

She released a sigh and wandered farther away from the main house. It was a beautiful day, one she might have been more inclined to appreciate if not for the fact that her emotions were so raw. Passing the stable, she allowed her instincts to lead her toward the barn.

Suddenly, and without warning, someone moved to block her path.

A sharp, breathless cry of alarm escaped her lips as she drew abruptly to a halt. The man before her was quite dark, almost chocolate-colored, with a full head of wiry black hair and features that were like no others she had seen before. Although he stood only a few inches taller than she, his manner was quite imposing. He was clad in nothing more than a loincloth of sorts, and his skin was marked by strange white tatoos.

"Dear God! Who—who are you?" Alex gasped out,

fear gripping her heart when her eyes fell upon the spear he carried in one hand.

"His name is Jaga," Jonathan spoke behind her. She whirled at the sound of his voice.

"You mean to tell me you *know* him?" she demanded in startlement.

"Jaga and I are old friends." He smiled faintly and sauntered forward to slip a possessive arm about her waist. "This is my woman, Jaga."

"Her hair is the color of fire," the aborigine noted in a low, guttural voice.

"You speak English?" asked Alex, her gaze wide and incredulous.

"I speak English." His mouth curved into an unexpected grin as he told Jonathan, "She is much to look at."

"She is indeed."

"She will bear you many sons," Jaga added, his dark eyes falling significantly toward Alex's hips.

"Daughters would please me as well," said Jonathan.

"I beg your pardon!" Alex interjected at this point. Taking considerable exception at being talked about as though she were nothing more than a brood mare, she pulled angrily away from her husband and lifted her head to a proud angle. "I am honored to have made your acquaintance, Jaga," she declared, with all manner of civility. To Jonathan, she said, "If you will kindly excuse me, sir, I have far better things to do than listen to a discussion of my—my physical merits!"

As if on cue, Jaga murmured something in his own language and turned to leave. Jonathan answered, still in words Alex could not understand, and lifted a hand in farewell. The aborigine disappeared as suddenly as he had come.

"Mr. Muldoon told me the natives stayed in the wilderness now," remarked Alex, frowning thoughtfully in his wake.

"They do, for the most part," Jonathan replied. "But as I told you, Jaga is a friend."

"It is a curious friendship, is it not? You did, after all, settle on land that once belonged to his people."

"An apt description of British colonialism," he quipped wryly.

"The two of you behaved quite churlishly," she accused, indignant once more.

"Count yourself fortunate that you are my wife instead of his. Among the aborigines, women are treated with shocking brutality. A bride who makes the mistake of provoking her mate is likely to be met with blows and kicks, or even to find herself struck on the head with a club. It's said that a particularly vengeful husband will pursue his wife for days at a time with murder on his mind." His eyes held a devilish light of amusement when he concluded, "So you see, my love, your own husband is not such a savage after all."

"I am not 'your love'!" she said in denial, nonplussed at the way her heart leapt within her breast.

"What are you doing out here?" he asked, with infuriating calm. "Looking for me?"

"Certainly not." Feeling both awkward and lightheaded now that she was facing him again, she looked away and murmured, "I simply felt the need for some fresh air."

"I had not meant to neglect you for so long, but one of the wagons was in need of repair and there was no one else to do it." His gaze warmed, and his low tone was laced with passion when he vowed, "From now on, Mrs. Hazard, our Sundays will be spent in rest. There's every possibility we won't leave our bed at all."

"Why do you keep pretending that our marriage is a

normal one?" she demanded, rosy color staining her cheeks. It was impossible to erase the memory of his touch. And his words secretly thrilled her. "It is not at all normal, and well you know it."

" 'Extraordinary' is more what I had in mind."

"The wedding cannot have been legal," she proclaimed, trying another tactic. "I did not agree to honor the vows; I did not agree to be your wife."

"It was legal. 'Till death do us part,' remember?" He, too, was recalling the enchantment they had shared. She looked more beautiful than ever; he smiled to himself at the thought of what the night would bring.

"I shall see to it that my uncle arranges to have it dissolved. He is a member of Parliament, and as such will be able to find a way to—"

She broke off with a gasp when he suddenly seized her arms in a hard, punishing grip and yanked her close. His eyes glinted with barely restrained fury.

"By damn, there will be no divorce!" he ground out. "I don't care if your uncle is the king himself, I'll never give you up! *Never!*"

Stunned, Alex could only stare mutely up at him. She was certain he meant to kiss her. But he did not. As if realizing that their quarrel might be witnessed by others, he did nothing more than subject her to one last darkly quelling look before releasing her. She was startled when a faint smile of irony touched his lips.

"Perhaps I am something of a savage after all." He resisted the urge to drag her into the barn and show her just how primitive he could be. "You are my wife, Alexandra. Now and forever. I'll hear no more talk of divorce."

She was unable to offer a suitable retort as he strode past her and disappeared behind the stable. Rubbing at her arms and glaring resentfully after him, she turned her own steps back toward the main house.

The workers returned to the plantation shortly before sunset. Their voices drifted into the kitchen, where Alex was busy preparing the evening meal. She smiled at the sound; oddly enough, it filled her with a certain contentment. Although she had been at Boree only a short time, she was beginning to care very much about those who lived here. They were, she mused idly, rather like a family. With Jonathan Hazard their handsome, all-powerful patriarch.

Her smile quickly turned into a frown, her eyes clouding at the sudden thought of her own family. She had not yet completed the letter to Uncle Henry. Why the devil was she finding it difficult to do so? It *wasn't* difficult to imagine what his reaction would be when he discovered that she was married, and that her husband was—of all things—an American. Finn Muldoon had told her that Jonathan had actually captained a naval vessel throughout the War of 1812. So, it seemed he was not only an impossible rogue, but an enemy as well. And since her uncle had served as a military adviser for his own country during the conflict—saints be certain, she told herself (employing one of Muldoon's favorite idioms), the two of them would not be at all compatible. Of course, it was highly unlikely their paths would ever cross.

Her gaze traveled back to the window. It would be dark soon.

Thoughts of the coming night made her heart pound erratically. She muttered an oath and whirled about, marching to the sink. Her hand reached for the handle of the pump, and she began to move it up and down with such angry vigor that the sound of the back door opening was drowned out.

"Impatient for my return?" drawled Jonathan. His mouth twitched with wry amusement when she rounded on him.

"You, sir, may go to the devil for all I care!"

"Is that any way for a wife to greet her lord and master?"

"You'll never be that," she countered, the fire in her eyes a perfect match for the state of her emotions. "And you can get your own supper!" She stormed from the kitchen and into the dining room, only to call a halt to her temperamental flight when she discovered Finn Muldoon sitting at the table.

"Sure now, Mrs. Hazard . . . I'll not be troubling you for a meal this night," he said apologetically, rising to his feet and doing his best to suppress the grin tugging at his lips.

"Stay put, Mr. Muldoon." She sighed, coloring guiltily. Jonathan entered the room now as well, taking his own place at the head of the table. She folded her arms across her chest and refused to meet his gaze.

"I'll see what I can do about finding another housekeeper," he promised. His eyes glowed warmly. "Perhaps I should send Muldoon this time."

"Aye, Captain. It could well be I'll find meself a bride." He smiled and looked at Alex, who appeared anything but appreciative of their raillery. "Begging your pardon, Mrs. Hazard," he said as he quickly sobered again, "but maybe I should be leaving—?"

"Nonsense." She drew herself proudly erect. "You shall remain and have your supper." She swept back into the kitchen and soon reappeared with the meal. As soon as she had lowered the platter of food to the table, Jonathan stood and gently grasped her arm.

"Sit down, Alexandra."

"No." She shook her head and tried to pull away, but he held fast.

"You'll join us, I say."

"I will not."

"By heaven, woman! *Sit down!*"

She might have made the mistake of further defiance, but a quick glance at Finn Muldoon served to change her mind. Capitulating, though with obvious reluctance, she moved to the other side of the table and sank stiffly down into the chair opposite the Irishman's.

"I'll be fetching the coffee," Muldoon was quick to offer.

Throughout the course of the meal, Alex ate little. The two men, however, helped themselves to generous portions and talked of business matters—the fall harvest, plans to breed new stock, the purchase of additional plows and other farm implements. They made frequent attempts to draw Alex into their conversation, but she gave only brief responses. Finally she stood to clear away the dishes.

"Leave them," Jonathan directed.

"Leave them?" she echoed in surprise. "Why, I cannot—"

"You are mistress of the plantation now, Alexandra," he pointed out. If she had known him better, she would have realized that he was baiting her. "I'll not have my wife acting as a servant."

"For heaven's sake, would you have me do nothing but sit with my tea and embroidery all the day long?" she challenged indignantly, planting her hands on her hips.

"Isn't that how highborn English ladies are expected to pass the time?" He leaned back in his chair and folded his arms across his chest. His green eyes twinkled up into the luminous turquoise depths of hers. "Well, Lady Alex?" His tone was soft and mocking.

"Perhaps that is true, but *I* have never been content to let my behavior be dictated by others."

"I can well believe it." He rose leisurely to his feet and tossed his napkin to the table. Alex felt a sudden knot of alarm tighten in her stomach. Finn Muldoon's gaze shifted from one to the other, and he waited no longer before standing and announcing his departure.

"I'll be going now," he said, with a respectful nod and another hidden grin. "Many thanks, Mrs. Hazard, for the fine meal."

"Please, Mr. Muldoon ... Would you not like to accompany me into the parlor for a glass of brandy before you go?" Alex impulsively suggested. She dreaded the prospect of being alone with her husband again—*for good reason.*

"Well now," he replied, wavering indecisively for a few moments. His eyes traveled to Jonathan once more. What he saw there prompted him to decline Alex's kind invitation. "Thank you all the same, mistress, but I've things to see to this night. Things, I fear, that cannot wait. Yes, indeed. No matter how strong a thirst I—"

"Good night, Muldoon." Jonathan cut him off firmly.

"Good night to you, Captain. And to you, Mrs. Hazard." He gave another nod and beat a hasty retreat.

"The hour grows late, my love," Jonathan pronounced as soon as their guest was gone.

"It is still quite early," Alex bravely disputed. Turning her back on him, she headed into the parlor. She was not at all surprised when he followed, but she did not acknowledge his presence as she wandered across to the table on the other side of the sofa and turned the flame higher.

"Do you fear the dark, Alexandra?" teased Jonathan,

his voice low and vibrant. He stood framed in the doorway, and he made no move as yet to advance upon her.

"I fear nothing." It was a childish response, and she groaned inwardly as soon as she had uttered it. Folding her arms beneath her breasts again, she found herself torn between the urge to declare that she would spend the night alone in the parlor—and the more cowardly impulse to bolt for the front door.

"Perhaps you'd like to talk."

"The only thing I'd care to discuss with you, Jonathan Hazard, is my freedom!" Her eyes flew wide open when he started toward her.

"I warned you against that," he reminded her, with a dangerous half smile playing about his lips. "I'll never let you go." He had reached the end of the sofa; she darted behind it.

"Do you think I would ever wish to stay with a man who treats me as you do?" she demanded, backing away. Her throat constricted with alarm at the look in his eyes.

"How is it I treat you, Alexandra?" He continued to advance, his movements slow and steady and purposeful. "Like a wife perhaps? Like a woman whose passions run as hot as my own and whose mind and spirit are more than equal to her beauty?"

"Save your compliments. You use them only because you want me in your bed again." She cast a desperate glance toward the doorway.

"I'll not deny my desire. But I will have all of you," he vowed softly. "Heart and soul."

"I shall never love you," she insisted, then was dismayed to feel herself trembling. "I shall never feel anything for you other than—than anger and distaste."

"Shall you not?" His gaze burned across into hers with compelling intensity as she rounded the other end of the sofa. He stopped and gave her a smile that was thoroughly disarming. "I think, my dearest bride, that you already do."

"No!" Afraid of the sudden, wild stirring of her heart, she shook her head and exclaimed breathlessly, "I still know nothing about you. Why, it is as though I were married to a stranger."

"What is there to know? I am Jonathan Hazard, formerly of Baltimore, Maryland. I've a mother and father still living, and one sister, of whom I am very fond. There are other assorted aunts, uncles, and cousins, all happily back in America. I was on the seas before coming to Australia two years ago. And the rest is of no importance."

"You neglected to mention that you fought against *my* countrymen."

"The oversight was unintentional, I can assure you." Another glimmer of amusement lurked within his eyes. "What else did Muldoon see fit to tell you?"

"Only that he thinks we are perfectly suited to each other," she blurted out.

"So then, the old rascal is perceptive as well as loyal."

"Everyone here seems completely *besotted* with you. How can they be so blind to your faults?" She crossed her arms beneath her breasts again, then felt her legs weaken when she observed the way his eyes strayed downward to feast hungrily upon her rounded, creamy flesh. "Why do they not realize what a scoundrel you are?" she lamented, her mind screaming at her to run, but her body refusing to obey.

"Perhaps you should ask them." His gaze caught and held hers once more. "But not now. I've been patient long enough. By heaven, you've filled my mind all day," he told her, his words a simple statement of fact rather than a complaint. "Just as you've done since the first time I set eyes on you at Parramatta. I knew even then that you would be mine."

"You promised that my job as housekeeper would entail nothing more than the traditional duties," she reminded him.

"You're no longer the housekeeper." He started forward again.

"And will you offer the same assurances to the next woman who accepts the position? Will you give her the same 'personal' attention? Perhaps, once you've tired of me, you'll turn to *her* for—"

"I'll never tire of you, Lady Alex."

"You—you cannot be certain of that."

"You're wrong."

The way he said it provoked her to action at last. She shook her head again and spun about, racing for the doorway. A cry of defeat escaped her lips when he caught her and pulled her back against him. Her hand came up to land a stinging blow to the side of his head. Undeterred, he carried her to the sofa and flung her down upon it, but she immediately rolled to the floor. Scrambling up onto her hands and knees, she suffered a sharp intake of breath when he knelt behind her and slipped an arm about her waist.

The next thing she knew, he had tossed her skirts above her waist and was yanking her drawers all the way down to her knees.

"Jonathan!" She crimsoned at having her bottom bared to him.

"You've a beautiful backside, Mrs. Hazard," he murmured huskily.

Shocked and outraged—and more feverishly excited than she would ever admit—she tried to squirm free, but he pulled her back against him once more. His hand moved between her thighs, his warm fingers stroking the silken flesh there with a mastery that was both sweet and savage. His other hand plunged within the rounded neckline of her bodice.

"No, please . . . don't!" she gasped out, her arms lifting traitorously upward to his neck.

It was much too late, of course. Within minutes, he was urging her back down to her hands and knees. He unfastened his breeches. She wondered how he meant to take her when he had as yet to turn her around, but her bewilderment was answered in a most satisfying way when he thrust into her from behind. She moaned to feel his hardness sheathing perfectly within the moist warmth of her feminine passage. The position was wicked and shocking—*and wonderful.* She arched her back and welcomed his lips upon the tempting curve of her shoulder, her hips matching the sensuous rhythm of his as the blending of their bodies took them to a level of pleasure that was, in truth, heaven on earth.

Afterward, Jonathan took a seat upon the couch and cradled her across his lap. Alex was quite flushed and breathless as she rested within his arms. Her bodice was sadly askew, her breasts threatening to spill over as they rose and fell. She attempted to push her creased skirts back down into place, but her loving captor would not allow it. His hand smoothed appreciatively over her naked derriere, and he dropped a soft, caressing kiss upon her forehead when she stirred and heaved a sigh.

"How is it you know so much about . . . well, about what we've just done?" she asked in a small voice. He gave a low chuckle of delight and gathered her even closer.

"A wifely question if ever I heard one."

"Are you by any chance evading it?"

"Not at all." His features grew solemn, and his eyes

were gleaming dully when he confessed, "I've not lived the life of a monk, Alexandra. And after the war ... Suffice it to say, I spent a number of years wandering without any real direction or purpose."

"Why?" Seized by the sudden, fierce desire to know all she could about him, she frowned and lifted her head to meet his gaze. "What happened to fill you with such restlessness?"

"The reason no longer matters." Another brief smile touched his lips. "It was long ago and best forgotten."

"Why have you never returned to America?" Her heart fluttering anew, she lowered her head back to his chest and traced a finger along the opened edges of his shirt.

"Because I found what I was seeking."

"And what was that?"

"A new life. A new land. A place where a man's true worth is judged on his character and ability, not his past. Even those who have been sent here against their will can find a freedom that's all the sweeter for having been hard won." He released a sigh of his own and trailed his hand upward to entangle gently within her lustrous, flame-colored curls. "Australia is my home now—and yours as well."

She opened her mouth to deny it, but the words would not come. Her eyes swept closed, and she did not protest when he finally carried her upstairs. . . .

Chapter 12

Two days passed before storm clouds gathered on the horizon again. They foretold of more than rain.

Just as Alex had envisioned, she was treated differently by the workers at Boree once news of her marriage reached their ears. There were many congratulations but few questions; it seemed no one dared risk the captain's wrath by casting any aspersions upon his bride. Indeed, everyone was quite respectful, even distant, and she realized with a touch of sadness that things would never be the same again. Whatever she had been before, she was mistress of the plantation now.

Tilly continued to approach her with at least some of the old friendliness. Coleen and Agatha, however, were reluctant to work alongside her anymore, although they did not mind taking orders from her. Their attitude was not completely unexpected. They had left England far behind, yet they had brought with them the long-bred sense of class structure. Alex could only hope that time would bring an easier acceptance of her new position.

Acceptance. The word, she reflected with an inward sigh, was one she would prefer not to dwell upon. The past two days (and nights) with Jonathan Hazard had thrown her into more of a quandary than ever. He was passionate and demanding, tender and charming . . . and she was absolutely powerless to resist him. But his ap-

209

peal extended far beyond the bedroom. She took undeniable pleasure from the sound of his voice and each smile he gave her, she secretly looked forward to seeing him at mealtimes and whenever they "chanced" to meet elsewhere throughout the day, and she even found herself counting the hours until sunset, for only then would they be alone with each other.

Thoughts of escape were growing increasingly rare, a fact that provoked a sharp twinge of guilt within her. What had happened to her determination to be free? And why did she find it more and more difficult to remember the faces of all her friends back in London?

These troubling questions, and perhaps a dozen others, tumbled chaotically about in her mind as she wandered outside to the front porch late that Tuesday afternoon. Her preoccupied gaze drifted skyward, and she smiled softly at the sight of the thick gray clouds waiting to release their bounty upon the sun-baked earth. The fresh scent of rain already filled the air. She took a deep, appreciative breath and closed her eyes.

The sound of approaching hoofbeats caused her eyelids to fly wide open again. She watched as two riders, a man and a woman, came into view just beyond the row of cottages. They slowed their horses to a walk as they neared the main house, then reined to a complete halt when Jonathan suddenly strode forth from the smaller of the two barns. The woman did not wait for her companion's assistance in dismounting, but hastily swung down and whirled to face Jonathan with a tearful, joyous smile of greeting.

"Jon!"

"Gwendolyn?" he murmured in stunned disbelief. His brow creased into a frown, his gaze darkening as it traveled swiftly over her. She had changed, he noted—her hair was a deep, burnished gold instead of the light

blond he remembered, her figure was fuller, more voluptuous, and her face was etched with lines that had
not been there before. But she was still Gwendolyn, still
beautiful, and he was relieved that he felt nothing more
than surprise at seeing her again.

"Oh, Jon ... I've missed you so very much!" Concealing her disappointment at his less than impassioned
welcome, she flung herself dramatically upon his chest.

Alex, meanwhile, had overheard their brief exchange.
And now, as she witnessed the woman's outpouring of
affection, she felt a burning pain slice through her heart.
She was tempted to call out, to protest the embrace, but
she did not. Folding her arms tightly beneath her
breasts, she descended the front steps at a slow, measured pace.

"What the devil are you doing here?" demanded Jonathan, disentangling his former fiancée's arms from
about his neck. His reaction would have been no different even if he had been aware of his wife's approach.
"Why didn't you let me know you were coming?"

"Don't scold me, dearest Jon," Gwendolyn pleaded.
She was quite tall, her head reaching past his shoulder,
and she smiled once more as her brown eyes gazed
adoringly into the fathomless green of his. "I know I
should have written, but I was afraid you would forbid
me to come. It has been so long, after all, and we *did*
part bitterly."

"Did your husband make the voyage with you?" His
mouth curved into a faint smile of irony.

"No. No, my—my husband is dead." Looking every
inch the grieving young widow, she drew a handkerchief from the pocket of her blue velvet riding skirt and
raised it to her nose. "It has been more than a year
now."

"Has it?" There was an astonishing lack of sympathy

in his voice. His eyes moved significantly to where her guide stood waiting with the two horses.

"I'd best be getting back to Sydney, Mrs. Wilcox," the young, well-dressed stranger announced, setting her carpetbag on the ground. He responded to Jonathan's curt nod of acknowledgment with one of his own.

"Yes, of course," said Gwendolyn. Releasing a sigh, she pivoted about and told him, "Many thanks, Mr. Fitzpatrick, for your kind escort." Her smile was almost coquettish, and his face reddened before he swung back up into the saddle and rode away, leading her borrowed horse behind his.

Jonathan's gaze softened when he finally caught sight of Alex. Closing the distance between them, he gently grasped her arm. She stiffened at his touch, but he appeared to take no notice of it as he led her forward to make the introductions.

"Alexandra, I'd like for you to meet an old friend of mine from America, Mrs. Gwendolyn Wilcox."

"Surely not 'old,' nor merely a friend," Gwendolyn corrected him with a throaty laugh. Her eyes glittered and narrowed while they flickered disdainfully over Alex. "Who is she, Jon? One of your little convicts, perhaps? Your mother told me how they are the only ones available to work—"

"I am his wife," Alex declared on sudden impulse, then colored and looked away when she felt her husband's warm, amused gaze upon her. His arm slipped about her waist.

"His wife?" Gwendolyn echoed, incredulous. She looked mutely from one to the other for several long moments. Finally she rounded on Jonathan in a burst of barely controlled anger. "How long have you been married?"

"Only a few days," he answered, with maddening equanimity.

"Well then, that would certainly explain why your family said nothing of it to me!" Struggling to maintain her composure, she forced another smile to her lips. "I can imagine they will be quite as surprised as I was. It was no doubt a whirlwind courtship—much the same as *ours*, perhaps?"

"Yours?" It was Alex's turn to widen her eyes in amazement.

"Of course! Why, hasn't Jon told you?" She heaved another highly eloquent sigh and recalled, "We were so desperately in love with each other. If not for the war—"

"That was a long time ago." Jonathan cut her off in a voice that was whipcord sharp. His fingers tensed about Alex's arm; the look in his eyes was guarded. "You haven't yet told me what you're doing here, Gwendolyn."

"I am here because I had to see you."

"Why the sudden urge after all these years?"

"You know why." Her eyes glistened even more brightly with unshed tears when she asked, "Did you truly plan to stay away forever, Jon? Is that why you never answered any of my letters?"

"It would have served no purpose."

"You're so very wrong," she exclaimed. The tears spilled over from her lashes now, and she shot a quick glare toward Alex before entreating him, "Please, I—I must speak to you in private. I have come so far, Jon. The least you can do is hear me out."

Jonathan swore inwardly. He was reluctant to grant her request; he wanted nothing more than to send her packing. But he told himself that no matter what she had done, she was undeserving of such cruelty.

"Let's go inside the house," he said quietly.

Alex's throat constricted with a sudden, inexplicable dread. She held back when Jonathan took her arm again and attempted to lead her along with him.

"*I* shall remain outside," she proclaimed in a low, simmering tone.

"Alexandra, I—"

"You and Mrs. Wilcox desire a private conversation, do you not?" Her eyes blazed reproachfully up into his.

"I'll explain everything to you later," he promised.

"That will not be necessary," she retorted. Her fiery turquoise gaze shifted to Gwendolyn. "Once you have finished with your 'discussion,' Mrs. Wilcox, I shall see that you are made comfortable in one of the guest rooms."

"Thank you," the other woman murmured, with little attempt at warmth. She dabbed prettily at her eyes and untied the strings of her silk taffeta bonnet.

Alex watched as Jonathan turned away, caught up the single carpetbag, and escorted their unexpected guest across the grounds to the house. The two of them soon disappeared inside.

Wondering why the discovery that her husband had once been betrothed to another should be so upsetting, she frowned and tried to ignore the ache deep within her. *We were so desperately in love with each other.* Gwendolyn's words returned to taunt her, to provoke emotions so intense that she felt a wave of nausea.

A man like Jonathan Hazard had probably known a great many women, she mused as she drew in a deep, ragged breath. Why, he himself had admitted to her that he had lived a less than saintly life. She could well imagine that he had left a trail of broken hearts throughout his many travels.

But Gwendolyn Wilcox was no figment of her imagination. No, by heaven, the statuesque young widow was all too real. And she had journeyed halfway around the world to see Jonathan. *For what purpose?*

A rumble of thunder sounded overhead; the wind began to whip and howl through the trees as the storm approached. Clutching at her skirts, Alex glanced indecisively back toward the house. She had no wish to be caught in another cloudburst. Faced with the choice of seeking shelter in the barn or returning to the front porch, she settled upon the latter. But in so doing, she found herself unintentionally privy to every word drifting through the parlor's open window. . . .

Jonathan, meanwhile, had taken up a stance before the fireplace. Gwendolyn sat on the sofa, arranging her velvet skirts about her and unbuttoning the jacket of her riding habit to reveal a fitted, white lawn blouse underneath.

"Will you not at least offer me some refreshments, Jon? The ride was long and tiring. I fail to see how you can stand this awful heat." She drew off the jacket and tossed it aside, then lifted a hand to make certain her hair was still securely pinned in its fashionable chignon.

Moving to the sideboard near the doorway, Jonathan poured a glass of water and took it to her. He was normally a more congenial host, but he was not pleased to welcome this particular visitor to Boree.

"When did you arrive in Australia?" he asked.

"Three days ago." She drank thirstily before elaborating. "I wanted to call upon you right away, but I was quite exhausted after the voyage."

"The truth, Gwendolyn—why have you come?" He resumed his position in front of the fireplace, his eyes gleaming dully as they bored across into hers. "Would you really have me believe you traveled so far merely for old times' sake?"

"I told you, I had to see you! Five years I've waited, five long years without so much as a word—"

"You were married, remember? I doubt your husband would have allowed you to correspond with a former lover."

"You're still angry with me, aren't you?" she charged, with more than a hint of triumphant satisfaction. "For heaven's sake, Jon. I've paid for my mistakes. My life with Henry was unbearable."

"You should have considered that beforehand."

"How could I have known he would turn out to be so mean and selfish? After all, I was quite young, and so terribly lonely. I loved you, of course, but I—I was confused. I feared you would never return from the war, and Henry seduced me with his promises of devotion. If only you had never gone away!"

"You could have waited, Gwendolyn," he pointed out, another faint, mocking smile playing about his lips. "Other women did."

"I was different," she argued feelingly. "You know how vulnerable I was, how easily influenced I could be. My nature has always been most passionate." She raised the handkerchief to her nose again and lamented, "Oh, Jon. How can you be so cruel? After all we meant to each other—?"

"What does any of that matter now? What's past is past." His handsome features were inscrutable, and there was no discernible warmth in his gaze when he told her, "If you've come all this way to apologize, then you've achieved your purpose and can book passage homeward."

"I *did* come to beg your forgiveness." She rose abruptly to her feet and hastened across to lay an imploring hand upon his arm. Her eyes were soft and seductive as they met his. "But there was another reason as well, one you must have already guessed. I've never stopped loving you, Jon. And I cannot believe you no longer feel anything for me."

"Have you forgotten that I have a wife?" he challenged, his deep-timbred voice brimming with wry amusement.

"Ah, yes. Your blushing bride," she spat out contemptuously. "I'll wager the little redheaded vixen trapped you into marriage somehow." Whirling about, she swept across to the sideboard. She poured herself some brandy this time, and downed the fiery amber liquid in a single gulp. Bright, angry color suffused her face when she rounded on him again. "She isn't woman enough for a man like you. But *I* am, and well you know it. You cannot have forgotten the hours we spent in each other's arms, my dearest love, nor the fact that we could scarcely contain our passions. Surely you must remember how I would steal away to meet you, how I—"

Alex had heard more than enough by now. The realization that Jonathan had shared with Gwendolyn what he had shared with her provoked a white-hot surge of mingled pain and jealousy. It was one thing to be curious about her husband's past; it was quite another to have that curiosity satisfied with such terrible, shocking clarity. The color drained from her face. Sick at heart, she raced down the steps and across the yard. She headed aimlessly toward the fields, oblivious to the fact that the storm was threatening to break at any moment.

In her wake, the confrontation grew increasingly unpleasant.

"Can you honestly say that you no longer desire me?" demanded Gwendolyn, moving close again. She lifted her hands to his shoulders, only to have him seize her wrists in a firm grip and force her arms back to her sides.

"I can. And the 'happy' memories of which you speak have long since faded."

"No!" She shook her head in a vehement denial, her ample bosom heaving beneath the clinging fabric of her blouse. "You swore you would love me forever."

"I was wrong to do so," he readily admitted. He folded his arms across his chest and encountered no real difficulty in preventing his eyes from straying downward. "And what of your late husband, the much maligned Mr. Wilcox? You said he had only been dead for a year. It doesn't require the mind of a scholar to deduce that you cannot have mourned for long. You must have set sail within a few short months of his death."

"Why should I brand myself a hypocrite? He was unforgivably cruel to me!"

"So you have claimed."

"Your mother will bear out the truth of my story. She was only too happy to lend a sympathetic ear. I will be forever grateful to her for her kindness." She sighed again, and her eyes shone with what she hoped was a thoroughly captivating radiance. "She showed me your letters, Jon. I devoured every word of them. That's when I knew I had to come."

"My mother's heart has always been soft." He smiled to himself and remarked, "Strangely enough, she's made no mention of you in her letters to me." His sister had done so, he recalled silently, but that had been years ago, when she had taken it upon herself to inform him that Gwendolyn's marriage to Henry Wilcox had proven to be a much-talked-about disaster. There had been rumors of indiscretions on the part of both husband and wife, of a scandalous amount of money spent on clothes and parties and furnishings, and of violent quarrels.

While the news had given him no pleasure—he had been well past both heartache and revenge by that time—it had not been all that surprising.

"I suppose she wanted to spare you any further pain." Gwendolyn sighed, wandering back to the sofa. "And then, when Henry died, I asked her not to tell you. I think I always knew that I would come, that I would find you and we would finally be together again." She turned to face him once more, and did not try to stop a fresh wave of tears. "Please, Jon. I have suffered enough. Surely you cannot doubt the sincerity of my desire to make amends, not after all I have endured to seek you out."

"It's too late, Gwendolyn." There was neither affection nor regret in his voice, only pity. "I'm sorry your life has not turned out as you might have wished, but there can be no going back. You could have saved yourself the trouble and expense of the voyage if you—"

"You wish to punish me, don't you?" she accused. "I cannot in all honesty blame you, for I know I hurt you. It was because of me that you've stayed away these past five years. But don't you see? That only proves how deep and inescapable your feelings for me are. Why else would you leave behind all that you hold dear and settle in this dreadful, godforsaken country?"

"In the beginning, you *were* the reason I stayed away," he confessed. "But only in the beginning. And it so happens that I consider this 'dreadful, godforsaken country' my home now."

"You cannot mean that! Return to Baltimore with me." She flew back to lift her hands to his arms again, her expression one of purposeful cajolery. "You don't belong here. You're an American, for heaven's sake!"

"So my bride keeps reminding me." Drawing away, he crossed to the window. His eyes filled with a harsh gleam when he demanded, "Doesn't it matter to you that I am married now? Damn it, Gwendolyn! Can you really be so lost to shame?" Another rumble of thunder split the air. He frowned, his thoughts returning to Alex.

"I have no shame when it comes to you. I never have! You still love me, Jon. I know you do! Since you've only been wed for a few days, it cannot be so difficult to set aside this ridiculous marriage of yours and—"

"*Enough!*" he ground out. His features were dangerously grim when he turned his head and met her gaze.

"Do you think it a mere coincidence that I've come now?" she demanded, afraid of what she read in his eyes, yet unwilling to abandon her scheme after only one attempt.

"I think it an inconvenience, nothing more." A flash of lightning suddenly lit the sky. His concern for Alex prompted an end to the reunion at last. "You can stay here at Boree until I've arranged your passage back to America." He strode toward the doorway.

"I will not accept defeat so easily," she avowed, her voice rising shrilly after him. "I will not leave Australia unless you come with me!"

Jonathan swore underneath his breath, but he did not slow his pace. The first raindrops stung his face as he headed down the front steps and across the yard. His search led him first to the stable, then to each of the barns. There was no sign of Alex.

His worry increased along with the wind's turbulent fury. His gaze darkened as it swept the grounds. The workers and their families had already taken shelter from what promised to be a violent summer storm. The heavens were dark and boiling, the air positively electrified.

"Captain!"

He jerked his head about, watching as Finn Muldoon hastened forward. The Irishman's face wore an unusually grave look.

"Have you seen Alexandra?" demanded Jonathan, raising his voice to be heard above the deepening howl of the wind as it chased leaves and dust across the ground.

"Aye, Captain, that I have," Muldoon confirmed with a nod. He flung an arm outward and pointed to where the cattle were bawling and moving restlessly about in the near distance. "The poor girl's making her way along the east pasture. I tried telling her it was no time to be having a stroll, but she would not listen. You'd best—"

"Get inside the house and stay with the lady there," Jonathan directed tersely. He was already on his way to find Alex.

"Lady, Captain?" the other man called after him in bewilderment.

"Just do as I say!"

The rain began to fall in heavy, near blinding torrents as he followed the fence line eastward. A terrible apprehension gripped him when he thought of all the possible dangers Alex was facing. She could lose her way and wander far into the bush; she could be struck by any of the bolts of lightning that continued to streak across the blackness of the sky; or she could even be swept away by a flash flood if she had the misfortune to try and cross the river.

He cursed again and quickened the chase, offering up a silent prayer for Alex's safety. *And* a silent promise to rake his beautiful, headstrong bride over the coals once she was in his arms again. The thought of anything happening to her was unbearable. By damn, never in his life had he expected to fall so completely and irrevocably in love. . . .

Unaware of his pursuit, Alex stumbled back to the fence and gripped the top railing. Her wet muslin skirts kept tangling about her legs, threatening to send her facedown into the mud, and she could see very little as a result of the rain lashing at her face. She regretted the impulse that had led her so far, though the discovery that had sparked it still twisted at her heart.

Feeling considerably more wretched than the last time she had been caught in the midst of a thunderstorm, she lifted a hand to shield her eyes against the downpour and peered back the way she had come. The main house and outbuildings were no longer visible. She turned and cast a desperate glance ahead. A sob rose in her throat, but she choked it down and continued on her way, holding fast to the railing for support as well as guidance. Relief welled up within her when she suddenly spied a small, tin-roofed cabin; she remembered asking Muldoon about it and being told that Jonathan had built it himself when he had first come to the wilderness two years ago.

Gathering up her skirts, she bent her head against the storm's fury and made her way over to the cabin. The door was unlocked. She slipped inside, closed the door, and stood breathing heavily while her eyes adjusted to the darkness. What little light there was streamed in through a narrow, uncurtained window, revealing a single room that was devoid of any furniture save a rough-hewn table and chairs and an old sea chest in one corner.

Alex raked the dripping auburn curls from her face and looked toward the stone fireplace. She was pleasantly surprised to see wood stacked beside it. Hurrying forward, she dropped to her knees on the dusty floor, placed several of the split logs in the fireplace, and then searched about for matches. Her eyes lit with triumph when they fell upon the tinderbox, and she wasted no time in striking a spark with the flint and steel. She coaxed the fire to life, blowing gently on the pile of kindling she had stuffed beneath the pyramid of logs. Her efforts met with success; the ensuing blaze began to chase the chill from the room as she rose to her feet again and released a sigh.

A shiver ran the length of her spine. Her gaze moved back to the sea chest, and she swiftly crossed to open it. Following a brief search through its contents—old clothing, navigational charts, and three leather-bound volumes of what appeared to be captains' logs—she pulled out a shirt. She removed her own sodden clothes and exchanged them for the shirt. It was much too large and smelled musty, but was at least dry. Spreading her gown and undergarments across the table to dry, she pulled a chair before the fire, took a seat, and held her hands toward the warmth.

A disconsolate frown creased her brow as Jonathan's image rose unbidden in her mind. Gwendolyn's followed immediately thereafter. *You cannot have forgotten the hours we spent in each other's arms,* the woman had said. Why should the discovery of their long-ago love cause her such pain? Dear God, why?

He was with Gwendolyn now; the widow was no doubt making yet another pretty declaration of her undying love and devotion. Would he be tempted to resume the intimacy he and his former fiancée had once shared? Was it possible that he could forget his marriage vows so soon?

Her eyes clouded as they reflected the fire's bright and flickering dance. A look of utter anguish crossed her face.

The door suddenly opened, startling her from her torturous reverie. She gasped and sprang to her feet.

"Jonathan!"

"Damn it, Alexandra! Have you taken complete leave of your senses?" he demanded irefully. His eyes smoldered across into hers as he strode inside and slammed the door behind him. "Surely even in England, they warn you against the perils of gallivanting about in a storm!"

"They warn us against other things as well," she retorted, giving an angry, defiant toss of her head. Her gaze sparked and blazed, and her voice was laced with bitter sarcasm when she queried, "Have you left your ladylove to her own resources then? In truth, I am surprised you could tear yourself away from her side long enough to concern yourself with *my* welfare!"

"It was not difficult," he bit out, scowling darkly. "Nor is Gwendolyn my ladylove." He waged a fierce, unseen battle with his temper. "Why the devil didn't you return to the house when it began to rain?"

"Because I had no wish to intrude upon your happy reunion." She turned to the fire again and blinked back another sudden wave of tears.

Jonathan's eyes raked hotly over her. His fury diminished somewhat when he finally took note of her attire. The faded blue cotton shirt reached all the way down to her knees. She looked like a child dressing up in her older brother's clothes, except that there was nothing the least bit childish about her figure. The fabric clung to the curve of her breasts and the roundness of her hips, while her shapely legs were bare.

"Gwendolyn and I have known each other since we were children," he disclosed in a much calmer tone. "Still, she has arrived as both an unexpected and uninvited guest."

"But you were delighted to see her, were you not?"

"I was surprised. Nothing more than that."

"I don't believe you!" She was loath to confess how she had eavesdropped upon their conversation, yet she could not resist an indictment of his far too placid response to Gwendolyn's blandishments. Whirling to confront him again in the soft firelight, she suggested, "I expect you were profoundly flattered to discover that *her* heart and soul were still yours!"

"You heard?" he demanded sharply. His suspicions were confirmed when a guilty flush crept up to her face. "By heaven, woman! Could you not have trusted me to—?"

"How can I trust a man whose past is such a mystery to me? You never told me of your betrothal to the alluring Mrs. Wilcox, nor that it was she who drove you from America!"

"I didn't think it important." He moved closer now, his own rain-drenched boots and clothing leaving a trail of water on the wooden floor. "I've always preferred not to look back at the past."

"I am all too aware of that," she countered in a resentful tone as he paused mere inches away. "Indeed, you still refuse to hear anything of mine."

"That is a different matter entirely."

"How so?"

He did not offer an immediate response. Instead, his steady, gold-flecked emerald gaze burned down into the brilliant turquoise of hers; he appeared to be struggling with something deep within himself. When he did speak again, it was in a voice edged with raw emotion.

"Because I fear the truth."

It was Alex's turn to fall silent. She stared up at him, her breath catching in her throat. It was startlingly uncharacteristic of Jonathan Hazard to admit to anything less than supreme confidence. . . .

"I had long since forgotten about Gwendolyn," he told her, firmly steering the quarrel back to its origins.

"How could you forget the woman who was to have been your wife?" she argued while her head spun. "You loved her once—you must have. For heaven's sake, you were *intimate* with her." She dashed impatiently at the tears that stung her eyelids.

"I thought I loved her, yes. And I'll not deny that we shared a mutual passion, though I only gave freedom to it once. We were betrothed. But that was many years ago." He paused for a moment, and his visage looked quite somber when he explained, "There was a war going on, and I was like any other young man away for months at a time—lonely and homesick and not at all certain I'd live to see another day. Still, I did not seek to take advantage of Gwendolyn. She offered her affection to me, just as I later discovered that she'd offered the same to another beforehand. As she herself pointed out, she possesses a highly passionate nature. In the end, she did me a kindness by marrying someone else. I realized that eventually."

"Then why is she here now? Surely she did not travel all this way just to have her conscience salved by your forgiveness."

"Her motives were always difficult to understand," he recalled, with a faint smile of irony.

"Not in this case," she disputed, shaking her head and folding her arms against her chest as the ache returned full force. "She has come to rekindle what was between you, in spite of the fact that you are wed to another, and if you have any thought to cooperating with her despicable little scheme, you had best be forewarned that I—"

"Your jealousy is unfounded, Alexandra." Secretly, of course, he was delighted by it, for it only served to bear out what he had always believed to be true—that her feelings ran as deep as his own. She loved him, he was convinced of it, and perhaps, he reflected with more than a twinge of satisfaction, Gwendolyn's appearance on the scene wasn't so inopportune after all.

"Jealousy? I—I am not jealous!" sputtered Alex, her eyes first growing very round and then bridling with indignation. Hot, angry color rode high on her cheeks as she uncrossed her arms and battled the powerful urge to strike him. "*I* wanted none of this marriage, remember?"

"I do. But you've not found your wifely duties all that distasteful," he expounded, thoroughly unrepentant. His gaze brimmed with wicked and loving amusement now, which made her all the more furious.

"Why, you conceited, insufferable rogue," she said seethingly. She was still smarting as a result of being confronted with his former inamorata. And she could find nothing the least bit humorous about being reminded of her own traitorous response to his lovemaking.

It was all too much for her.

She, who had always been high-spirited yet never particularly given to violence, now found herself caught in the throes of a fury that owed a good deal more to the "green-eyed demon" than she was as yet willing to admit. With her temper and emotions flaring beyond control, she raised her hand and brought it slapping across the clean-shaven ruggedness of her husband's cheek.

Immediately ashamed at what she had done, she released a sharp gasp and clamped a hand to her mouth. She stared up at Jonathan in breathless anticipation, her eyes wide open as she took note of the faint, reddened imprint of her fingers on his skin.

She expected him to be angry. She expected him to subject her to a fierce tongue-lashing, or (heaven forbid) to turn her across his knee as he had once threatened to do. But his response was in direct contrast to her expectations. While his mouth curved into a slow, triumphant smile, he reached for her at last, his strong hands gliding gently up her arms.

"God help me, I've gone and fallen in love with a regular English spitfire," he proclaimed. His tone was low and vibrant—and so wondrously compelling that it sent another chill down her spine.

"Fallen in love?" she echoed, thunderstruck.

"Yes, Mrs. Hazard. Fallen in love." His eyes glowed with an undeniable warmth as he pulled her toward him. He looked rakishly handsome with his wet hair curling upon his forehead, and she could feel the heat of his virile, oh-so-masculine body even before they touched. But it was his words that provoked a wild stirring of her heart. "Why else do you think I insisted upon our marriage?"

"I thought it was because—because you desired me," she stammered, her fingers spreading upon the drenched fabric of his white linen shirt, where it clung transparently to his chest.

"That was but a part of it. If I had given my name to every woman I'd found attractive, I would have been charged with bigamy a thousand times over. No, Alexandra," he concluded, with another brief, disarming smile, "it was much more than desire. And it began the moment I saw you standing so proud and beautiful in that blasted prison cell at the Factory."

"But, love at first sight is nothing more than romantic nonsense. It is a fantasy, a—a myth." Her protests, while vehement, were nonetheless woefully inadequate. She shivered anew as her breasts pressed against him. The wetness of his shirt spread to her own.

"Is it?" His arms encircled her with their sinewy hardness; he gazed deeply into her eyes while the firelight played across his face. "I love you, Lady Alex. What does it matter when or how it took hold?"

"Why did you not tell me this before the wedding?" she demanded, feeling perilously light-headed. Her hands crept up to his shoulders.

"You swore you would not believe any such declarations."

"And yet you expect me to do so now?" She swallowed hard and realized in amazement that her spirits were soaring heavenward. Filled with a sudden, inordinate jubilance, she clung to him and asked tremulously, "How can I know you are not saying this simply to appease me? It might well be that you want me to continue sharing your bed—while you are at the same time planning to share Gwendolyn's!" The notion both pained and infuriated her, bringing her crashing back to earth. She choked back a sob and stormed, "As God is my witness, Jonathan Hazard, if you think to—"

"We share *our* bed," he corrected sternly, though his gaze lit with fond amusement once more. "And I've no wish to share it with anyone save you."

Alex's glistening eyes searched his face. The rain pounded noisily on the roof above, and the wind threatened to shake the very walls, but she was oblivious to the storm. Jonathan's arms were about her, holding her close, making her feel safe and secure. For now, nothing else mattered.

I love you. His words echoed in her mind . . . and drove out all thought of Gwendolyn Wilcox.

He swept her higher in his embrace and bent his

head. She welcomed the touch of his lips upon hers. The kiss was by far the sweetest they had ever shared; it was but a promise of the splendor to follow. . . .

Chapter 13

The storm's fury had abated somewhat by the time they returned to the main house nearly an hour later. Gwendolyn, still waiting impatiently in the parlor with Finn Muldoon, called out to Jonathan as he led Alex across the entrance foyer. He frowned at the sound of her voice and reluctantly paused to speak with her.

Alex cast him one last dubious glance before hurrying up the stairs to change. Surprised to realize how desperately she wanted to believe his declaration of love, she could think of little else as she stripped off her damp clothing and crossed to the washstand. Her own feelings demanded an examination; she could no longer deny that she felt more for Jonathan Hazard than an acute physical attraction. A great deal more.

She recalled his accusation of jealousy, recalled her own denial of it. *Yet it was true.* She tensed and whirled to face her reflection in the mirror.

"Merciful heaven!" she whispered, her eyes growing enormous within the delicate oval of her face. She *was* jealous of his past relationship with Gwendolyn. The very thought of the two of them together filled her with rage. In spite of her confusion, in spite of the uncertainty of her future, she could not bear the possibility that Jonathan might love another.

But why? she asked herself as she picked up a towel

and began to rub absently at her hair. Was it merely because he had made her his wife, because of what the
two of them had shared? There was no wisdom to it.
After all, she still planned to return to her former life in
England, didn't she? If she had no intention of remaining in Australia, then it should not matter if he sought
comfort in the arms of Gwendolyn, or even someone
else. It should not matter—*but it did.*

A long, ragged sigh escaped her lips. She closed her
eyes and felt a sudden lump rise in her throat. Nothing
made sense any longer.

That evening, she prepared supper as usual and tried
to ignore the chaotic state of her emotions. She accepted
Muldoon's generous offer to help her carry the food to
the table in the dining room, then took her usual seat
beside Jonathan. Gwendolyn sank down into the chair
to his left, while Muldoon, presented with the choice of
sitting beside either one of the ladies, chose to settle
himself nearest Alex. He and the Widow Wilcox had
spent a disagreeable hour in each other's company that
afternoon; he had no real desire to repeat the agony. *To
be sure, the woman was a snake in silk skirts,* he mused
to himself.

"Jonathan told me you are an excellent cook,"
Gwendolyn remarked, smiling coolly at Alex while she
helped herself to a minimal portion of the fresh buttered
peas, boiled potatoes, and corn bread. She regarded the
bowl of beef stew with a faint—albeit visible—grimace
of distaste.

"Did he?" murmured Alex. She stole a look at him,
only to hastily avert her gaze when she glimpsed the
light of utter bedevilment in his. The memory of their
storm-tossed idyll in the cabin sent warm color flying to
her cheeks.

"How long have you been in Australia, Alexandra?"

Gwendolyn now began an interrogation. She was wearing a stylish, low-cut gown of rose silk. Her gaze had already swept disdainfully over Alex's simple white muslin.

"Not very long."

"You are from England?"

"Yes."

"And what brought you to this country?"

"A transport ship."

Jonathan's mouth twitched at that. Muldoon's appreciation, however, was not so subtle. His deep rumble of laughter filled the room, then ceased abruptly when Gwendolyn shot him a quelling glare.

"A transport ship?" she echoed, her features hardening as she turned her attention back to Alex. "I'm afraid I don't understand."

"The convicts are sent here on transport ships, Mrs. Wilcox," Alex explained, with a composure that belied her inner turmoil. It was difficult to be civil to the woman, especially when she recalled everything she had overheard. "The journey itself is an absolute nightmare, and the circumstances waiting at the end of it are often even more terrifying." She could feel Jonathan's eyes upon her again, but she stared down at her plate.

"You are a *convict*?" Gwendolyn breathed in astonishment.

"I was, yes." Her blue-green gaze met the dark, scornful condemnation of the widow's, and she found herself adding impulsively, "But I committed no crime."

"Indeed?" drawled Gwendolyn. She cast a knowing smile in Jonathan's direction before telling Alex, "I am not at all surprised to hear you make such a claim. Why, I doubt you would want your 'husband' to know the truth."

"I know the truth," Jonathan interjected quietly. His

remark earned him a quizzical, wide-eyed look from Alex.

"As do I," the old Irishman beside her saw fit to proclaim.

"Oh, Jon. What can you have been thinking?" asked Gwendolyn, turning to him now with an impassioned plea for reason. "How do you think your family will react when they discover you've married a woman of such questionable character? Surely you cannot mean to persist in this folly? Why, how could you ever hope to—?"

"I thought I made myself clear this afternoon." He cut her off brusquely.

"Do you truly expect me to stand by and do nothing while you ruin your life?"

"My life is no longer your concern."

"It will always be so." Her glaze sliced back to Alex. "Did he tell you that we grew up together? Since we were children, our families planned to see us wed."

"Gwendolyn," Jonathan said, the tone of his voice carrying a warning.

"I will not be silenced—not when it is a matter so close to my heart," she countered dramatically.

"I'm quite sure you and Jonathan have very old ties," Alex remarked in a low and level tone. It was a studied attempt to diffuse the volatile situation. She disliked the widow intensely (how could she not?), yet she was anxious to avoid a full-scale confrontation. Battling the urge to meet fire with fire, she smiled faintly. "Indeed, Mrs. Wilcox. I have little doubt that you—"

"*I* have little doubt that he was tricked into this marriage," Gwendolyn said accusingly. "He cannot have been in his right mind to take a common criminal to wife. What did you do? Entice him into your bed first— and then offer the lie that you were virginal?"

"Blast it, Gwendolyn! I'll hear no more of this!" Jonathan ground out. His handsome face was thunderous, his eyes glittering harshly. "You are a guest in my house—and therefore deserving of every courtesy—but speak to my wife like that again and I'll damned well forget the rules of hospitality!"

"I have every right to seek the truth."

"If you've not much of an appetite, Mrs. Wilcox, it's more than happy I'd be to show you about the place," Finn Muldoon hastened to submit. His own stomach was far from appeased, but he was willing to go hungry in order to spare his mistress any further strikes of the adder's tongue.

"No, thank you, Mr. Muldoon," Gwendolyn declined coldly. She shot Alex another venomous look. "Although the fare is much too simple and heavy for my taste, I would prefer to remain and visit with Jonathan. We have a lot of catching up to do."

"Catching up?" Alex repeated, frowning in suspicion. "And what exactly is it you intend to 'catch up' on, Mrs. Wilcox?"

"Why, the usual, of course." She beamed engagingly at Jonathan again. "After all, we do have a lifetime of shared memories. Very special memories ... which cannot be obliterated by something so insignificant as marriage to another."

"Do not judge other unions by your own," he cautioned, raising a glass of wine to his lips.

"Has he told you of our betrothal, dearest Alexandra?" she challenged, turning her unwanted attention to Alex once more. "I daresay, in the eyes of God, we *are* man and wife."

"Then how is it you took another man as your husband?" parried Alex. Jealousy set her temper to raging; her palm itched to slap the woman's face.

"It was wartime," Gwendolyn replied, with an eloquent shrug. "Nearly a year had passed without any word from Jonathan, and I, like many others, mistakenly assumed he had been killed." It was not quite the truth, but it made her appear more the tragic heroine. "I wed Henry Wilcox out of grief and loneliness."

"Have you any children?"

"None. I fear—Well, my late husband was unable to sire . . ." Her voice trailed away; she heaved what was intended to be a pathetic sigh.

" 'Tis a pity, to be sure," Finn Muldoon murmured in a show of sympathy, then grinned irrepressibly while predicting, "I expect the captain and his bride will suffer no such misfortune."

His remark prompted Jonathan to smile in wry amusement, Alex to blush hotly, and Gwendolyn to glower. Silence fell for a brief time after that. It was broken by Jonathan, who announced that he wanted to check on any possible damage from the storm before Mother Nature took it in mind to rage again. Finn Muldoon accompanied him from the room. Alex found herself in the unenviable position of entertaining their guest. Since it was a matter of pride for her to play the dutiful hostess, she had little choice but to let the dining table remain uncleared as she stood and led the way into the parlor.

"How long are you planning to stay, Mrs. Wilcox?" she asked, with forced politeness, taking a seat on the far end of the sofa. The other woman settled herself on the chair immediately opposite.

"I have made no definite plans."

"Then perhaps—"

"Come now. Why should we waste time on pleasantries?" Gwendolyn suddenly demanded. Her mouth curled into a sneer. "We both know why I have come."

"Do we?" said Alex, tensing.

"You little fool! Do you really think you can hold on to him now that I am here? He loves me, he has always loved me, and nothing you can say or do will make any difference."

"There is the small, 'insignificant' matter of our marriage," Alex pointed out, with more than a touch of bitter sarcasm.

"Jonathan Hazard is a man of means," the widow informed her. "His family name is among the most respected in all of Maryland. Surely even you can see how preposterous this marriage of yours is. He deserves better than a woman who is in all probability a liar and a whore!" Her eyes narrowed into mere slits. "Just how *did* you come to be sent away from England?"

"I am not a liar. Nor am I a whore." It was on the tip of her tongue to remark that either one would be preferable to an adulteress. "And as I told you before, I was falsely accused and convicted. After that, I had very little choice. There was no chance of escape."

"And so Jonathan took you in. It isn't at all surprising that he would be swayed by a pretty face. He was ever hot-blooded."

"It was no case of charity," Alex declared. She was particularly stung by the last comment, for it served as a reminder of his past intimacy with Gwendolyn. "Nor was it the way you imply. I was hired to be the housekeeper."

"The housekeeper?" the haughty blonde echoed, then gave a trill of soft, scornful laughter. "Is that what they call it here in Australia? We have a far different term for it in America."

"Believe whatever you please. The fact remains that I am Jonathan Hazard's wife, and I'll be hanged if I'll allow you to usurp my place in either his heart *or* his bed!" The words burst forth of their own volition. She was as shocked as Gwendolyn at the sound of them.

"Well, my dearest Alexandra, if we're going to be blunt," the widow hissed, leaping up from the chair with an expression of pure malevolence on her face, "then you might as well know that I have no intention of sailing home without Jonathan. I'll do whatever it takes to convince him that we belong together— *whatever it takes!*"

"Is that a declaration of war, Mrs. Wilcox?" Her manner was one of deceptive calm as she, too, rose to her feet.

"You may be certain of it. And you may also be certain that Jonathan has never stopped loving me."

"Do you really believe these many years have not changed him? Is it so difficult to fathom that he is not the same—?"

"Why do you not return to England?" Gwendolyn startled her by demanding. She abruptly closed the distance between them. "You've said yourself that you were brought here against your will."

"I was indeed, but—but so much has happened since my arrival," stammered Alex. The question, of course, was one she had asked herself more than once these past few days.

"I can help you," the other woman proposed, the light of triumph growing in her eyes. She raised her hands to Alex's shoulders. "Listen to me, Alexandra, I can see to it that you are on the first available ship bound for England. I still have a bit of money, and I would gladly put it to such use. You can go where you belong. And so can Jonathan. He owes it to his family to return; he owes it to himself!"

"He will never let me go." *Dear God, did she even want him to?*

"Never fear. I can persuade him," Gwendolyn assured her confidently. "Once you are gone, there will be nothing left to distract him from—"

"No!" She pulled away and shook her head in an adamant denial. Her eyes blazed when she uttered in a tone of barely controlled fury, "I will not listen to any more of this. You had no right to come here. You had no right to assume that Jonathan would welcome you back into his life with open arms. And in truth, it amazes me that you could be so lost to reason and decency as to throw yourself at a man who has not only made it clear that he wants none of you, but who has also recently taken a bride he professes to love." Her heart soared anew at the memory of his avowal.

"You cannot win, you redheaded bitch," Gwendolyn reiterated acidly. "Jonathan Hazard is mine—and always will be."

"That claim might have held more meaning if you had not become the wife of another man," said Alex. "The mistake was of your own doing. You have no one to blame save yourself."

With her head held high, she swept past the wrathful, red-faced woman and returned to the dining room. It was left to Jonathan to escort Gwendolyn upstairs to one of the guest rooms when he returned a short time later. Try as she would, Alex could not prevent herself from envisioning the two of them together as she tidied the kitchen. And that night, when she finally lay sleeping beside her husband in the warmth of the big bed, she was plagued by horrible dreams in which she was back in the prison cell at Parramatta, calling in vain to Jonathan as he walked away with a smirking Gwendolyn at his side.

The situation offered no evidence of improvement the following day. Alex busied herself about the house all morning long, grateful as always for Coleen's and Agatha's company. The two of them were of the same opinion regarding the plantation's American visitor—"a pasty-faced scorpion" was Coleen's assessment following their first encounter with Gwendolyn after breakfast. Fortunately the buxom widow spent the better part of the morning upstairs, in the privacy of her room. Whenever she and Alex did come face-to-face, scarcely a word passed between them. But there was an understanding—one that provoked determination in Gwendolyn and an awful uneasiness in Alex.

By early afternoon, Alex was feeling the need to escape outdoors. She set out on her customary turn about the grounds, raising her face gratefully to the sun's rays as she pushed the long sleeves of her work dress above her elbows. The storm had left several broken limbs, mangled leaves, and patches of thick mud in its wake, yet it had also left the air fresh-smelling and cooler by several degrees.

She was soon wandering impulsively along the fence line, farther than usual—toward the cabin where she and Jonathan had shared a passionate, highly illuminating hour the day before. Her eyes shone with the remembrance of their lovemaking; she felt her body grow warm. The desire to believe his vow of eternal devotion was stronger than ever, as was the temptation to consider a future far from England's shores. She sighed, and a soft smile of irony touched her lips at the thought of how the London tongues would wag when it became common knowledge that Lady Alexandra Sinclair was living in the untamed wilderness of New South Wales as the wife of an American.

But as she drew closer to the cabin, the smile vanished, for her ears had detected the sound of voices— *Jonathan's and Gwendolyn's.*

Her throat constricted with sudden dread. Quickening her approach, she arrived at the open doorway. She paused beside it and peered surreptitiously around the corner, into the cabin. Her gaze widened when it fell upon the two people there.

Jonathan stood tall and angry near the fireplace, his back turned toward the doorway. Gwendolyn was directly in front of him. She gave no indication of having seen Alex.

"I knew it was true," she exclaimed, her mouth curving into a smile of certain victory. "I knew you could not have forgotten me so easily!" In the next instant, she threw her arms about Jonathan's neck and pressed her lips to his.

Alex inhaled upon a sharp gasp of mingled pain and fury. Jonathan heard her. He roughly seized Gwendolyn's wrists and forced her arms away, then spun about to confront his bride.

"Alexandra! Why the devil didn't you let me know you were there?" he demanded, a silent curse rising in his mind.

"What, and disrupt your *catching up* with Mrs. Wilcox?" she retorted irefully. Trembling with the force of her outrage, she fought against the impulse to launch herself at him. Her voice was dripping with vengeful sarcasm when she said seethingly, "Pray, sir, do not let me keep you from your discussion any longer!"

She whirled and sped back the way she had come. Hot, bitter tears sprang to her eyes, and there was such anguish twisting at her heart that she found it difficult to breathe. Jonathan started after her, only to be detained when Gwendolyn clutched at his arm.

"Let her go." She raised her arms to his neck again and pushed her voluptuous curves against him. "Please,

Jonathan. Can't you see it's just as well this happened? We'll be together now, and—"

"I have never before struck a woman, Gwendolyn," he ground out, "but you'd best be forewarned that in your case I am sorely tempted to make an exception!" With that, he thrust the calculating widow away from him and set off after Alex.

He caught up with her just as she reached the grove of trees near the workers' cottages. His hand curled about her arm to pull her to a halt, but she jerked free and plunged into the forest shadows in an effort to escape him. He gave chase.

"Damn it, Alexandra! Stop!" he commanded.

"Go back to your paramour," she flung over her shoulder. She cried out when she felt his arm snaking about her waist. He yanked her back against him, but she was far too hurt and infuriated to surrender. With her arms and legs flailing, she writhed violently in his grasp. "I hate you, Jonathan Hazard! Would to heaven I had never set eyes on you!"

"What you saw was—" he tried to explain.

"I know very well what it was!" She clawed at his arms, then shrieked again when he suddenly tumbled her down to the cushion of thick, moist grass and imprisoned her body with the hard-muscled weight of his own. He caught her wrists in a firm grip, pulling her arms above her head while his gaze burned compellingly down into the blue-green fire of hers.

"I neither wanted nor invited Gwendolyn's embrace," he stated in a cold and clear tone.

"How could you?" she stormed, sounding for all the world like the affronted wife she was. "And in the very place where you ... where we ..." She choked back a sob and squirmed furiously beneath him. "Let me go! I don't ever want to see you again. I want none of you!"

"You'll have me all the same," he declared, his features dangerously grim. "I love you, you little shrew! I love you and no one else. And by heaven, it's time you realized I'll let nothing come between us!"

"Nothing except your own selfish desires," she countered hotly.

"Selfish?" He smiled faintly. It was a mocking smile, and also one of wicked, amorous intent. "I think not, Lady Alex."

Before she could ask him what he meant, he tugged up her skirts and moved his hand purposefully downward to the apex of her thighs.

"Jonathan, *no*," she gasped out, her eyes growing very round. It was broad daylight, and even though they were concealed within the forest, there was always the possibility that someone would come along. Besides, she mused dazedly, how could she even think of submitting to him after what she had just seen? "No, damn you! I won't let you put between my legs what you've put between hers!" She crimsoned at her own bluntness.

"Well spoken, my love," he murmured in a husky tone brimming with humor. "But many years have passed since that time. And I seek no renewal of it."

He was through talking. Alex suffered another sharp intake of breath when his warm fingers delved within the opening of her drawers and began a gentle, masterful stroking of the silken flesh between her thighs. Her hands came down to curl upon his shoulders; she pushed weakly at him, but the familiar yearning was already blazing upward.

Her eyes swept closed when his mouth descended upon hers. He kissed her deeply, ardently, his lips and tongue ravishing the sweetness of hers. She kissed him back and arched beneath him, her stockinged limbs parting wider as the delectable heat spread. There was a faint sound of fabric ripping when he impatiently tore the seam of her drawers to get at her better, and she was only dimly aware of the cool dampness of the grass against her back as their mutual, white-hot desire flared beyond control.

A soft scream of pleasure broke from her lips when he plunged into her. She entangled a hand within the dark thickness of his hair and pulled his head down to hers once more, her mouth demanding and receiving the loving possession of his. Higher and higher their perfectly matched passions soared, until the tempestuous, anger-heightened blending of their flesh, male and female, reached its ultimate and satisfying conclusion.

They drifted slowly back to earth, their bodies still entwined upon the forest floor while life went on as usual all about them. Alex lay flushed and breathless in Jonathan's arms. He smiled softly down at her and trailed a hand along the curve of her breast.

"I've no particular wish to quarrel with you, Mrs. Hazard," he remarked in a low and vibrant tone, "but I'll be damned if I can regret it so long as we settle our differences this way."

"Why did you let that woman kiss you?" demanded Alex, a sudden shadow crossing her face when reality intruded once more.

"I had no idea she meant to do so," he answered honestly.

"Then what were the two of you doing at the cabin—alone?"

"Muldoon told me he had seen Gwendolyn heading toward the fields. I followed, intending to warn her against straying too far. She refused to come back until I had agreed to another private conversation."

"You—you are sure there was nothing more to it than that?" She held her breath and waited for his answer.

Relief washed over her when he did not hesitate before replying in the affirmative. Once again, she wanted desperately to believe him.

"Gwendolyn is little more than—"

Before he could say anything else, they heard Muldoon call his name in the near distance. Jonathan reluctantly climbed to his feet, fastened his trousers, and drew Alex up beside him. She shook her skirts back down into place. Her color deepened when she reflected that she would have to make repairs to yet another garment.

"I plan to ride to Sydney tomorrow," he announced, leading her back through the trees. His green eyes were brimming with fond amusement as he plucked a blade of grass from her flame-colored tresses. "The sooner Gwendolyn Wilcox is on her way back to America, the better for us all."

"I still find it odd that she should surface again after so long," murmured Alex, her brow creasing into a mild frown of bemusement.

"As do I. But I suspect there's more to it than she is willing to admit."

"What do you mean?"

"Her marriage was a disaster. Henry Wilcox was a wealthy man, but it seems his fortune diminished with astonishing haste after he took Gwendolyn as his wife. My mother allowed her to read my letters, so she knew of my success here." He had already made himself a silent promise to take his interfering parent to task for the betrayal of confidence. But he would do so gently.

"Perhaps her finances *were* a contributing factor, but it might well be that she does still care for you," Alex suggested unhappily.

"It would make no difference." He paused and drew her in front of him, his arms encircling her. They were midway along the row of cottages now. Finn Muldoon stood waiting amid a group of women and children only a few yards away.

"Jonathan!" she protested, blushing as she took note of their rapt audience. "What will everyone think?"

"What they know to be true—that their master cannot keep his hands off his bride." He gave her a quick, hard kiss, then spun her about and landed a playful slap upon her backside. She gasped and shot him an indignant look, but he merely smiled. "I have work to do, Mrs. Hazard." He sauntered away to join Muldoon.

She opened her mouth to fling a suitably scathing retort after him, but thought better of it. Her eyes sparkled as she watched him, and she could not suppress the smile that rose to her lips.

"Are you aware of the fact, Alexandra, that you have mud on your gown?" Gwendolyn suddenly remarked behind her. She cast an angry, exasperated glance heavenward before pivoting to face the woman.

"Henceforth, Mrs. Wilcox, you will stay away from my husband," she cautioned, "or else face the consequences."

"Oh? And what might those 'consequences' be?" the widow challenged mockingly.

"I learned a great deal from my sister convicts during our many months at sea. Including, of course, the various methods by which one can inflict pain upon another." Her blood boiled anew at the memory of Gwendolyn's lips meeting Jonathan's. At that point, she knew it would require little more provocation for her to snatch the woman bald.

"How dare you threaten me!"

"It is no threat." Her gaze kindled with vengeful fire, and she frowned darkly before adding, "It is a promise." While Gwendolyn hurled a blistering curse at her head, she turned and walked away.

The rest of the afternoon passed pleasantly enough, for Gwendolyn, complaining of the heat and dust and smells, sought the privacy of her room once more. Supper, however, proved to be every bit as much of an ordeal as the previous evening's had been, with the still determined widow alternately flirting with Jonathan and taunting Alex. Finn Muldoon remained silent this time; he had no wish to go hungry again. And he had little doubt that his mistress could hold her own against the "hussy" who had been fool enough to betray the captain all those years ago.

Since the night was clear and calm, Jonathan insisted that they gather on the front porch instead of the parlor afterward. Alex had endured more than enough by that time, so she offered the excuse of a headache and retired upstairs. She could hear the deep resonance of Jonathan's voice drifting up from below through the open window, and she felt her heart flutter at the sound of it.

I love you and no one else, he had told her. Why was she seized by such a deep yearning for those words to be true? And why in heaven's name had she still not finished that letter to her uncle?

She lay beneath the covers of the bed, pretending to be asleep when Jonathan entered the room less than an hour later. With a crooked smile playing about his lips, he undressed quietly, blew out the lamp, and slipped into bed beside her.

For the first time since their wedding night, he did not pull her to him. She was surprised when he rolled onto his side with his back toward her. Her eyes flew wide open, and she frowned with a mixture of perplexity and disappointment. Solely on impulse, she rolled over as well and pressed her thinly clad curves against his naked, hard-muscled warmth.

She was given an immediate reward for her boldness. Jonathan turned upon his back and swept her close, his mouth curving upward in wholly masculine triumph. Alex heaved a soft sigh of contentment and closed her eyes again.

Chapter 14

Jonathan left for Sydney shortly after breakfast the next morning. Gwendolyn did her best to dissuade him, but to no avail. He was determined to arrange her passage homeward, and he would also see what he could do about finding her suitable accommodations until the ship sailed.

The day promised to be another of the country's infamous scorchers. In spite of her anger toward Gwendolyn, Alex could not help feeling a twinge of sympathy when she saw how the widow was suffering in the heat. She advised against more than one petticoat and offered the loan of a cooler gown, but Gwendolyn scornfully declined to accept either the advice or the loan.

The hour of noon approached when Finn Muldoon suddenly came rushing inside the kitchen with the news of visitors. Alex, exchanging a startled glance with Tilly, hastily dried her hands on her apron and turned to the Irishman.

"Visitors?" she echoed, a thoughtful frown creasing her brow. "But who—?"

" 'Tis the governor himself," Muldoon revealed. He gave her a nod and a wink. "You'd best be getting yourself to the front porch, mistress, else he'll be thinking the captain's gone and married himself a poor, witless creature ashamed to show her face."

"Governor Macquarie is *here*?"

"He and the captain be old friends," said Tilly, smiling. "He's not a true ogre, though there be many who would say so."

"Good heavens," Alex said breathlessly. Her hands were shaking as she untied the strings of her apron and drew it off. Fate had played yet another trick. The very man she had been so desperate to find was actually waiting on her doorstep. It was beyond belief!

"I'll be finishing the meal," Tilly pronounced kindly.

"Thank you," Alex murmured, her head spinning. She whirled about and hurried from the room, her face flushed and her eyes bright as she made her way to the front porch.

Two well-dressed men had emerged from the trees a few minutes ago to travel along the road leading to Boree. They had set a leisurely course for the main house, in no particular hurry to return to the boat—and the entourage—they had left waiting on the riverbank a short distance away.

Alex held her breath as they drew closer to where she stood at the top of the steps. Her heart pounded fiercely within her breast, and her mind raced to think of the words she would use to explain her circumstances. Without warning, her husband's face swam before her eyes. *Jonathan.*

"Good day to you, Mrs. Hazard!" the older of the two men called out when he had reached the yard in front of the house. Wondering how he could be so certain of her identity, Alex could manage nothing more than a weak smile in response. "Please allow me to introduce myself," he said, his voice holding evidence of his proud Scottish heritage. He was quite tall, and attractive in a rather down-to-earth way, with a lean body and a full head of bright red hair. "I am Lachlan Macquarie, Governor of New South Wales. And this gentleman you see at my side is Lord Montfort, who is at present visiting our fair shores."

"I am honored to make your acquaintance, Mrs. Hazard," intoned Lord Montfort. He looked to be somewhere near thirty, and he held himself like a true gentleman—stiff and haughty. His light blond hair, well-trimmed mustache, and gray eyes gave him an almost delicate appearance, a far cry from that of his robust companion's.

"How do you do, Governor Macquarie," Alex finally said. "Lord Montfort." She clasped her hands tightly together in front of her and took a deep, steadying breath as the two visitors climbed the steps.

"Is your husband within the house, Mrs. Hazard?" the governor asked, tossing a swift glance about the grounds. He drew a handkerchief from the pocket of his dark blue waistcoat and mopped at his forehead.

"No, I—I am afraid he is not. He has gone to Sydney."

"To Sydney? Aye, then we'll have to wait to interrogate the slippery young rascal!" He gave a low chuckle and remarked, "Jonathan Hazard was ever the one for missed opportunities. Until he clapped eyes on you, I daresay." His blue eyes twinkled down at her, and it was obvious he approved of what he saw. "My wife is anxious to meet you as well. In truth, I think she wants to make certain our American friend has not been taken in by some cold-hearted adventuress. Never mind that the good Reverend Stockbridge held forth that you were no she-wolf in lamb's clothing. No, she'll not be satisfied until your husband brings you to our home in Sydney for a visit, which he must be commanded to do in the not too distant future."

"Would you care to come inside for some refreshment?" Alex offered, with only a slight, telltale quavering in her tone.

"That we would, Mrs. Hazard. We've just floated down from Parramatta, and we've still some distance to go. A drink would be most welcome."

"Something cool, perhaps?" Lord Montfort saw fit to appeal. Sweat poured down his pale, aristocratic features, and he frowned as he patted gently at his temples with his own handkerchief.

"Of course." She turned and led the way inside, showing them into the parlor before hastening back to the kitchen. Tilly and Muldoon were waiting for her.

"Well, mistress?" the Irishman probed, grinning like a Cheshire cat. "To be sure, Macquarie's not what you expected, is he?"

"Not at all," she confirmed, numbly shaking her head. How convenient that Jonathan was away; this was the chance she had been waiting for. Dear God, would her ordeal finally come to an end now?

"He's not half bad, for a Scotsman," Muldoon allowed magnanimously.

"Will the gentlemen be staying for dinner?" Tilly asked.

"I don't think so," replied Alex. "But they *do* intend to remain for a bit." Wasting no more time, she loaded a tray with a pitcher of fresh lemonade and some glasses. She carried it into the parlor and set it atop the sideboard, then proffered each man a full glass of the tart, honey-sweetened liquid.

"You are kindness itself, Mrs. Hazard," the governor remarked as she took a seat on the sofa. He sank down beside her, while the young English nobleman perched on the edge of the chair.

"Governor Macquarie, there is something I wish to

discuss with you," Alex announced in a breathless tumble of words.

"Indeed?" He raised the glass to his lips again, took a long drink, and cast her a mildly quizzical look.

"Yes, it concerns my presence here." She drew in another uneven breath and was dismayed to feel a sudden, strange reluctance to continue. "Not just here at Boree, of course, but—"

"Say no more, lass." He cut her off with a benevolent, almost paternal smile. "I know of your unfortunate past. And I am also aware of your less than traditional courtship and marriage. It matters not. We are a country full of ghosts, so to speak. Everyone has something, some small part of their lives they wish to bury. You'll not suffer any lasting judgment because of it. But then, your husband would have seen to that in any case," he concluded, another mellow laugh escaping his lips.

"You don't understand." She opened her mouth to explain, but found herself struck speechless. A sharp, inexplicable pain gripped her heart, and she caught her lower lip between her teeth as Jonathan's image rose unbidden in her mind once more.

"Since this Hazard fellow is an American, there can be little objection to his taking a convict bride," Lord Montfort was obliging enough to interject.

"American or not, he is among the finest men you'll ever have occasion to meet," the governor proclaimed in Jonathan's defense. He drained his glass and frowned before adding, "Aye, 'tis a pity we've not a hundred more like him."

"You are from England, Mrs. Hazard?" Lord Montford inquired of her, though with only a casual interest in the subject.

"Yes. From London," she murmured. *What the devil was the matter with her?*

"Have you any family there?"

"An aunt and uncle." The answer was far more evasive than she had intended. And she did not elaborate.

"Oh." He took another drink and looked bored.

"Alexandra?" Gwendolyn's voice suddenly rang out in the entrance foyer. Alex muttered an oath underneath her breath and frowned in displeasure as the widow sailed into the room. The two men stood politely.

"Oh! Oh, my dearest Alexandra; I had no idea you were entertaining visitors," lied Gwendolyn. She had heard them talking on her way to the dining room.

"Governor Macquarie, Lord Montfort." Alex had no choice but to make the introductions. Each of the men nodded in turn. "I should like to present Mrs. Wilcox. She is . . . an old friend of my husband's. From America."

"How do you do, Mrs. Wilcox," the tall Scotsman was the first to respond. "And a hearty welcome to our beloved country."

"Charmed, madam," Lord Montfort declared. Immediately smitten by this blond Amazonian beauty, he moved forward to raise her hand to his lips. She flashed him a winsome smile, her eyes captivating his.

"You will quite turn my head with your gallantry," she drawled. "I fear my late husband was not so attentive."

"You are a widow then?" he asked, hope springing to his breast.

"Yes. For more than a year now." She drew her hand from his at last and swept forward to the other chair. Sinking gracefully down upon it, she waited until the two gentlemen had resumed their own seats, then smiled at the governor. "I heard a great deal about you when I was in Sydney, sir."

"I fear my name is much bandied about." His own

smile did not quite reach his eyes. There was something about her that troubled him. He glanced at Alex, whose tenseness did not escape his notice.

"I am a visitor as well, Mrs. Wilcox," Lord Montfort disclosed.

"Then perhaps we should commiserate with each other. *I* find the heat unbearable, don't you?"

"Most assuredly. And I cannot comprehend why the locals see fit to retire so early in the evening, for it is only after darkness falls that one can hope to breathe. Why, in London, we do not dine before the hour of nine, and it is not at all unusual for us to indulge in any manner of entertainment until well past midnight."

"We are much the same in Baltimore." She paused and released a soft, dramatic sigh before adding, "Although, I must say, there is little enough to do."

"Would you be agreeable to a turn about the grounds before we leave, Mrs. Hazard?" Governor Macquarie suddenly asked, tiring of the inactivity and anxious to be on his way again. "Though it pains me to confess it, I have not visited Boree in a matter of months now. I've a desire to see the improvements your husband has made."

"Yes, of course," she agreed, trying without much success to steer her thoughts away from Jonathan.

The four of them rose to their feet and proceeded outside. Alex paired off with the governor, while Gwendolyn was only too happy to drape herself over Lord Montfort's arm. The heat was evidently no longer such a tribulation.

They moved leisurely across the front yard and toward the outbuildings. Governor Macquarie made several comments regarding the plantation's neat and prosperous appearance. Alex managed to offer a response to most of his remarks, and she did her best to answer the few questions he tossed her way. Finally, after Gwendolyn and the Englishman had wandered some distance ahead, her own escort gently pulled her to a halt.

"What is troubling you, lass?" he asked, his eyes full of such kindness that she found herself tempted to reveal everything. Though it made no sense, she held back.

"I . . . nothing."

"Could it be that you're homesick?"

"At times, yes," she admitted. Her gaze fell beneath the steady compassion of his. *What are you waiting for?* her mind's inner voice stormed. She closed her eyes for a moment and hastily averted her face. Why wasn't she pleading with the governor for help? Why wasn't she pouring out the whole incredible story and demanding that he see justice done?

"Your aunt and uncle in London—do they know of your whereabouts?" he continued. "What are their names? Perhaps I can see that they are informed of your marriage. I might even be able to arrange a visit."

"I fear they will not approve of my marriage."

"How could they not approve of a man such as your husband, Mrs. Hazard?" he responded, with a smile of wry amusement. "Come now. Surely they will see that your situation has improved greatly. And your marriage to an American cannot be so repulsive to them. I intend no insult, but Lord Montfort was correct when he implied that a woman in your circumstances could scarcely hope for better." He frowned thoughtfully before persisting. "Is your uncle engaged in an honest profession? If not, then—"

"My uncle is Lord Henry Cavendish!" It was done. But instead of feeling as though a weight had been lifted, she felt the awful heaviness of her heart increasing.

"Lord Henry Cavendish?" the governor echoed, visibly taken aback. The name was not unfamiliar to him. "You say that your uncle is a peer of the realm?"

"I know it sounds farfetched in the extreme, but it is true all the same." Her throat constricted painfully as sudden tears gathered in her eyes. "My name is Lady Alexandra Sinclair, and my uncle *is* Lord Henry Cavendish!"

"How can that be?" His expression had grown cold and distant.

"Someone, seeking revenge against my uncle, arranged to have me falsely accused and imprisoned. I was convicted and transported before I could summon help from either my family or my friends."

"And does your husband know of your 'misadventure'?"

"I have told him of it, but he— I am not at all certain he believes me," she stammered weakly, then heaved a ragged sigh and dashed at her tears. Her tone was plaintive when she added, "I cannot blame him, of course. I am a convict. I was imprisoned at Parramatta when he found me."

"If your own husband does not believe you, then why should you expect me to do so?" he challenged dispassionately. His gaze bored down into the luminous depths of hers. "I have heard many a claim of innocence and mistaken identity since assuming the post of governor in this colony of lost souls. But I must say, yours is the most unexpected. It seems that Jonathan Hazard has fallen victim to questionable judgment after all."

"He is not to blame for what has happened."

"Precisely." He scowled and shook his head, then

challenged, "What did you hope to gain by pressing me with this information?"

"I had hoped that at the very least you would send word to my uncle. Or perhaps that you would even go so far as to correct the injustice by granting me my freedom."

"But you are Jonathan Hazard's wife now."

"Yes, and I—"

"Is it your desire to leave him and return to England?"

"It *was*," she murmured tremulously. "But now, I— God help me, I don't know what I want anymore."

"I will make inquiries on your behalf," the governor startled her by promising. Her eyes flew up to his again, and she was almost certain she glimpsed a renewed spark of clemency in them. "Tell Jonathan to come and speak with me about it."

"He will not agree to do so," she expounded, with another sigh. "He is determined to hold me to the marriage."

"Then I would say, Mrs. Hazard, that you are a very fortunate young woman indeed."

She inhaled sharply. His words provoked a wild stirring of her emotions. Before she could offer a reply, however, the sound of Gwendolyn's ear-piercing scream rent the air. The governor immediately raced forward to investigate, with Alex following hot on his heels. They came upon Gwendolyn and Lord Montfort just beyond the stable. Before them stood Jaga, his features stoic, but his dark eyes virtually dancing with ironic humor.

"Dear God, he'll kill us all," cried the widow, cowering behind her escort.

"Stand fast, you murdering savage!" Lord Montfort shouted bravely, in spite of the fact that he had no weapon with which to back up his enjoinder.

"Stop it, you imbecile!" Alex snapped at him. She hastened to the aborigine's side. "Jaga, I am sorry."

"No harm," he said. He looked to the governor, who greeted him with a curt nod.

"It's good to see you again, Jaga."

"You mean you—you are acquainted with this heathen?" sputtered Gwendolyn, rounding on the governor in stunned disbelief.

"Aye. Jaga's well known to Captain Hazard."

"He is Jonathan's friend," Alex clarified pointedly. She directed an apologetic smile at the half-naked visitor. "Would you care to come inside? I'm afraid my husband is away at the moment, but—"

"I will come again," he stated. Just as before, he soundlessly turned and disappeared around the corner of the building.

"The natives are harmless, Mrs. Wilcox," Governor Macquarie assured Gwendolyn, with more than a hint of annoyance.

"Nevertheless, I should think this unpleasant little episode lends credence to my proposal," Lord Montfort opined.

"And what proposal is that?" the older man demanded.

"A lady such as Mrs. Wilcox does not belong here in this ghastly, bug-infested outpost. She should return to Sydney with us."

"But we are leaving *now*, William. I am set on a journey's end before nightfall."

"Dash it all, Lachlan. A few more minutes won't make any difference."

"Aye, perhaps not. But it could be Mrs. Wilcox is not anxious to tear herself away from her friends. She has, after all, traveled a great distance to—"

"It so happens, sir, that Captain Hazard is at this moment arranging my passage homeward," Gwendolyn saw fit to inform him. She cast another beguiling smile at the young Englishman—the *wealthy* young Englishman, as she had recently discovered. Though she hated to admit defeat, it had become clear to her that Jonathan would never be swayed. Besides, she could console herself with the determination of a new pursuit. One which might very well reward her with both a title and a desperately needed fortune. "I am not at all averse to accepting Lord Montfort's kind invitation."

"What about Jonathan?" Alex queried, her voice laced with sarcasm. "I seem to recall, my dear Mrs. Wilcox, that you were set upon a 'prolonged' visit with my husband."

"He is not the man I remembered."

"I am glad to hear of it."

"Come along, Mrs. Wilcox," said Lord Montfort, drawing her arm possessively through the crook of his once more. "I shall assist you in gathering your things."

"We haven't much room in the boat," Governor Macquarie cautioned sternly.

"I brought nothing more than a carpetbag," Gwendolyn replied. To Lord Montfort, she boasted, "I am quite an able traveler."

The four of them returned to the house. Alex led the way in preoccupied silence, feeling both pleasure at the prospect of her rival's departure and trepidation over her long-awaited disclosure to the governor. When it came time to bid Gwendolyn and the two men farewell a short time later, she was able to manage only a wan smile.

"Good-bye, Governor Macquarie. Lord Montfort." Her turquoise gaze filled with a certain measure of triumph when it moved to the troublesome widow. "I hope you enjoy a safe journey back to America, Mrs. Wilcox."

"Do you indeed, Alexandra?" retorted Gwendolyn, haughty as ever. Her mouth curved upward in satisfaction. "Please tell Jonathan I am sorry to have missed the opportunity for a personal leave-taking. I'm quite sure he will understand."

"As am I."

"Good-bye, Mrs. Hazard," Lord Montfort said, though his eyes remained on Gwendolyn. He took her carpetbag and escorted her down the front steps. Governor Macquarie tarried briefly on the porch.

"Even if your story should prove to be true," he told Alex, "the confirmation of it will take months to receive."

"I know." She looked away, her cheeks suddenly growing warm. "I—I suppose I shall simply have to make the best of things until then."

"You have the best of things already, lass."

With that last bit of wisdom, he placed his hat atop his head and turned to follow the others. Alex stared after him. She stood watching until both he and his two companions had disappeared into the concealing darkness of the forest at the top of the hill. Then, folding her arms across her chest—and wondering why in heaven's name she should feel so melancholy—she moved to join Tilly in the kitchen once more.

She was grateful for the other woman's company. After they had finished with the meal, she accompanied Tilly back to her cottage. Seth and the three boys were delighted with the generous "leftovers" she had brought them, and she remained to visit for a while before setting off toward the stable.

Since the workers were still enjoying the customary, well-earned respite from their labors, there was no one to either try and stop her or offer her assistance as she slipped inside the stable and saddled one of the horses there. She had not ridden since the day Jonathan had brought her back from Sydney. The memory of that wild and frightening trek through the storm, and of her confidence that Jonathan would see her safely home, caused a sudden lump to rise in her throat.

Soon she was on her way, the animal beneath her racing like the wind along the road. She didn't want to think. She didn't want to plan or ponder, didn't want to reflect or examine. Desperate to escape the turbulence of her own mind, she didn't even care about her destination. The sunlight filtered down through the trees while she rode farther and farther from Boree, her uncharted course leading her deeper into the forest, as it had done the night she had tried to escape. The night Jonathan Hazard had first held her in his arms.

She bent low in the saddle and allowed the horse to find its own way among the trees and thick tangle of undergrowth. The road, she noticed, was barely discernible now, and she could not deny a growing apprehension as she became aware of how truly alone she was. Jonathan had warned her against traveling beyond the plantation's boundaries.

"Jonathan," she whispered, his name an endearment on her lips. In spite of her resolve, she could not prevent herself from contemplating everything Governor Macquarie had said. Perhaps he was right—perhaps she *did* have the best of things already. . . .

A flash of white suddenly caught her eye. Before she could urge her mount to take flight, a burly, coarse-featured man materialized beside her, his rough hands pulling her from the saddle. She screamed, then found herself tumbled to the ground while the terrified horse reared up on its hind legs. The reins were grabbed by another man, who steadied the animal and looked to where Alex was being hauled to her feet by his cohort.

"Well, now. We've gone and caught ourselves a flash piece of mutton, we have," her captor remarked, his foul-smelling breath making her nauseous as he brought his face close to hers.

"Take your hands off me, damn you!" she spat at him in wrathful defiance. He merely chuckled and tightened his grip upon her arm until she winced with pain. She balled her other hand into a fist and landed a punishing blow to his face. He growled an oath, his eyes glittering menacingly down into hers. "You little bunter." He raised a hand to strike her.

"Leave her be, Ollie!" A third man strode forward to intervene. He was younger than the other two, and not nearly so sinister-looking. All three men wore the clothing given to convicts forced into labor on the road gangs. "We've got the horse; now let's be on our way."

"The soldiers'll be comin' this way soon enough," advised the man holding the reins. He glanced nervously about.

"We'll take her with us. She'll fetch a pretty penny once we're back in Sydney."

"Are you daft, man?" the youngest escapee charged. "We can't go back to the city, and we can't take the woman! They'll hang us for sure if—"

"I'm for Sydney." The burly leader of the trio cut him off. "Do as I say, or you're on your own."

"Maybe Shaughnessy's right," the second man dared to suggest. "Maybe we'd have a better chance if we made straightaway for the bush."

"You'll have little chance at all if you do not let me go," Alex proclaimed, with far more bravado than she was actually feeling. Furiously, belatedly, lamenting the fact that she had disregarded Jonathan's warning, she offered up a silent prayer for a way out of her peril. "My absence will be noticed soon. Release me, and I shall forget I ever set eyes upon you."

"Shut your crack," the man called Ollie bellowed. He dragged her over to the horse.

"No!" She fought him with all her might, but was unable to keep him from tossing her up on the horse's back. The saddle had already been discarded, so that he was able to swing up behind her. His arm clamped brutally about her waist.

"I'll not hesitate to slit your throat, girl," he threatened. He scowled down at the other two runaways. "We'll find mounts for you soon enough. Till then, keep up or find your own way!"

"I'm not going to Sydney." The youngest escapee dissented once more. He cast Alex a look of helpless remorse, then abruptly whirled about and plunged back into the undergrowth.

"Follow him if you like, you bastard!" Ollie rasped to the other man.

"No, I—I'll stick with you," he stammered fearfully.

Alex struggled for breath as her captor reined about and delivered a ruthless kick to the horse's flanks. They rode back the way she had come, with the convict on foot trying in desperation to follow close behind.

Jonathan! her heart cried out in anguish. But she knew it was hopeless to think he could save her. He had not yet returned from Sydney, no one knew of her whereabouts. Dear God, there had to be some way she could escape before it was too late!

She fought against another wave of nausea as the horse thundered beneath them. Although sickened by dread, she would not allow herself to give in to despair. There had to be something she could do. The thought of what awaited her in Sydney was unbearable; the possibility of what might happen before then was even more so.

A strange whirring sound filled the air. Alex tossed a startled glance overhead, then gasped when she heard a man's cry of pain rise in the near distance. Her captor jerked the horse to a sudden halt.

"Thomas?" he called out. He turned his head, frowning in angry bewilderment when there was no answer. "Blast your eyes, Thomas. What—?"

Before he could finish, the odd sound came again. There was a swift flash of movement among the canopy of branches overhead, then a loud, sickening thud. Alex felt the man behind her tense, but he did not cry out as his fellow runaway had done. His grip about her waist suddenly loosened. She grasped at the reins and twisted about—just in time to watch him tumbling downward. While he lay sprawled unconscious on the ground, she took note of the small amount of blood trickling from a wound on his head.

Her wide, incredulous gaze shot to where a lone man, characteristically stoic and wraithlike, stood a scant twenty yards away.

"Jaga!" she said, breathing raggedly. Flooded with relief, she slid from the horse's back. She turned to face her rescuer with an expression of profound gratitude while he moved soundlessly toward her. "Oh, Jaga. I—I—*thank you!*" she stammered.

Pale and shaken from her ordeal, she could not prevent her legs from buckling beneath her. She sank to the grassy earth and watched as the aborigine approached the fallen convict. He bent and retrieved his weapon, which was nothing more than a slender, deeply curved stick.

"What—?" Alex started to query in bafflement.

"Boomerang," supplied Jaga. He straightened, and

the merest hint of a smile touched his lips. "You must
go home now."

"But what about him?" she asked, unable to suppress
a shudder as she climbed to her feet and glanced down
at the man who had tried to carry her off. "And the
other one as well? Have you—have you killed them?"

"Perhaps." His dark eyes lit with macabre humor.

"Should we not make certain?"

"Leave them." He was already turning away. "You
are a good woman. But your husband should beat you."
Without another word, he was gone, disappearing into
the eerily beautiful shadows of the forest while she
shook her head in wonderment.

Averting her gaze from the runaway's prone body,
she hoisted herself onto the horse's back once more and
rode homeward. Jonathan had still not returned from
Sydney when she reached the plantation, but Finn
Muldoon greeted her with a worried demand to know
where she had taken herself off to. She poured out her
story, and appealed to him to lend aid to her assail-
ants—or to provide them with a Christian burial, if they
were past help.

The Irishman, after first reassuring himself that his
young mistress had suffered no lasting harm, hurriedly
summoned three of the workers to help him fulfill her
wishes. It was his stated intent to take the escapees to
Parramatta if they were still alive; he advised to Alex to
prepare herself to face the brunt of "the captain's fearsome wrath" when she explained her troubles and the
workers' absence.

She watched the four men ride away. Then, stricken
with a combination of remorse and self-directed anger,
she plodded wearily inside the house. It was only after a
hot, soothing bath and a cup of tea that her frayed nerves
began to heal. But her tranquility was short-lived.

She sat curled up on the sofa in the parlor, trying to lose herself within the pages of a volume of Shakespeare's sonnets, when Jonathan strode inside at half past three. One look at his face told her that someone had already met him with the news of her assault.

"What the devil is this about your being accosted?" he demanded, his voice taut with simmering rage.

"I am quite all right, in the event that you care!" she flung back resentfully. She scrambled to her feet and lifted her head to a proud, defiant angle as he came forward to grasp her about the shoulders.

"I care a great deal," he ground out, his eyes smoldering down into hers. He was furious with her for having placed herself in such danger. Wavering between the desire to sweep her close and the urge to beat her pretty bottom, he settled for giving her a hot, reproachful glare. "However, since I have already been apprised of your well-being, I want to know why you disobeyed me and went out riding alone. By all that is holy, woman, you might have been killed!"

"Do you think I am not aware of that? If Jaga had not come along when he did—"

"Jaga?"

"He rescued me." She swallowed hard, and a shadow of remembrance crossed her beautiful, heart-shaped countenance. "He was here at Boree earlier today. I am not certain whether he followed me, or simply happened to be nearby when I was abducted. But he struck down two of the convicts. A third had already parted company with them. Mr. Muldoon and several of the others have gone to see if they are still alive. They were going to take me to Sydney. I—I would have found a way to escape them," she insisted, though her words lacked any true conviction.

"Damn it, Alexandra!" His arms encircled her with

their strong, comforting warmth at last. She closed her eyes and surrendered willingly to his embrace. "Thank God you weren't harmed," he murmured, his tone low and vibrant now, brimming with emotions far beyond anger. He held her as though he would never let her go.

"I will not ride alone again," she promised tremulously a few moments later.

"If anything had happened to you . . ." He left the sentence unfinished, but his meaning was clear. Alex offered no protest as he bent his tall frame down upon the sofa and settled her upon his lap. She raised her arms to his neck, an audible sigh escaping her lips when his hand moved to clasp her about the hips.

"I know my actions were reckless, but I felt the sudden need to get away," she confided.

"Because of Gwendolyn?"

"No. Because of . . . other matters."

"After tomorrow, we'll no longer have to worry about Gwendolyn's intrusions."

"You have arranged her passage homeward?" Her eyes flew wide open, and she cursed the fact that the volatile subject had come up immediately after the resolution of the other. She would have had to tell Jonathan about the startling turn of events sooner or later, of course—how else to explain the widow's absence?—but she would have preferred to wait until his temper had had more time to cool. Now, there could be no postponement.

"I have," he replied in satisfaction. "She'll be aboard the *Sandpiper*, scheduled to weigh anchor in only five days' time. I've also booked a room for her at my friend Tanner's inn."

"And will you be sorry to see her go?" Alex couldn't help asking.

"Not in the least." He swept her closer and tossed a

brief glance up toward the ceiling. "Is the meddlesome Mrs. Wilcox in her room?"

"I am happy to say she is not."

"Then where is she?"

"Your guest is at present on her way to Sydney."

"She is traveling there alone?" He tensed in displeasure again.

"No," she hastened to assure him, then finally disclosed in a small voice, "she was fortunate enough to have the escort of Governor Macquarie."

"What the—?" muttered Jonathan. He broke off and drew her away a bit so that he could search her face for the truth. "The governor has been here?"

"Yes." She gave a reluctant nod of confirmation. "He and a gentleman by the name of Lord Montfort came to call while you were away. Gwendolyn was invited to accompany them on their journey back from Parramatta. She asked me to convey her apologies for—"

"What of yourself?" he demanded, his features taking on a dangerously grim look once more. "I suppose you seized the opportunity to impart your tale of mistaken identity?"

"How could I *not* do so?" she countered defensively. Her eyes flashed across into his. "It was the truth, after all. And I had every right to seek his help."

"And what was his reaction?" His mouth curved into a faint, humorless smile.

"He promised to make inquiries."

"His promise was unnecessary."

"Unnecessary? Blast it, Jonathan Hazard. How—?"

"I have already taken steps to untangle the mystery of your past."

"*What?*" She gazed at him in stunned disbelief.

"That same day you took it in mind to play the role of stowaway aboard the wagon, I dispatched word to a highly placed associate of mine in London. I charged him with the task of finding out all he could about Lord Henry Cavendish. And about a young woman named Lady Alexandra Sinclair."

"Why in heaven's name did you not tell me?"

"It will take months to receive a reply," he pointed out with maddening calm.

"Perhaps so, but I—I could have had the pleasure of knowing *something* was being done," she sputtered indignantly. Her own temper blazing, she pushed herself from his lap. She folded her arms tightly beneath her breasts while he rose to his feet before her. "Since you had gone that far, why did you not tell the governor of my plight?"

"I think you know the answer to that."

"Nevertheless, please enlighten me."

"There was always the chance, however slim, that Lachlan Macquarie would decide to grant your request of asylum. And I could not give you up. Even then, I knew I would never let you go."

"If you truly loved me, you would not have put your own desires before mine," she choked out.

"I love you," he avowed quietly, his gaze darkening as it raked over her stormy, upturned features. "If you would but be honest with yourself, you would admit that our desires are the same."

"No!" She shook her head, as if she could somehow deny what was in her own heart. More than ever, she was tempted to abandon the struggle altogether. "I . . . Heaven help me, I don't know what to do," she confessed, her voice quavering while her head spun anew.

"You are my wife, Alexandra. Now and forever." He reached for her again. And in spite of her confusion, it was heavenly to be in his arms.

Chapter 15

Alex was relieved to learn that the two escaped convicts had survived their wounds. Finn Muldoon told her that the men had been safely returned to the road gang's camp near Parramatta, where they would receive medical attention before being clapped in irons as punishment for their flight. The colony's methods for dealing with its transgressive inhabitants were harsh, often cruel, but they were for the most part highly effective. Still, Alex was glad that the third man, the one she had heard called Shaughnessy, had not been apprehended.

The next two days dawned cooler and overcast, though there was little evidence of coming rain. Alex spent the better part of both mornings indoors with Coleen and Agatha, who had leapt at the prospect of earning extra wages for helping her make two new work dresses. Recalling all the elegant, expensive gowns she had worn back in London, she was surprised to realize that she missed them very little. Simplicity suited her best now. She had grown accustomed to wearing far less clothing than in the past, and she reveled in the sense of freedom it gave her.

Thoughts of Jonathan invaded her mind with their usual bold frequency throughout each day. The nights were filled with tenderness and passion. She was a willing participant in the sweetly rapturous enchantment that took place in the massive four-poster. But there was still a small part of herself she held back. She prayed for an end to the awful uncertainty that bound her heart. No matter how hard she tried, she could not forget that she would eventually be faced with the decision of either returning to England or staying with the man who claimed to love her—*and vowed never to let her go.*

On the third day following Gwendolyn's departure, she sat on the wicker porch swing with Finn Muldoon at his leisure in a chair nearby. It was still early in the afternoon, and the two of them had just enjoyed an idle, pleasant discussion regarding her plans for the fall garden. The sound of approaching hoofbeats (a great many horses, if their ears were to be believed) suddenly drifted to them on the warm, aromatic breeze.

"Would you be listening to that?" the old seaman murmured, his eyes meeting hers.

They rose to their feet, watching in mingled surprise and puzzlement while more than a dozen riders came into view. Jonathan, who had been engaged in conversation with Seth near the barn, broke off and quickly strode forward. He reached the front yard just as the double column of uniformed horsemen reined to an abrupt halt before the house.

The soldiers were led by a man Alex immediately recognized as Governor Macquarie. But it was the gray-haired gentleman to his left who caught and held her attention.

Her eyes widened in profound amazement. The color drained from her face; she felt her heart turn over in her breast.

"Uncle Henry!" she gasped. Her thunderstruck gaze moved instinctively to Jonathan, then back to the rather portly, well-dressed older man.

"Alexandra!" Lord Henry Cavendish swung down

and hastened to close the distance between them. "Dear God, it *is* you!" He opened his arms to her, and she hesitated only a moment before flying into his joyful, warmly affectionate embrace.

Watching them, Jonathan found himself beseiged by several conflicting emotions. He looked toward the governor, only to offer up a silent curse for what he read in his friend's eyes.

"Uncle Henry, wha—what are you doing here?" Alex demanded unsteadily, still suffering from shock as she drew away to peer up at his face. "How did you know where to find me?"

"It was not so very difficult," he replied enigmatically. He smiled and kept an arm draped about her trembling shoulders. "But I shall explain everything to you soon enough, my dear."

"I suggest you take your uncle inside, Mrs. Hazard," Governor Macquarie put forth somberly. He dismounted, but the red-coated men under his command remained astride. "And your husband as well."

"Husband, indeed," Lord Henry Cavendish muttered, with a gesture of contempt. Yet he had little choice but to comply with the governor's request. He had given his word that he would hear Jonathan Hazard out—in spite of the fact that he was already of the opinion that the fellow was both a scoundrel and a fortune hunter.

Struck speechless, Alex allowed herself to be led inside the house by her uncle. Jonathan followed a few steps behind. She was acutely conscious of his eyes upon her, and she resisted the sudden, sharp impulse to whirl about and cast herself upon his chest.

The three of them headed into the parlor. Lord Henry drew Alex down beside him on the sofa, while Jonathan took up his customary stance before the fireplace.

"I still cannot believe you are here," Alex said, shaking her head as her eyes met her uncle's once more.

He clasped her hand with his and frowned darkly at the thought of what she must have endured throughout the past eight months. She had changed; her physical appearance was considerably altered from what he remembered. And there was something else as well, though he could not yet put a name to it. Still, she was the same beloved niece he had traveled so far to see restored to him, and he thanked Providence that they had been reunited at long last.

"I learned of Arneson's treachery the very day your aunt and I returned to London," he told her.

"Arneson?"

"The devil's spawn who arranged your abduction." His scowl was furious and vengeful. "If not for the benevolence of an anonymous informant, I might never have discovered your fate. I was clued to Arneson, who was thereupon 'persuaded' to reveal the whole diabolical scheme he had set in motion. It required only a few days' time in which to arrange my affairs, and then I set sail to find you."

"And Aunt Beatrice?" she queried anxiously. "Is she well?"

"Quite so. She wanted to accompany me, but I would not hear of it. Her health is a trifle delicate, as you know—yet I anticipate a miraculous recovery once you are home again."

"Home?" She swallowed a sudden lump in her throat. Her gaze clouded as it moved to Jonathan. He had said nothing, yet she knew what he must be thinking. And feeling. "I beg your pardon, Uncle Henry," she murmured, turning back to the man beside her again, "but I have not yet properly introduced you to—"

"I am Alexandra's husband," Jonathan provided for

her. A faint smile played about his lips, and his own gaze was filled with an intense, strangely foreboding light. He gave a curt nod in the Englishman's direction. "Captain Jonathan Hazard, to be precise."

"I know who you are. And the marriage is not valid," Lord Henry disputed in a gruff, ireful tone.

"Uncle Henry, would you care for something to—?" Alex hastily sought to intervene.

"Governor Macquarie has told me how you rescued my niece from a prison cell, and for that alone I am grateful," he said, his scowl deepening. "But you took advantage of her afterward, you damned American rogue, and for *that* I could well see you hanged!"

"Alexandra is my wife," Jonathan reiterated in a deceptively low and level tone. "The marriage is legal."

"Did you think to get your hands on her fortune?" Lord Henry accused, his face reddening with anger. "If so, you will be sadly disappointed. You'll not get a penny of it, do you hear? Not a blasted farthing!"

"Jonathan did not marry me for that reason," Alex exclaimed breathlessly. She looked toward her husband again, only to color at the wry, loving amusement in his eyes.

"She told you who she was, did she not?" Her uncle continued to rage at him. "If you'd had so much as a shred of decency in you, you would have taken her straightaway to the governor for protection."

"She was in no danger here."

"The devil you say!"

"Oh, Uncle Henry, please," Alex entreated, her head spinning. She stood abruptly and swept across to the window. A frown creased her brow when she gazed outward and saw the soldiers waiting at attention beneath the trees, but she was too preoccupied with other, far more urgent matters at the moment to consider the significance of their presence. "Jonathan did not believe my story, so how could he have been intent upon seizing my fortune?"

"It matters not," Lord Henry pronounced stiffly, rising to his feet as well now. "I have already taken steps to have the marriage dissolved."

"What?" She rounded on him in another burst of astonishment.

"Upon my arrival in Sydney, at first light this morning, I wasted little time in seeking out Governor Macquarie. You can imagine my surprise when he confessed that he not only knew where you were living, but that you had recently become the wife of the same unscrupulous colonial who had forced you into servitude." He paused and flung Jonathan another narrow, belligerent glare. "The petition has already been filed. With my signature on it, you can be certain it shall be granted forthwith!"

"There will be no divorce," Jonathan decreed. His green eyes darkened to jade, and his handsome features became a grim mask of determination. "Alexandra is my wife in every sense of the word. And I mean to hold what is mine."

"The governor warned me to expect little cooperation from you," the older man replied scornfully. "But it so happens I took the precaution of anticipating difficulty upon these godforsaken shores. I have brought with me a document, signed by the prime minister himself, stating that my niece's conviction has been overturned and that I am hereby granted full guardianship of her once more!"

"What are you saying?" demanded Alex, her voice quavering again. "Do you actually mean to—?"

"I am saying, my dear, that you will be returning to Sydney with me this very day, and that we will be sailing for England by week's end!" To Jonathan, he confided,

"The governor was reluctant to offer his assistance, but he had little choice when I showed him the document. I demanded, and received, a military escort, and I will not allow my niece to spend one moment longer under your roof!"

"Merciful heaven," Alex whispered. Filled with a sudden, awful dread, she gazed at Jonathan and felt the color drain from her face once more. The moment of truth had finally arrived. And God help her, she could take no joy in it.

"I'll not let her go," Jonathan vowed, with deadly calm.

"Your opinion, sir, does not matter," Lord Henry countered. Before Alex could guess his intent, he moved to join her at the window. "*Now*, Governor!" he called out.

"No!" Alex vehemently protested, her eyes widening in horror. "Please, Uncle Henry. You—you cannot do this!"

"I can and shall!" He placed an arm about her shoulders again. "You have been through a terrible ordeal, dearest Alexandra. You must now trust me to decide what is best for you."

"But I am married to Jonathan!" Her bright, anguished gaze flew back to her husband's face. He looked ready to spring into action at any moment.

"You were forced into the marriage," argued her uncle.

"In the beginning, perhaps," she allowed, "but—"

"Alexandra will not be going with you, Lord Henry," insisted Jonathan, his temper flaring to a dangerous level. "You can produce all the documents you please, but they will change nothing. She is mine. And by damn, I'll not let you or any other man take her from me."

"You'll not dare to interfere, if you value your own rascally head," the Englishman warned. "It would take very little provocation for me to kill you myself."

Six of the soldiers were on their way inside by this time, with Governor Macquarie preceding them. Their boots drummed noisily on the wooden floor while they moved into position in the parlor doorway. One of them, a dark man with a hawkish gaze, was belatedly recognized by Alex. Her eyes widened anew at the sight of him, and she felt her throat constrict with increasing alarm.

"Major Beaton!" she gasped. No one save Jonathan appeared to hear her.

"I am sorry, Jonathan," the governor said earnestly as he came forward. "But no matter how much I value your friendship, I could not refuse Lord Cavendish's request."

"He has no right to do this, Lachlan," Jonathan replied. There was an almost savage gleam in his eyes now, one that struck apprehension in the other man's heart. "And you know she belongs with me."

"I can understand how you must feel, but the man *does* have a document—"

"I will not give her up." His gaze burned across into Alex's.

"Perhaps we can settle this better in a day or two," the Scotsman suggested. "Until then, I'm afraid Alexandra will have to return to Sydney with us."

"No, Lachlan."

"Damn it, Jonathan. I've my duty to see to!"

"Enough of this nonsense," Lord Henry growled impatiently. He seized Alex's arm and began forcing her toward the doorway.

Jonathan moved to stop them. Major Beaton was the first to intervene. He was knocked aside with a well-placed blow to the chin, but there were five others to take his place. They immediately set upon Jonathan.

"No!" screamed Alex, jerking her arm free. She instinctively tried to rush to his defense. "Jonathan!" Her uncle slipped an arm about her waist and pulled her back.

"Take him and hold him fast!" the governor commanded, though it pained him to do so. "You're not to release him until we're well on our way." Muttering an oath, he strode outside to make sure there was no danger of interference from the workers.

The sound of Alex's scream brought Finn Muldoon running from the kitchen, where he had gone to eavesdrop upon the conversation. He did not hesitate before throwing himself into the fray. Lord Henry tried to force Alex from the room, but she continued to resist his efforts.

Everything happened with such dizzying swiftness, there was no time to plan or reason. In the end, Jonathan was simply too far outnumbered to succeed against the men who overpowered him and bound his hands behind his back. The loyal, hapless Muldoon had been knocked unconscious within seconds of his own arrival upon the scene.

Still struggling within her uncle's grasp, Alex watched in horrified disbelief as Major Beaton suddenly advanced upon Jonathan with the light of vengeance in his eyes.

"So, Captain, we meet again," he drawled, then raised his fist and smashed it forcefully against Jonathan's face.

"Jonathan!" cried Alex.

In that moment, the truth flashed into her mind with startling clarity. She shook her head, the hot tears gathering in her eyes.

"Here now, Major. The governor'll not like it—" one of the soldiers said, starting to object.

"Hold your tongue, you bastard!" he rasped. His gaze sliced to Alex. The corners of his mouth turned up into a slow, malevolent smile. "I've an old score to settle with our American friend!"

"No!" Alex screamed again, only to suffer a ragged intake of breath when her uncle suddenly bent and scooped her up in his arms. She looked back in desperation toward Jonathan. Her eyes met his for only an instant, but it was long enough for her to glimpse an unspoken promise in those deep, gold-flecked emerald orbs. She knew she would never forget the terrible sight before her—that of a strong and proud and fiercely unyielding Jonathan Hazard being restrained by five soldiers whose faces bore the marks of his defiance.

She called his name again. But her uncle quickly bore her out of the house and down the front steps. A crowd had gathered just beyond the yard. The soldiers waited with guns held in readiness should anyone try to prevent them from leaving with Alex. Although she fought him as best she could, she found herself tossed up onto the saddle of a waiting horse. One of the red-coated men mounted behind her, his arm clamping about her waist to hold her prisoner while the governor bit out the orders for departure.

"Please, Governor Macquarie," she begged, choking back sobs. "Jonathan is—"

"It's out of my hands, lass." He cut her off. Then he reined angrily about and led the procession toward Sydney.

Alex glanced back at the house before she was spirited away. She felt as though her very heart was breaking, as though half of herself remained behind in that room where she had become Jonathan's wife ... and where she had been so cruelly torn from his side.

Chapter 16

Night was fast approaching by the time Alex stood alone in her room on the second floor of the governor's house in Sydney.

The large whitewashed building lay within a stone's throw of the Tanners' inn—an irony that was completely lost on her. Weary and disconsolate, she was in no mood to admire her surroundings, in spite of the building's impressive, early Georgian columns, intricately carved woodwork, and elegant furnishings. The ride from Boree had been long and exhausting, and there had been no opportunity for her to speak privately with her uncle.

Governor Macquarie's wife, Elizabeth, had been there to greet them upon their arrival. She was a handsome woman, several years younger than her husband, and possessed of such a sweet nature that Alex had been tempted to pour out her troubles on the spot and plead for help. She might well have done so, if not for the presence of her uncle, who had let it be known that his own mood was dangerously cross-tempered.

A ragged sigh escaped her lips. She wandered over to the bed and sank heavily down upon the embroidered silk coverlet, battling a fresh wave of tears as Jonathan's face swam before her eyes. Try as she would, she could not forget the blow he had suffered. Nor could she forget the look of pure malevolence on Major Beaton's face. Had the coward struck again? Had Seth or any of the other workers braved the soldiers' armed defense to aid their master?

"Oh, Jonathan," she whispered brokenly. Another desperate, heartfelt prayer for his safety rose in her mind. She choked back a sob and drew herself up from the bed again. After pacing distractedly to-and-fro for a brief time, she moved to the window and turned her glistening, anguished gaze outward.

The harbor stretched before her in the near distance, its unusually calm waters reflecting the moon's bright, silvery glow. The lights of the city were just beginning to find life in the gathering twilight, while the few clouds marring the endless blue of the sky above were blown about by a wind that was both gentle and cool. The coming night promised to be what the locals called "a soft one"—the thought of it caused a painful knot to tighten in Alex's stomach. This would be the first night since their wedding that she and Jonathan had been apart ... the first night she had not slept contentedly within the strong, loving warmth of his arms.

An insistent knock sounded at the door behind her. Dashing hastily at her tears, she whirled to face her uncle as he stepped inside the room.

"I'm sorry to disturb you, my dear, but I felt we should talk before supper. Mrs. Macquarie was kind enough to send you the appropriate attire." He indicated the stylish, primrose silk gown draped over his arm. When Alex offered no immediate response, he crossed to the bed and placed the gown upon it, then turned back to her with a conciliatory smile. "Perhaps our reunion was not as either of us might have wished, but—"

"How *could* you, Uncle?" She finally found voice

enough to storm at him. "How could you do such a thing?"

"I sought only what is best for you," he insisted, with an exaggerated patience, almost as though he were speaking to a child. "My methods may have been a trifle unconventional, but they were nevertheless quite effective."

"Jonathan Hazard did not deserve such churlish treatment!"

"Did he not?" He frowned and shook his head. "The scoundrel took advantage of you, Alexandra."

"That isn't true," she denied hotly.

"Are you saying that you married him of your own free will?" he asked, obviously skeptical.

"No," she had to admit, then hastened to add, "but only because I was not yet aware of my true feelings."

"And what are your 'true feelings'?" His tone was underscored by sarcasm.

"I love Jonathan Hazard!" She took a deep, shuddering breath and folded her arms beneath her breasts, her heart stirring wildly as she put words to her love at last. "I suppose I knew it all along, but I—I did not want to acknowledge it. Indeed, the last thing I ever expected was to fall in love with the impossible, infuriating man who hired me as his housekeeper, refused to believe my story of false imprisonment, and then wasted little time in wedding and bedding me. But I *did* fall in love with him, and I think I must have done so the very first time we met. I should have realized it long before now. He tried telling me," she murmured, heaving a deep sigh of regret. "He tried to make me face the truth, but I would not listen. If only I had not been so blasted stubborn! Oh, damn my own obstinance!"

"Alexandra!" Lord Henry admonished sharply. His frown deepened, and his eyes filled with a dull gleam as he raised a hand to her arm. "What you feel for him is not love, my dear."

"Oh, but it *is*, Uncle Henry." She pulled away and resumed her pacing. "And that is why I cannot leave."

"You have led a sheltered life," he reminded her, his concern over the state of her emotions increasing tenfold now. "Thank God, we have never had occasion to speak of such things before. But it is necessary that we do so now."

"I must go back," she exclaimed, paying him little mind. "Don't you see? I cannot—"

"Listen to me, Alexandra!" He seized her arm in a firm grip once more and forced her to a halt before him. "The rogue seduced you. He stole your innocence. He's left you confused and deluded."

"No!" She shook her head in a vigorous denial. "You are wrong."

"Do you think you are the first to be so deceived?" His mouth twisted into a knowing gesture of contempt. "The situation is all too commonplace among our peers. You were forced to play the role of the man's servant, were you not? It was precisely because you were in such a vulnerable position that he was able to take advantage of you."

"Then how do you account for the fact that he married me?" she challenged.

"You are an heiress. He recognized the opportunity to—"

"Stuff and nonsense!" With the proud spirit of defiance Jonathan had admired from the very beginning, she lifted her head and declared, "I cannot return to England with you, Uncle Henry!"

"You'll forget about him soon enough once we're back in London," he opined, with smug, maddening assurance. "Once you are among your friends again, restored to the world where you belong, you will be able to put this unfortunate episode behind you and concentrate on making a match that will bring you far more happiness than you could ever imagine. The divorce might prove to be a somewhat delicate matter, but I shall take pains to keep it as quiet as possible. Even if a scandal should threaten to ensue, your family name and fortune, and your connection to me, will no doubt smooth any ruffled feathers among the ton."

"Have you not been listening to a word I've said?" Alex demanded in growing exasperation. Her eyes kindled with their brilliant, blue-green fire. "There will be no divorce. I am going to stay with my husband!"

"What is there for you here?" His fingers tightened about her arm, and his aristocratic features were flushed angrily as he brought them close to the willful beauty of hers. "Do you really believe you could ever hope to find happiness in this harsh, uncivilized land, a far-flung colony inhabited by the very dregs of society? Can you truly imagine yourself as the wife of a man who is not only an American, but a villain and an outcast as well? What do you think your mother, God rest her soul, would say about your choice of a husband?" He released her arm and heaved a long, troubled sigh of his own. "I love you as I would my own daughter, Alexandra. Thus, I cannot allow you to ruin your life on the basis of some passing infatuation. You *shall* return to England with me!"

He spun about on his booted heel and strode from the room. Alex stared after him, feeling more wretched than ever.

She loved her aunt and uncle. They had been exceedingly kind and generous these many years past. And her life in London had been one of ease and comfort and privilege—a far cry from the hard work at Boree. Yet, how could she even consider returning to England now that she knew she loved Jonathan? The prospect of life without him was unbearable; the very thought of never seeing him again was enough to bring a sharp pain knifing through her heart. Dear God, she could not leave him!

"What am I going to do?" she murmured, casting another desperate glance heavenward. There had to be some way to convince her uncle of the truth. There had to be some way to prevent him from forcing her to accompany him on the return voyage to England.

She crossed to the window again. Her eyes suddenly lit with a clear and certain determination.

Of course! she thought, her pulse racing feverishly as a plan (employed with some degree of success once before) took shape in her mind. It would be dark soon. She could climb out of the window, lower herself to the ground, and then take flight. God willing, she would follow the river all the way back to the plantation. *Back to Jonathan!*

Tossing a quick, anxious look over her shoulder, she eased the window all the way open and whirled toward the bed. She knew her uncle would return to fetch her for supper soon; she hurried to wash and dress.

She spoke little during the course of the meal. Fortunately she and her uncle were the only guests that evening. The governor and his wife seemed to understand her reticence, for they made few attempts to include her in the conversation. Once again, she was tempted to appeal to Elizabeth Macquarie for help, but she told herself the woman would not defy her husband. Their relationship was obviously a warm one.

It was nearing nine o'clock by the time she was finally allowed to return to the privacy of her room. She bid her uncle good night in the hallway—taking care

not to arouse his suspicions by doing so *too* warmly—
and swept inside, closing the door behind her. Her eyes
fairly danced with excitement as she sped across to the
window and peered into the darkness below.

She saw no one. Her spirits soaring, she gathered up
her skirts.

Suddenly a hand clamped across her mouth. She
tensed, a scream of alarm rising deep in her throat when
she felt an arm slipping about her waist from behind.

"Quiet, my love, or I may well have to take on the
whole blasted regiment," a familiar, splendidly deep-
timbred voice sounded close to her ear. Her heart leapt
with joy. She turned within his embrace, her eyes wide
and luminous as they shone up into the loving amusement of his.

"Jonathan!" she whispered tremulously. "How—?
Where—?"

"I told you I'd never let you go."

"How on earth did you get into this room?"

"Never underestimate a Hazard."

"But, good heavens, I cannot believe you are actually
here," she said with excitement. "What if someone had
seen you? You are in far too much danger here! Please,
Jonathan. You must leave at once."

"Not without you." He raised his hands to her shoulders. His handsome face, only slightly bruised and bat-
tered, wore an expression of mock severity when he
demanded, "Will you come with me of your own free
will, Mrs. Hazard? Or do I toss you over my shoulder
and carry you away?"

"Did you not notice that I was preparing to escape?"
she parried saucily, tossing a nod back toward the window. She turned serious in the next instant. "Oh, Jonathan. Are you all right? Major Beaton—"

"Is at present enjoying the fruit of his 'labors' in a

tavern at Parramatta." He did not add that he had exacted a more personal revenge beforehand; the good major would be sporting bruises of his own come morning. "Seth and two of the others were obliging enough to provide him with escort there. His superiors will not take kindly to his being found drunk and disorderly while still on duty." He battled the urge to kiss her, consoling himself with the thought of a proper reunion once they were away from Sydney. "But none of that matters now. Come, Lady Alex," he said, reluctantly setting her from him but taking her arm in a firm grasp. "We've no more time to waste. Our ship lies ready to weigh anchor just as soon as—"

"Our ship?" she echoed, her eyes clouding with bewilderment. "What are you talking about? Are we not returning home?"

"No. We are sailing for America."

"America?"

"Your uncle will not allow you to remain here. The governor has made his own position clear. We've little choice but to leave."

"But what about the plantation? What about—?"

"Later!" he commanded.

He quickly pulled her across the room with him, opened the door, and made certain that the dimly lit hallway was deserted. Once again cautioning her to keep silent, he slipped from the room.

Alex went obediently along with him as he headed for the staircase. It occurred to her that he had not asked *why* she was willing to defy her uncle and surrender all hope of returning to England. If not for the fact that her nerves were already strung tight as a bowstring, she would have bristled at his presumption. But she still would have gone with him.

Her anxious gaze darted about, and she held her

breath while he led her down the wide, carpeted steps. She suddenly found herself plagued by a terrible vision of her uncle's interception, of the alarm being sounded and the governor's troops descending upon them. The vision, however, did not become a reality. Jonathan urged her down a narrow corridor to a back door. They emerged into the cool darkness outside.

"Why were there no guards?" she whispered, her head spinning at the ease with which they were able to escape. "Surely the governor—"

"I've a friend inside," Jonathan confided, with a faint smile of irony as he closed the door behind them.

"A friend?"

"Elizabeth Macquarie was ever a hopeless romantic." His smile briefly deepened at her expression of surprise. "This way," he directed, pulling her forward again.

They hurried along the quiet, moonlit streets, down the hill to the more raucous atmosphere of the waterfront. Alex was struggling for breath when they finally reached the harbor. Jonathan pushed her through the crowd, then down one of the wharves to where a three-masted schooner waited for them.

"How were you able to—to arrange passage so quickly?" she stammered, her eyes bright and her cheeks flushed as she gathered up her skirts to climb the gangplank.

"The *Prospero* is mine, Alexandra."

"Yours?" She gasped in startlement. "But, I thought—"

"I was too many years upon the sea to abandon it altogether," he commented wryly. "And in the event that you were tempted to share your uncle's suspicions regarding my avarice, you should know that I have other ships as well."

"So you have no need of my fortune after all," she

teased, her eyes sparkling with triumphant satisfaction at the thought.

"To hell with your fortune." He steadied her as she stepped from the gangplank onto the schooner's deck. "Make ready to sail, Mr. Muldoon!" he ordered in a brusque, authoritative tone.

"Aye, Captain!"

Alex spun about to observe the old Irishman standing upon the quarterdeck above. He grinned broadly down at her.

"We're that happy to have you aboard, Mrs. Hazard!" he said, tipping his hat.

She watched in fascination as the crewmen scrambled about to prepare for departure. Her gaze continued to stray apprehensively back toward the wharves, for she dared not yet believe that she and Jonathan were in the clear. She knew her uncle would stop at nothing to get her back. She could well imagine him demanding that Jonathan be hanged for attempting to spirit her away.

An involuntary tremor shook her. She looked farther, toward where the revelers were spilling out of the taverns and gaming houses. Her worst fears were realized when she spotted her uncle and the governor pulling up in a carriage at the end of the dock. A column of soldiers, their escort insisted upon by Lord Henry when he had discovered his niece's absence, had been summoned from the nearby barracks. They marched close behind the carriage.

"Jonathan!" Alex cried hoarsely, her throat constricting in alarm. He was beside her again in the next moment. His face became a grim, furious mask of determination as his piercing gaze followed the direction of hers. "Dear God, what are we going to do now?" she choked out.

"Whatever it takes." At a signal from him, Muldoon

and the other crewmen assembled in defensive readiness behind him. All were armed. And all were prepared to fight, even if it meant facing off against the governor's own troops.

"Alexandra!" Lord Henry Cavendish called out to her as he raced angrily down the lamplit darkness of the wharf to confront her. He stopped at the foot of the gangplank, his narrow, vengeful gaze shooting to Jonathan. "Let her go, you black-hearted rogue!"

"He is no rogue, Uncle," Alex flung back. "Jonathan is my husband, and there is nothing you can do to prevent me from going with him."

"I am your guardian. You'll do as I say. Now come down at once, *or else!*" he warned.

"Damn it, Jonathan! Have you lost your mind?" Governor Macquarie charged when he reached Lord Henry's side. The soldiers had moved into position on the dock, awaiting his command. "The man has a perfect right to take Alexandra with him."

"She is my wife, Lachlan," he stated quietly. His eyes were filled with that same dangerous intensity Alex had come to know so well. "As I told you before, I'll not give her up."

"Are you willing to risk bloodshed?" Lord Henry challenged in scornful disbelief.

"I am willing to risk my very life."

"*No,*" Alex cried, her horror-stricken gaze moving from Jonathan to her uncle, then to the governor. "For heaven's sake, Governor Macquarie. Surely you cannot mean to—?"

"I am afraid, lass, that the decision rests with your uncle." He was bluffing, of course. He had no intention of resorting to violence; both his conscience and his wife had raked him over the coals for his part in that afternoon's unpleasantness at Boree. But he had to make a convincing show of force just the same. "If Lord Cavendish will but agree to work this out in a civilized manner, we can all go home to our beds."

"There is nothing to work out," the Englishman replied. He glared at Jonathan again. "I might have known you would attempt to steal away like a thief in the night."

"We are sailing to America," Alex revealed.

"The devil you say!"

"Yes, Uncle Henry, I *do* say! And I also say that you will never see me again if you persist in this nonsense!" She felt hot tears stinging against her eyelids, but she resolutely blinked them back. "I love you and Aunt Beatrice very much. Truly, I am grateful to you for all you have done. But I am Jonathan's wife now. No matter what you say or do, no matter how much you want things to be as they were before, you cannot change what was meant to be." She drew in a deep, unsteady breath before declaring, "I love him, Uncle. I love him with all my heart. And if what you feel for Aunt Beatrice is one-tenth of what I feel for Jonathan Hazard, then you cannot help but understand why I must stay with him!" She felt the strong warmth of Jonathan's hand closing about her arm once more, and her cheeks colored rosily when her eyes lifted to his.

"Better late than never, Lady Alex," he murmured, his low, wondrously vibrant tone for her ears alone.

"What has happened to you, Alexandra?" her uncle asked, frowning in hurt and angry bemusement as he reflected that she had changed even more than he had thought. He had never seen her quite so unyielding and steadfast about anything. He had never heard her speak with such fiery determination. "You were always high-spirited, but—"

"I fear I am even worse now," she admitted, with a

sigh. Her expression became soft and entreating, and her voice was full of hope when she said, "Surely you must see that Jonathan is worthy of your acceptance? He has shown himself willing to give up everything he has here in order to be with me. He has pledged his undying love and devotion to me. Please, dearest Uncle. Will you not grant us your blessings?"

"She's right, Henry," Governor Macquarie saw fit to interject at this point. He lifted a hand to the other man's shoulder and stared solemnly across at him. "Would you allow your pride to break her heart—and your own? Aye, man. You may well lose her entirely if you deny her this chance at happiness."

"What happiness can there be in such an ill-favored union?" Lord Henry replied, his heart warring with his head. His gaze softened at the look on his niece's face.

"More than you can imagine."

Alex turned her face up toward Jonathan's again. Drawing strength from what she saw in his eyes, she moved away and walked slowly down the gangplank. She stood before her uncle, her hand reaching for his.

"Please, Uncle Henry," she implored. "I love him."

"So you would have me leave you in this wilderness?" he asked, his voice thick with emotion. "So far from home? So far from all you hold dear?"

"Except for you and Aunt Beatrice, all I hold dear is here in this wilderness," she assured him, her eyes sparkling anew.

"Are you sure, Alexandra?" He searched her face closely. "There can be no turning back. Once you have chosen your course, you will have to follow it through to the end. You must be certain."

"In truth, I am more certain than I would ever have believed possible." She looked back at Jonathan, who strode down the gangplank now to join her. He extended his hand in a gesture of conciliation toward the older man.

"You've my word, Lord Cavendish, that I will make sure she has no regrets," he vowed somberly.

"And why the devil should I believe the word of an American?"

"Because American or no, I am the man who will hold her forever." The merest ghost of a smile played about his lips as he continued to wait with his hand held steadily outward.

Lord Henry Cavendish was faced with a dilemma unlike any he had ever known before. It galled him to think of his niece married to someone so inferior, so thoroughly unsuitable. He had always envisioned her as the bride of a wealthy nobleman, or perhaps even one of the crown princes of Europe. Yet what choice did he have? He could still insist upon exerting his rights as her guardian. He could seize her now, and, with the help of the governor, make certain she sailed for England with him at the end of the week. But in so doing, he feared the Scotsman's warning would be well-met; he would lose her entirely.

"I cannot deny that I am entrusting her to your care with great reluctance, Captain Hazard," he said, though he finally accepted the offer of Jonathan's hand. His expression was stern, his eyes full of begrudging resignation. "Treat her with gentleness, young man, or as God is my witness, I shall see you in hell!"

"I'll keep that in mind," drawled Jonathan, his own eyes magnificently aglow.

"Thank you, Uncle," Alex murmured. Flooded with a mixture of relief, gratitude, and affection, she threw her arms about his neck and hugged him tight. "Tell Aunt Beatrice I have found my heart's desire at last. She will understand!"

"For my own sake, dearest Alexandra, I certainly hope so."

Later than same night, after the crewmen had been given leave to go ashore and Governor Macquarie had taken his soldiers and his guest away to seek the comfort of their own beds once more, Alex and Jonathan lay together in the *Prospero*'s cabin. Finn Muldoon remained at watch on the moonlit deck above, celebrating the end of the crisis—and the promise of a bright tomorrow—with a well-earned bottle of spirits.

"Would you really have done it, Jonathan?" Alex wondered aloud. She snuggled closer to him in the warmth of the three-quarter bed, her naked curves fitting with perfection against his virile hardness. "Would you have sailed all the way to America?"

"I'd have sailed to the ends of the earth if need be." He glided a strong, possessive hand down to the curve of her hip. "Do you not yet realize, Mrs. Hazard, that I love you more than life itself?"

"I am beginning to." She sighed blissfully, then frowned while her eyes filled with sudden contrition. "I—I am sorry I allowed my foolish pride to overpower what was in my heart. You were right, of course. I *was* jealous of Gwendolyn. And today, when I saw Major Beaton strike you, I could escape the truth of my feelings no longer."

"If I had known it would require so little, I'd have let him hit me that night at The Roost," he teased. He sobered in the next instant, his own gaze briefly darkening when he admitted, "It was wrong of me to doubt your story. I wanted you so much . . . By heaven, I knew you were not like the others. I knew it the first time I set eyes on you. But it was too late. I had already been bewitched." A soft smile of irony tugged at the corners of his mouth.

"As had I," she was quick to point out. "I suffered the most dreadful guilt over my inability to resist you. I was certain I had become a veritable harlot, a woman of such easy virtue that you had merely to touch me in order to tumble me into your bed."

"The notion is an agreeable one. So long as you play the harlot with no other man save me."

"You can be certain of that," she promised, coloring delightedly.

Another sigh of contentment escaped her lips before she stirred within his arms. She lifted her head from his shoulder and gazed down at him. His ruggedly handsome features were set aglow by the lamplight, while his deep green eyes held an intoxicating mixture of tenderness and desire. She saw her future in them. A future full of love, with no regrets for what she had left behind.

"And so shall we stay in Australia forever, my dearest Captain Hazard?" she asked, her voice scarcely more than a whisper.

He smiled up at her, and she felt her heart melt.

"Forever and a day, Lady Alex," he confirmed, pulling her back down to him. Their lips met in a kiss so sweetly passionate that all else was forgotten once more.

Bestselling author

CATHERINE CREEL
Wild Texas Rose

Callie Rose Buchanan had a face and figure that would tempt any man—but also a fierce independence that no man could challenge. A trip to Europe was arranged to land this fiery cowgirl a husband with enough gumption to tame her. What she got was Ian MacGregor, a devilishly handsome Scotsman determined to possess her, first with angry lust, then with a searing yet tender passion that branded her soul and bound them to a heated and turbulent future—as vast and storm-tossed as the seas spanning the Highlands and the blazing skies of Texas.

Published by Fawcett Books.
Available in your local bookstore.

Call toll free 1-800-733-3000 to order by phone and use your major credit card. Or use this coupon to order by mail.

__WILD TEXAS ROSE   449-14785-1 $4.99

Name _____
Address_____
City_____ State_____ Zip _____

Please send me the FAWCETT BOOKS I have checked above.
I am enclosing $_____
   plus
Postage & handling* $_____
Sales tax (where applicable) $_____
Total amount enclosed $_____

*Add $2 for the first book and 50¢ for each additional book.

Send check or money order (no cash or CODs) to:
Fawcett Mail Sales, 400 Hahn Road, Westminster, MD 21157.

Prices and numbers subject to change without notice.
Valid in the U.S. only.
All orders subject to availability.   CREEL